here
groan
the
dead

here
groan
the
dead

a novel by
auric adams

The Artless Dodges Press

Here Groan the Dead
by Auric Adams
ISBN 978-0-9819939-0-4
© 2009 Artless Dodges, Inc.
Published by The Artless Dodges Press
Cleveland, Ohio.

Cover design by T. Maven
www.TrashMaven.BlogSpot.com

This is the place of woe, here groan the dead;
Huge Tityus o'er nine acres here is spread.
Fruitful for pain th' immortal liver breeds,
Still grows, and still th' insatiate vulture feeds.
Poor Tantalus to taste the water tries,
But from his lips the faithless water flies:
Then thinks the bending tree he can command,
The tree starts backwards, and eludes his hand.
The labour too of Sisyphus is vain,
Up the steep mount he heaves the stone with pain,
Down from the summit rouls the stone again.
The Belides their leaky vessels still
Are ever filling, and yet never fill:
Doom'd to this punishment for blood they shed,
For bridegrooms slaughter'd in the bridal bed.
Stretch'd on the rolling wheel Ixion lies;
Himself he follows, and himself he flies.
Ixion, tortur'd, Juno sternly ey'd,
Then turn'd, and toiling Sisyphus espy'd:
And why (she said) so wretched is the fate
Of him, whose brother proudly reigns in state?
Yet still my altars unador'd have been
By Athamas, and his presumptuous queen.

-Ovid, Metamorphoses

AURIC ADAMS

I.

Back then I was working the blotter at the Daily News with Doug Finnerty and Ray Greene. We had the week divided up so that we each took two days and cycled through who took the seventh. It was a pretty good setup. We each had a desk in there, and we could smoke in the office, and with the door closed you could barely hear the noise from down on the floor. The work wasn't bad either, if you want to know the truth. It sort of fit me. A lot of guys can't work there for very long, because you have to go out and hang out at crime scenes and look at some pretty gruesome stuff. But I didn't really mind it. My parents died when I was a pretty little kid, and so that kind of stuff never really bothered me. I mean it did for a while, and everybody said it would get easier, and it never did, but after a while I got too tired to care, and I figured that was just as good. My dad died in the war and then my mom drove our car onto the train tracks, so it was pretty gruesome all the way around. After I got too tired to care about that there wasn't much else that bothered me, so the work kind of suited me. My uncle used to tell me that police reporting was one step above grave robbing, and that may be true. I guess everything is grave robbing if you look at it that way. But in any case it was a pretty good job.

Anyway it was a Tuesday in early February, and I got the call while I was asleep at home. It was my day to be in at the paper, but the day was slow and I went home early, thinking that probably nothing was going to happen, and even if it did happen nobody could blame me for leaving early, if they could even figure out that I was gone. The main floor was always a madhouse. But somehow somebody figured out that I wasn't around and they called me up and told me to get to this address out in one of the neighborhoods. I got dressed, but I couldn't find a cab that would take me that far. It was freezing out. I ended up walking around the block for thirty minutes before I got one.

HERE GROAN THE DEAD

The cops were all parked in a big ring around this guy's driveway, with the ambulance backed right up the garage. The front of the house was all lit up. I walked across the driveway and onto the yard. It was so cold the grass crunched. That light, dusty kind of snow was falling, that kind that never seems to go anywhere but just hangs in the air around your face or gets caught in your hair. There was a cop outside the door, hunkered down inside his coat, and another one just inside, behind the tape. Lights were on in the windows of the houses along the street, and I saw a few people standing outside the light of the police cars. I nodded to the cop and ducked under the tape. He didn't move or seem to notice, but the one inside put up a hand. I told him who I was and he let me through. I went down the hall to the kitchen. There were a bunch of cops were standing around, drinking coffee and not saying much to each other. Somebody was crying somewhere. Not one of the cops, I figured, but I couldn't see who it was.

"Where is he?" I said.

"Through there," one of them said. He pointed at a doorway leading off the kitchen. "Why don't you take a second to prepare yourself."

"I'm fine," I said. I went inside. Everybody inside the room was tucked up tight against the corner near the door, so at first I couldn't get through. The police photographer was taking pictures a mile a minute, so the room kept flashing bright and then going black and then flashing again. They had the lights off to give better shadows in the pictures. Then someone said, "that's good, I think I got it," and someone flipped the lights back on.

"Ugh," said someone. "All right. That's enough for me," and somebody ducked out beside me. I slid into his place.

"Who the hell are you?" said a hollow-faced man beside me.

"Press," I said. I bumped into a couple coats hanging on a row of hooks on the wall behind me and they came loose and draped down over my shoulder. "I'm with the Daily."

"This is a closed crime scene," said the hollow-faced man. "Who let you in here?"

"I let myself in," I said.

"We're investigating a murder here," he said. "Everything in this room is evidence. You're tampering with a crime scene. That's a federal offense."

"Blow it out your ass," I said.

"Frank," said someone else, "it's fine. Let the man do his job."

"Excuse me," said the police photographer, coming out. "Have a ball, fella," he said to me. "You're not gonna believe the angles. The colors. If it weren't a corpse, it's be art." He went out into the kitchen. Frank waved a finger in my face.

"Don't touch anything," he said.

"Come on, Frank," said the other man, who had spoken up earlier.

"Yeah, come on, Frank," I said. Frank made a start at me, but the other man grabbed him around the shoulders, and then pushed him into the kitchen. It jostled me back into the wall, then sideways so that the coats on my shoulder fell off onto the floor. The other man was in front of me. Frank was outside.

"One minute, Christ," he said to Frank. And then, to me, "sorry about that." He bent down, picked up the coats, and hung them back on their pegs.

"What's his problem?" I said.

"Frank gets moody around the dead," he said. He checked his watch. "I can give you five. Then the medics want to wheel him out. It's going to be better for the family to have him out of here as soon as possible." He looked back over his shoulder, and shook his head. "Poor bastard," he said.

"I guess you've got to say something," I said.

"Five minutes," he said. He left and I pulled the door closed behind him.

HERE GROAN THE DEAD

The body was sunk down against the far wall. There was a big fan of blood on the wall above him, starting where the head used to be. His shoes were sitting next to him. The shotgun was across his body, the butt resting on the tile between his legs. The room smelled heavy with sweat and the close heat from the cops and the photographer and gunpowder. I took a couple of shots of the body from a couple of different angles, but I left the lights on because I forgot my flash. Then I left and went out into the kitchen. Frank was there, making coffee. He looked at me but didn't say anything.

"Well Christ," I heard somebody say, "can I at least see him?"

"It's probably better that you don't," said somebody else. "He looks pretty bad."

"How bad?" said the first voice.

"Bad," said the second. "He looks pretty bad."

"Goddamnit," said Frank, spilling water onto the floor. "Son of a bitch."

"Easy Frank," said someone else.

"Fuck," said Frank.

"Why don't you go have a cigarette," one of the cops said. "I'll finish making the coffee." He took the coffee from Frank. Frank nodded and then looked at me as he moved past the man who had asked to see the body.

"Christ's sake," said the cop who had taken the pot from Frank, "he didn't even take the old grounds out. He just put in new ones on top. Christ," he said again, scooping it all out.

"He's cracking up," said one of the other cops. He yawned. "Hurry up with that, will ya?" he said. "I gotta get home."

"I'll tell you what," the cop talking to the new man was saying, "there's a newspaper photographer here. Why don't you talk to him, and see if he can send you some pictures after he's got them developed, if you want to see him so bad." He was steering the man over to me, pulling him by his elbow. The cop was the one who told Frank to take it easy. I hadn't seen the other man on the way in.

"All right," said the cop making the coffee.

"About damned time," said someone else.

"Hey," said one of two medics, "you guys finished yet?"

"I'm sorry," said the cop who had stopped Frank, "what was your name?"

"Elliot Poulain," I said.

"Right," he said, shaking my hand, "and you're with the…"

"The Daily News," I said.

"Right," he said. "I'm Detective Franklin. This is Mr. Canasson."

"Arthur," said Canasson, putting out his hand. "You can just call me Arthur." We shook hands.

"You want some pictures of the corpse," I said. "I understand." I held up a hand, to tell him that he didn't have to explain himself. He didn't seem like he was about to, but some people do. "I charge five apiece for prints, but I'll do five for twenty."

"You already saw him?"

"Yeah," I said.

"How did he look?"

I laughed. "How did he look?" I said. "He looked bad, that's how he looked."

Canasson looked at the floor. He said, "They let you in to see him. Do you think you could tell them that you didn't get all the shots you wanted, that you've gotta go back in and get a few more, then take me in with you?".

"They only gave me five minutes," I said. "I already used it up."

"I'll give you a hundred," he said.

I kind of laughed at that. Then I said, "Why do you want to see him?"

Canasson shrugged. Then he sort of ran his hands over his face and said, "I don't know. What difference does it make?"

I said, "One hundred and fifty."

"Sure," he said.

"All right," I said, "I'll see what I can do." I went over to Franklin. He was standing in the doorway leading off the kitchen into the living room. Most of the cops in the kitchen had gone in to wait for the coffee. I tapped him on the shoulder. "Say," I said. "I've been thinking about it, and there's one shot more I'd still like to get. Is it all right with you if I pop back in?"

He looked back over his shoulder at me, then turned and leaned to look farther around to the closed laundry room door. He shrugged.

"You got a job to do," he said. "So do the medics. When they show back up, I want you out of there. Otherwise it's fine with me."

"Thanks," I said. "I owe you one."

"Try not to pick a fight with Frank on your way out and we can call it even," he said.

"Sure," I said. I went back over to Canasson. "All right," I said. "Lets go."

He followed me to the door and we went inside. I went in first and stood between him and the body. He closed the door behind us. Then I turned sideways and let him pass me. He knelt down in front of it and looked it over. Then he started wiping his face with his hands again.

"Jesus Christ," he said.

"It's a bitch, isn't it?" I said.

"They're going to ask me to speak at his funeral," he said. He rubbed his face again. "Jesus."

"How did you even hear about it?" I said.

"Someone on our board knows the chief of police. Jesus." He didn't look at me.

"You worked with him?"

"Yeah," he said. "Sort of indirectly." He laughed, but you could tell he didn't mean it. He wiped his face again.

Then there was a knock on the door and when I opened it one of the medics was standing there.

"All right," I said to Canasson. "Time to go."

He got up and we went out into the kitchen. The medics left the door open, and I watched the two of them hoist the body up onto the stretcher. First they took the shotgun from his lap. Then they slid him along the wall and across the floor until he was laying on his back. Then they folded his arms across his chest, and one lifted him under the armpits and the other lifted him by the backs of his knees. The stretcher didn't fit through the door, and so they carried the body out into the kitchen. The stump of his neck dripped blood across the tile, and what was left of his jaw moved back and forth until it finally fell back to cover the stump as they dropped him onto the stretcher. Then one of them went back inside and took a towel from the shelf and wiped up the blood trail. They put the ruined towel on top of the body, then covered them both over with a sheet. The sheet touched the stump and soaked through and one of the paramedics cursed and lifted the sheet back off. He covered the stump with the towel and then covered them both with the sheet.

We followed the stretcher down the hall and out the door and then watched it down the front walk to the ambulance. Canasson stood with his hands in his pockets, watching them load it up. A few of the neighbors were still standing out around the police cars, but most of them had gone back inside. The houses across and down along the street were mostly dark. Then the medics slammed the doors and climbed into the cab. I yawned again and checked my watch.

"Christ, it's late," I said. I looked over at Canasson. He was standing on the step behind me, his hands in his pockets, watching the ambulance. "Aren't you cold?" I said. He didn't say anything, so I turned back around. "I'm fucking cold," I said. "I'm fucking freezing."

We watched the ambulance until it was gone, then Canasson tapped me on the shoulder. Most of the neighbors had gone back inside. I watched a pair of women in overcoats turn away and head down the street before I turned around. Canasson was digging in his pockets. Then he moved up into his suit jacket pockets, and came back with his wallet.

"Look," he said. "I don't have that much cash on me, but if you come to my office tomorrow with the best picture you've got, I'll give you a check for two hundred. All right?" He was holding his card out to me.

"This is up on the west side," I said, reading the address.

"Too much trouble?"

"It doesn't matter to me," I said. I shrugged and put the card into my pocket. "Do you have a cigarette?" He took out a pack and I took one and lit it. "Just ran out," I said. Behind me, one of the cops was ushering the widow and a pretty blonde - the guy's daughter - I guess, out the front door and down the steps. Canasson and I stepped aside.

"It's only a thirty or forty minute drive from here," the widow was saying. "I already called and she knows we're coming. Really it would be better if you just let us go. The lights and all would just upset her. She and my husband were very close." She was talking like she didn't realize it. His daughter was a mess, clutching at her shoulder. One of the cops took his coat off and put it around the blonde's shoulders. "Honey, say thank you," said her mother.

"That's all right," said the cop. He sounded sad and then he went inside because he had already started to shiver in the cold. "You can just give the coat back to Henry, there," he said from the doorway. "He can give it back to me."

"Come on," said Henry. "I'll give you a lift."

"It's really all right," said the widow, but she kept walking with Henry. They crossed the lawn. The blonde was still wearing her slippers, and stepped lightly on the frozen ground, like she was trying not to touch it. Henry closed the door behind them when they were inside. Then the widow tried to get back out. But the cop car doors didn't open from the inside, and she started pounding on the window. She started off pounding and looking at him, looking at Henry, and then she was just pounding, hard, and the reflected lights from the house were dancing on the glass. Henry jogged back around and opened the door. She tried to get out, but he stopped her. Then she said something and pointed and he nodded and then closed the door again, and jogged up to the house. He came out a second later carrying this mottled-looking cat in his arms. He carried it to the car and put it in the back seat with the blonde and the widow. Then he got in and we watched them drive away.

"Ok, gents," someone said from behind us, "we're closing up shop here."

The cop who had said it came out and then a half-dozen others came out after him. The last one pulled the door closed and checked the knob. We all stood around looking at each other for a minute. The snow was coming down heavier, now. It collected on the cops" shoulders. You could really see it against the blue.

"Christ, it's cold," someone said.

"You can say that again," someone else said. Someone pulled out a pack and asked me for a light. I gave him a book of matches. Then the cop offered me a cigarette. Then he passed the pack around. Canasson took one, and so did four of the other cops. We stood outside smoking and not saying much.

"Yipes," somebody finally said, "I gotta be getting home."

"One of you want to give me a lift?" I said.

"Where are you going?" asked one of them. I told him. "I can do it," he said. "Come on. You're on my way."

I followed the cop to his car. He kept the lights off. I took down some information about the body. He dropped me off at my building and I went upstairs and typed up my notes. After that I didn't feel tired so I shaved and walked to the newspaper. It was dark and cold and nothing was open.

HERE GROAN THE DEAD

While I was walking the sky went from black to deep blue to pink haze and then I was inside and everything was the off-white and yellow of the bulbs and that strange visceral feeling of nervous movement somewhere nearby from the few people still on the newspaper floor and the whir of the press through a half dozen walls, the big wheels going around and around. I went up to the beat office and called up Marty in obits, but nobody answered and so I sat down and smoked a few cigarettes. While I was doing that people started coming in. Then Greene came in. His red hair was combed flat down, plastered to his narrow forehead and still looked wet.

"What the hell are you doing here?" he said. "I got Wednesday and Thursday."

"Christ, it still feels like part of Tuesday," I said. "You want to take over on last night's suicide?"

"Heard about that," he said, shaking his head. "Not a chance. That's in your lap."

"Why don't you take it," I said. "That would put us even for the Gannett thing I covered for you."

"Goes around comes around," he said. "The universe will reward you for that one. No need to make more trouble for me. Besides," he said. "You're already in this one. I wouldn't know where to start."

"B-sides are the other halves of records," I said. "Save that line for the next time you find me fucking your wife."

"Fuck you," he said, laughing. "I got enough problems."

"Name the next one after me," I said. "It's just as likely mine."

I figured since I was already there I would get some work done, so I looked up the widow's sister's phone number. I called her, but she said that the widow couldn't come to the phone, and didn't have a comment. I asked to speak to the daughter, but then she hung up on me. So I called her back and asked if she had anything to say. She said it was a hell of a world to live in where a grieving widow and her family couldn't get a little respectful peace from vultures like me. I asked if I could quote her, and she hung up on me again. So I called the police station. They said the whole thing was still under investigation, but that they might have a statement by early afternoon. I said I'd call back, and then hung up. By then it was almost ten. I went to the photo lab and developed my negatives and then made prints of all of the pictures, and then made a couple copies of the best ones and hung them up to dry. Then I went and hung out with Greene and a couple other guys in the break room. When I came back the prints were dry and I put them in an envelope and left. It was just after eleven, but it was still cold as hell out. I walked for a block and then picked up a taxi, and gave him the address of Canasson's office. With the traffic it took half an hour to get there. We got caught in a roundabout and the dipshit cabbie couldn't get over to get off.

Canasson was in his office when I went up. He looked over the pictures and gave me a check. Then he invited me to lunch. I didn't have to go back to the newspaper, so I said sure. He said he was supposed to meet his wife, but that she had cancelled and he'd already made the reservation. We went down to the street and Canasson waved down a cab. We got in and he gave the name of the restaurant and the cabbie took off. Canasson watched out the window. I figured he was upset about seeing the pictures, and didn't feel like talking. But I also figured that he had only invited me to lunch because he wanted to know something about it. So I watched out my window and waited and didn't say anything. Then we pulled up outside of the restaurant, and Canasson paid the driver. The restaurant was through a wood and glass door and up a flight of stairs. The headwaiter led us to a booth that wrapped around a small circular table. Canasson ordered a drink and I did the same.

It was funny, because I figured that we wouldn't have a lot to talk about, but it turned out that we did. We liked the same books, for one thing. I had pegged him as a guy who

11

didn't read much, one of those well-off guys who got through school on their parents" money, but it turned out that he really read quite a lot. So we had that in common. We'd both been too young to fight in the war, too. We talked about that for a while. I didn't care about it that much, but Canasson said he felt like he'd missed something that couldn't be got back. He said it was probably because everyone else on the board had fought in it, and they all knew he hadn't. Then, after a while, we started talking about the other night, and about the guy, and the personal problems he was having, and Canasson said isn't it funny the way sometimes you see something coming, but you don't realize it until it's already happened? We both agreed that it was pretty funny, and then he said I don't know and I said I didn't either, and we let it drop at that.

After we ate I said I had some things to do. Canasson asked me to stay for another drink, but I said I really should get going. He said we should do it again some time, and I agreed. We shook hands and I left him in the restaurant. Then I took a cab back to the newspaper and got the rest of the prints and went home and went to bed.

I thought that I was pretty tired from not sleeping much the night before, but when I got into bed I couldn't sleep. I just lay awake, thinking. I started off thinking about how I didn't have to go back in to work until Monday, and what I would do until then. I had to have the story in on the suicide, but they probably wouldn't run it until the weekend anyway, and I figured I could bang it out in a couple of hours. I hadn't been able to track much down about it, and I so I decided to try the police again the next day and if they had anything, maybe try and use that on the widow or the daughter, maybe try and call and catch them when the widow's sister was out. Then I thought about how, after I got the calls made and the story finished up I was going to still have a lot of free time on my hands, and I started wondering what to do. There weren't any movies out that I wanted to see that I could think of. I thought about books that I wanted to read, but I had already read all of the ones I really wanted to read. Then I thought about rereading one of the ones I had meant to read over again, but thinking about that just made me tired. After that I started thinking about the girls that I knew, and which ones were around, and which ones might want to do something over the weekend. But every time I thought of one, I would just think about the way they chewed with their mouth open, or the way this one always asked a question about the part of what I was telling her that didn't matter, or the way another would interrupt me. Pretty soon I was through the whole lot of them, and so just out of boredom I started thinking about the widow's daughter. But I couldn't keep that up for very long without feeling like complete hell, so I gave that up. Then I got sort of upset at myself that I felt bad about thinking about her. I sort of remembered something the minister said at my father's funeral: *Wherefore I praised the dead which are already dead more than the living which are yet alive*, but thinking about that and about the church and the whole ceremony just made me angry and then I was more awake than I had been before I laid down. So I tried to stop thinking about it, but I couldn't. But after a while being angry and having no one to tell it to and nothing to do about it made me tired. For a little while I didn't think about anything, just sort of lay and thought about being tired. After a while I fell asleep.

HERE GROAN THE DEAD

II.

The next day I hung around my apartment all morning, then went down to the newspaper. It was Greene's day in again, and I figured if I could catch him before he went out for lunch we could eat together. It's funny. I don't like eating by myself. It's the only time I feel really alone. Most of the rest of the time, even if I'm alone I feel like people are all around me. When I'm eating alone its like I'm the only one in the room.

But I couldn't find Greene, and so I just went back to my apartment and called the police station. They said they hadn't turned up much. He had been covering up the losses on a business venture that had gone bust, and taken a good chunk of the company down with him. I asked if they'd been able to get anything out of the widow or the daughter, but the cop said that the widow's sister had been screening the calls and had only given them a statement, saying that the family did not see it coming and is in deep shock and mourning. Since I couldn't think of anything else to ask I thanked him and hung up. I figured I knew about as much as I was going to before my deadline, so I sat down and banged out fifteen hundred words. By the time I finished I was pretty hungry from missing lunch, and so I went down to the street and walked a block and a half to a restaurant I liked. It was too warm to snow, and so what came down from the sky was a light mist that sort of just hung in the air. I had the article in my pocket, and on my walk home I dropped it off at copy. It was late and the newsroom floor was almost empty. I felt hung-over and sick from the weather. I decided to go home and go to bed.

Then nothing happened for a few weeks. I mean nothing to do with any of this. It wasn't until about a month later that what happened next happened. I was sitting in McClafferty's bar with Doug Finnerty and a couple of the other guys from the newspaper. We were talking about golf. Somebody was saying they had gotten to the point that they could go out and shoot a buck ten for eighteen holes, give or take five, almost every time. Somebody else asked them how, and the guy who shot a buck ten, a guy named Ranks who worked on the floor and wrote a weekly column about local politics, said that it was through careful practice, discipline, and dedication. He said he went out every Sunday for eighteen, in the summer, and in the winter he kept it up at the indoor driving range and putted into a cup at home. I asked him how the hell he could keep doing that for so long, how he could keep going through it with any sort of investment, especially now that he knew how it was going to turn out every time, give or take a half dozen strokes. But he said he never thought about it. For him, being invested in it wasn't an issue. He just enjoyed it. I told him he couldn't pay me enough to golf every Sunday for the rest of my life.

"It would kill me," I said. "I'd slit my own throat, right there on the first green. Some caddie would go out some Sunday morning and there I'd be, soaking the grass, ruining the lie for everybody else." Everybody laughed except Ranks. "Lighten up," I said to him. "Look, I'll make sure my tee time is after yours. That way you can avoid the blood hazard."

"Seriously," he said, talking loud over the laughter and the noise from the bar. "There is something that you would like to do, every Sunday for the rest of your life. It's not like you can't understand what I'm talking about."

"The rest of my life is a very long time," I said, "and it only feels longer when I have to think of it in terms of Sundays."

It suddenly didn't feel funny anymore. Somebody else said something to Ranks, and Ranks turned away from me and started talking about golf again, and for a minute nobody outside the circle of his conversation said anything or looked at each other. There were three of us that weren't talking about golf, and we sat drinking and smoking. I didn't feel like being there anymore. But I didn't feel like going home, either. I thought about going somewhere else, but I didn't feel like standing up, so I lit another cigarette and pretended to watch a girl on the other side of the room. It's funny how you can suddenly feel like that. All of a sudden none of the things you used to think were good are worth anything anymore.

So we were sitting there, and Ranks was going on about golf, and this big crowd came in. I saw them coming in and then I checked my glass to see how much I had left. We were between the crowd and the bar, and I figured that I could beat them there. So I downed the rest of my drink and went over. They packed in tight behind me, and I pressed up close to the bar and yelled my order to the bartender. Somebody turned on the jukebox. Then somebody put a hand on my shoulder. It was Canasson. His face was red and he was standing sideways between a couple of people, his arm extended over someone's shoulder to reach me. He was grinning.

"Elliot!" he yelled.

"Arthur," I said. I grabbed his hand and pulled him forward. The crowd pushed us close together and he fell against me. I helped him back up and slid sideways, making room for him at the bar.

"Elliot," he said again. "Great to see you!" It was pretty easy to see that he was drunk but he was handling it well and was having a great time. Everyone he was with was the same way. "Elliot," he said, turning back into the crowd. "I want you to meet someone." He reached behind him, and I saw the hair and forehead and big eyes of a pretty brunette bounce up over someone's shoulder, disappear, and then bounce up and hold again, her eyes trained on Canasson. A thin white arm slid out between two close-pressed shoulders, and Canasson grabbed it and pulled and the girl came through, holding her dress in place with one hand.

"Goodness!" she said.

`Elliot," said Canasson, "this is Rose. Rose, this is Elliot Poulain. He's a reporter." He looked back at me, grabbed me by the shoulder, and leaned in close to my ear. "Rose is my secretary," he said, and then leaned back far enough to let me see his grin. "What are you drinking?" he asked. The bartender was coming back, holding my drink.

"Whiskey ginger," I said.

"Bartender," Canasson yelled, "give me another one of those, I'm sorry two more of those, and ring the three of them up together." The bartender put the drink onto the bar, and nodded to him. "Whiskey ginger," Canasson yelled to the girl. "You ever have that?"

"Never in my life," she said. She leaned in and reached for my glass. "Can I try a sip of yours?" she said.

"Be my guest," I said, holding it out to her.

"Ooh," she said, looking up at Canasson as she passed the glass back to me, "that is *good*. Mmm," she said again. "How did I ever live before that?"

"Who are all of these people?" I yelled to Canasson. The crowd had stopped pushing and turned in on itself. Everyone was trying to have a conversation while they waited for their turn at the bar, but everyone was yelling to be heard over everyone else and the noise from the jukebox. Someone started passing a silver flask.

"Friends of mine," said Canasson. He looked them over. "Jesus Christ, there are a lot of them." He laughed again. Someone passed him the flask and he took a long drink, then handed it to the girl. The girl sniffed at it, made a face, and then handed it to me. I took a sip and handed it back to Canasson, who handed it on to someone else. "Kind of makes you wonder where they all go," he yelled to me, "when the rent is due."

Our drinks came. Canasson paid the tab and we all clinked our glasses together and drank. Then we slid out sideways and someone else shuffled in to take our place at the bar. Somebody passed Canasson the flask again, but he shook it and then handed it back. The person he handed it to shrugged, then tipped it all the way back, and drained out what was left. He held it away from his mouth. You could see the last drops falling onto his tongue. We pushed out through the back of the crowd, into a narrow strip of floor between where the bar crowd stood and where the long row of tables began.

"Come and sit with us," Canasson said.

"All right," I said.

"Are you here all by your lonesome?" Rose said. But before I could answer Canasson brought her hand to his mouth and bit her on the knuckles, and she squealed and started giggling. We walked over to the far side of the room, to where a booth formed the corner. The table was crowded with empty glasses, but the seats were empty. Rose slid in across the leather and Canasson slid in beside her. I sat down across from them.

"I love this drink," said Rose. "What did you call it?"

"Whiskey ginger," I said.

"I love it," she said again. She was sucking it up through the little red straws the bartender had used to stir it. "So Elliot," she said, "how do you know Arthur?"

"We've just seen each other around," I said. "Been around enough to know each other."

"Elliot and I," said Arthur, but then he trailed off, and looked at me. "What happened? We were going to have lunch, but then something came up. At work. I had to cancel. It was horribly rude of me, and the thing that made it worse was that I meant to call him and reschedule, and I never did. I've been putting it off for a month now. Rose, make a note of this. First thing Monday morning, reschedule lunch with Mr. Elliot Poulain."

"Reschedule lunch with Mr. Elliot Poulain," she repeated into her drink. She looked up, confused. "Do you have a pen? Elliot, do you have a pen? I need. Hmm. I need to write something down."

Canasson laughed, and kissed her on the side of the head. "It's all right, darling," he said. "Never mind it. I'll remember." He looked at me. "I really have been meaning to call you," he said.

I could feel Rose looking at me, but I looked at Arthur

and said, "how did you say you knew all of these people?"

He waved a hand over towards the crowd standing by the bar. "Just business people," he said. "People. Business people. People I know from business. The club. That sort of thing."

"I never found out what you did," I said.

"I don't do much," he said. "I think you're looking at about half of it." He made a move for Rose's neck. She shrieked and giggled and shied away from it, then slowly melted towards him, relaxing her head back. I leaned back into the cushion and sipped my drink. Rose's eyes were closed and her mouth was open in a narrow slit that showed her teeth white against her very red lips. After a minute I turned away and watched the crowd standing at the bar. Most of them had drinks by now but they were still standing there, all facing in on each other in a tight clump. Then someone came out of the crowd, slipping his wallet back into his overcoat. It was Ranks. I looked over to the table. Everyone from the newspaper was standing and putting on their coats. I almost stood up to go with them. But my drink was still full and after the feeling I had had talking to Ranks about golf the whiskey was making me feel better and like there was no place else to be except where I was and that nothing mattered very much but that that was all right. I watched Ranks and the others go down past the booths to where the tables were, and then lost them as they moved towards the door. When I turned back Rose was curled against Canasson's shoulder, and Canasson was holding up his glass.

"I'm dry," he said. "How are you, Elliot?"

"I've got a bit left," I said. "But go ahead."

"I can wait," said Canasson. "Say, Elliot, what are you up to tonight? You have anything on?"

"Nothing," I said.

"Great," he said. "Why don't you come out with us? There's a new place just opened way uptown. We were there last week for the big hoopla opening, and the man said that if we came back next week there'd probably be enough room to dance. It took an hour to get a drink there, last week, even when I bribed a waiter." He laughed. Rose had her eyes closed and was leaning against his shoulder, and so he slipped his arm around her and then picked up her glass. He passed it to his free hand and drained off the last of it. He looked at me. "How are you coming on that?" he said. I drained it off and slid the glass into the center of the table. He grinned. "Wonderful," he said. "Rose, wake up, Rose. We've got to go to the bar."

He shook her and she opened her eyes, then stared first up at him, then at me, then down at her empty glass. She lifted it, tilted it to her mouth, but when nothing came she set it heavily down on the table and smiled.

"Oopsy," she said, looking at me and shrugging. "Guess you boys just. Can't keep up."

"Come on Sugar," said Canasson. He slid out and gave Rose a hand. She swung her legs around so that they were both resting on the seat cushion, and then gave Canasson her other hand and allowed herself to be pulled out. Her skirt came up, and as she slid off the cushion and her feet hit the floor I saw it come all the way up, saw her white legs going all the way up to her hip. Then her skirt fluttered down and she fell laughing against Canasson's chest. I followed them back across the room, and wove behind them through the crowd towards the bar. Someone took hold of Canasson's arm and he leaned down to listen. Then, he nodded. The man let go and Canasson moved on again, with Rose hanging on his arm. She reached back and wiggled her fingers at me, grinning wide.

We reached the bar. Canasson ordered three more whiskey gingers and the bartender went away to fix them. Then the man who had handed Canasson the flask earlier stumbled up and leaned against the bar. He had the flask in his hand. He reached across the bar and grabbed one of the bottles with the narrow pouring nozzle and began filling the flask. The bartender came back and slid the drinks down in front of Canasson, and then grabbed the bottle away from the flask man. The flask man set the flask down and held up one hand while with the other hand he produced a wad of money. The bartender looked him over, then looked left and right and took the flask and finished filling it. The flask man slapped the bills down on the wood and then took the flask and screwed the cap back on. The bartender put the bottle away and took the money without looking at him. Canasson put the money for the drinks on the bar and then turned around, facing me. He handed me my drink. Rose took hers and held it in both hands. She was tucked in against Canasson's chest, almost under his arm. I watched her suck the top film of the drink off and then wince as the whiskey hit her throat.

"Jack says one more drink, and then we'll go," Canasson yelled to me. "The band should be picking up right about now." He raised his drink to me and tipped it back, draining off half. I did the same. Rose was sucking hers up through the little red straw. "Drink up honey," Canasson said to her. "We've got to go soon. Everyone else is leaving." She looked at him with concern, then sucked harder, and I watched the level of the drink dropping. Canasson raised his glass to me, and we both finished ours. "Let's go," he said.

"I'm not finished yet," said Rose. There was still an inch of tan-gold liquid in her glass.

"We'll get you another when we get there," said Canasson. She looked at him, pouting. "Please darling," he said. "We have to go. I don't want to miss everyone." She shrugged and set her glass down on the bar. I moved in and set mine down next to it and Canasson did the same. He slipped a bill between two of the glasses and then moved off into the crowd. I fell in behind them. The crowd wasn't as tight anymore, and through them I could see a line of people standing at the door, putting on their coats.

"I'm going to go get the coats," said Canasson. "Hold Rose for me for a minute, would you?" He pressed Rose against me. I put my arm around her waist to steady her.

"Gentle now," I said. She nuzzled into my chest. Over her head I watched Canasson take the coats down off the hooks that lined the far wall. I watched someone in the crowd notice him do it, and move to get their coat as well. I put my other arm around Rose, and she pushed harder into me. I could feel the warmth between her legs against my thigh. "Gentle now," I said.

Canasson came back. He helped Rose into her coat and put on his own. I fetched mine from its hook by the table and we moved out into the street. It was drizzling cold and the clouds showed orange from the city glow. Canasson hailed a taxi and as it pulled up along the curb a half dozen more of Canasson's people came out. Someone got into the front, beside the cabbie, and then Canasson let a man and a woman in. The man climbed across the seat and the woman climbed up on the man's lap. Then Canasson got in and Rose followed and sat on his lap. Then I got in. Someone outside shut the door.

The back was tight and hot, and the girls were pressed up against the ceiling. Rose slid off the side of Canasson's lap and wedge her hip between us, leaning over me with her hair hanging in my face. The car started to move. Rose put her hand on my thigh to steady herself. I looked out the window, then leaned my head back against the cushion and closed my eyes, and felt her moving against me. The tires made a wet sound against the pavement. Rose came to rest with her back to me, half on my lap, leaning against Canasson with her arms around his neck. I opened my eyes and watched the lights through the rain hitting the rear windshield.

It took a while to get there, and I almost fell asleep. But when the cab stopped I woke back up. The guy in the front got out and held the door for the rest of us in the back. I slid out and then helped Rose out onto the sidewalk. She stumbled in her shoes. I could hear music coming through walls. Canasson slid out and put an arm around Rose, holding her up. The woman slid out, and then the man. I squinted through the rain. We followed Canasson inside.

Inside was hot and noisy and I couldn't see the bar. I took off my coat but couldn't find anywhere to hang it. The booths that lined the right hand wall were full, and so were the tables to the left. At the far end there was a stage and a big band playing. The horn section had moved up to the front of the stage, and were playing call and response with the singer, who stood off to the right. People were dancing below. Someone shoved me and I fell forward into someone else, and then fell sideways. The man who rode in the front of the cab pulled me up by my arm. I fell into him, then regained my feet. The song was reaching its climax, with the singer and the horns all holding the same note as the other instruments all cut out and the kick drum thumped behind them. Then somebody broke and the guitar picked back up and the bass, and the drum, and the people in front all cheered and clapped as the singer and the horns all drew out the last bars. The man who had helped me up was yelling something, but I couldn't hear him until the song ended.

"What?" I yelled.

"Arthur said he's got a table reserved for us," said the man. He pointed over towards the band. "Back there. By the way," he said, "I'm Tom."

"Elliot," I said, shaking his hand.

We made our way through the crowd and sat down at the table. Canasson and Rose were already there, with the man and the woman from the taxi. There were empty hooks on the wall beside the table and I hung up my coat. Then the band started a new song, and none of us tried to talk over the noise. Tom and I sat down across from Canasson and Rose. A waitress came over, and Canasson ordered a round of something by pointing at the menu, then around at us. The waitress nodded and went away. I leaned back into the cushion and felt the music and watched the people on the dance floor. I watched one couple dancing in front of our table and then watched them disappear around the front of the room, in front of the stage, and then reappear around the other side as the song ended. The waitress came back with a half dozen glasses and we passed them around. Rose looked very awake and clapped her hands when the drink was set down in front of her. Canasson paid the waitress, and she went away. The band started playing again.

"Pull the curtain, would you?" the man I did not know yelled to me. He pointed at a heavy black curtain I had not seen, running along a brass rail that crossed the front side of the booth, up above our heads. I reached back and pulled the curtain forward, over towards Canasson, who caught it and pulled it all the way across. The music went a little dull and muted behind the cloth.

"Finally," said Tom, "I can hear myself think."

"They are God awful loud, aren't they?" said the woman. "My goodness." She put her white-gloved fingers in her ears, and wiggled them. Her husband said something into her ear. "No, it's no good," she said. "Everything still sounds a million miles away. Hi," she said, turning to me. "Have we met? I'm Beverly, but everyone calls me Bev." She put out her hand and I shook it lightly. The man's hand went out beside it.

"Fritz," he said. "Everyone just calls me Fritz. Beverly is my wife."

"Oh," I said. "How do you know Arthur?" I was shaking Fritz's hand.

"Honey," he said, turning to his wife, "how do we know Arthur?"

"God," she said. "How does anyone know Arthur? I think someone sent him down the river to us in a bulrush basket." She laughed and lit a cigarette. She looked at Canasson and I did too, but Canasson pulled the curtain back and slipped out.

"Rose and I are going to go dance," he said, sticking his head back in. "See you all in a minute." He held his hand out to Rose, and Rose took it and slid out. He slid the curtain closed and the music went dull again. I accepted a cigarette from Fritz and then they moved around the booth so that Beverly was facing me. Fritz pushed the ashtray into the center of the table.

"I think we met Arthur," he said, "that night at the Ferguson's when you spilled Champagne on your coat. Wasn't that it? He gave you his handkerchief. No, yes, that was it. I remember because we couldn't find him, and you felt terrible that you weren't going to be able to give it back to him. Remember?"

"No, that isn't it," she said. "It was that night leaving The Grand. Remember? We shared a cab with him."

"That's right, that's right," said her husband. He looked confused. "Who was it who gave you their handkerchief?" he said. "What am I remembering?"

"Who knows," said his wife, drinking and winking at me. "It was Drew Porter," she said, suddenly remembering. "Don't you remember?"

He shrugged. "All those parties blend together for me," he said. He turned to me. "How do you know Arthur?" he asked.

"Well the funny thing is I don't, really," I said. "I met him once a month or so ago, and just happened to bump into him at the bar."

"That's Arthur for you," said Beverly. "I don't think we've ever gone out with him once without him running into somebody he knows and inviting them along. The man knows more people than God." She laughed again, blowing out short bursts of smoke. "We all came here last week, when this place opened, and Arthur ran into a dozen people he knew by name before we even reached the table. I think he probably ran into a dozen more before we left."

"What does he do?" I asked.

"A little bit of everything," said Fritz. "His people have loads of money, although he'd never tell you that. He's part owner of this place, among other things. He's also got a real estate concern and a rental conglomerate. He has people to run them all, of course. He just backs them." He took a drag on his cigarette. "Not a bad friend to have, really," he said. Beverly laughed. She raised her glass.

"Cheers to that," she said.

The curtain opened and Canasson appeared, red faced and grinning. He slid into the booth and took a long drink from his glass. He was sweating, and as he drank he undid his shirt collar and loosened his tie.

"My god," he said, lowering his glass, "it is hot out there. Elliot," he said, looking at me, "Rose wants to dance with you."

"With me," I said. Outside the curtain the band started up again.

"With you," he said. "You'd better get out there, before somebody snags her."

I crushed out my cigarette and slid out through the curtain. Rose was standing on the edge of the dance floor, facing the band and tapping her foot. I put my hand on the small of her back and she turned into me, and we moved out onto the dance floor. The floor was crowded and we danced close together. When she spun and rolled into me and wrapped my arms around her I could feel her through her dress. She held my hands with her fingers intertwined with mine and she kept her eyes closed and let me lead her. The people around us jostled and bumped into us and up on the stage the singer's face was bright red above his white collar and below his tie his shirt was soaked through and showed pink against the skin of his chest. I watched him wipe the sweat out of his eyes with his fingers. Rose's back was to me. I spun her back out and she came back facing me, her eyes open and looking up at me. I kissed her on the lips and she seemed to go limp everywhere but where our mouths met. I held her up. When I pulled away she was smiling and then she spun away again, and then spun back so that her back was to me and I could smell her hair. The singer was holding the long last note and she went tight and seemed to rise as the note went on and on, and then she fell back against me as the note broke.

"Oh my goodness!" she said. She led me back to the booth, then let go of my hand as she pulled the curtain open and dove onto Canasson. "Arthur!" she yelled. Canasson fell back onto Beverly and dropped his drink onto the table, where it spilled. Rose pulled herself back off of him.

"Hello," said Canasson, lifting the ice cubes off the table and dropping them into the empty glass. "And is our friend Elliot a good dancer?"

"A *wonderful* dancer," she said. She slid in beside him. "The very best." She fanned her face with one hand as she lifted her drink to her lips with the other. I slid into my seat and slid the curtain closed. Rose watched me and when I looked at her she winked at me. "Quite a dancer," she said.

The waitress came back, and Canasson ordered another round. The band started up again, a slow, instrumental number that was heavy on the horns and the bass. Fritz passed his cigarettes around and we all took one. I watched Canasson and Rose and felt tired and sober. The music went on and on. The waitress came back with our drinks. Fritz made a show of trying to pay, but Canasson beat him to it. The room was hot and I could feel myself sweating against the booth. We all raised our glasses, but nobody could think of anything to drink to. The song ended, and the bandleader announced that the next would be their last song of the evening. They launched into it. Canasson pulled Rose out onto the floor. Fritz and Tom had begun talking while we were all waiting for our drinks, and were still talking when the music changed. Beverly signaled to me, and we slid out and onto the dance floor. I could see Canasson and Rose, out ahead of us, and then the crowd moved in fast around them and I lost them. Beverly was pressed against me, her hips moving to the music. She'd left half-moons of lipstick on the edges of glasses all evening, and now in the light from the stage her lips showed pale and pink. I had thought that she was not much older than I was, but in the light I could see the fan of wrinkles around her eyes. She danced with her head up, facing me.

We moved into the crowd. I caught sight of Canasson, twenty or so feet away, through the crowd. His eyes were down watching Rose. Beverly was touching my face. I looked down at her, then over to the booth, but the curtain was still pulled all the way across.

That little girl, the singer said, *she drives me crazy*

THAT LITTLE GIRL, repeated the brass, holding their horns high and shining, *SHE DRIVES ME CRAZY*

Drives me crazy
DRIVES ME CRAZY
Get in my car
GET IN MY CAR
To pick her up
TO PICK HER UP
Ain't no one coming
NO ONE COMING
Just my luck
IT"S JUST HIS LUCK
She's got a big white house
BIG WHITE HOUSE
And I go round back
GO ROUND BACK
But Bobby's there saying too late Jack!
TOO LATE JACK!
I got a girl, said the singer, *she drives me crazy.*
DRIVES YOU CRAZY, said the band.
Drives me crazy, said the singer.
DRIVES YOU CRAZY, said the band.

The singer stepped back and the horns took over. Beverly was hanging on my neck. I looked over my shoulder, back to where I had seen Canasson and Rose, but she pulled my face around forward with the tip of her index finger. She gave me a closed-lipped smile. I could count the lines on her forehead. The horns stepped back and faded back into the band. The singer had already stepped off stage. The band dragged it out for a few more bars, each instrument getting louder and louder until the music turned into noise and the beat of the kick drum pulsed behind it. I spun Beverly around on the floor so that I was facing the center. Through the people I caught sight of Rose jumping with the beat, and Canasson caught her around the waist and pushed her higher. I caught a glimpse of the milk-white skin of her inner thigh and then I could only see her head and the top of her back as she rose up out of the crowd. Beverly was clinging to me, her arms beneath my arms and her hands wrapped up over my shoulders. She had her cheek pressed to my chest. The kick drum was coming fast and hard and the cymbals were crashing over it with the horns all blowing in unison and the guitar bending the same note over and over again. Then the beat broke and the horns and the guitar looped back into the main riff of the song. They cycled through the riff four times and then held off the last note, stretching the note before it long and thin and high in the horns and then the whole thing came crashing down with the cymbals.

Everyone stopped dancing and faced the stage and cheered. The band waved and left the stage. I watched the trumpet player, who stayed behind to disconnect the equipment. He was black and sweating and when he bent to disconnect the microphone cord his hat fell off and the lights shone off of his bald head. He ran a hand over his face and then shook sweat from his palm. I could feel Beverly looking up at me, but then she let go and walked away. I looked for Canasson and Rose, but the crowd was still thick on the floor. Then the crowd began to thin and I saw them. Rose had her arms wrapped around Canasson's torso, and was standing up onto her toes to kiss him. He held her lightly at the waist and stooped to meet her mouth. I watched them for a moment, then turned and went back to the booth. But I didn't go inside.

I leaned against the partition and smoked a cigarette. I could hear Tom and Fritz and Beverly talking inside, but I couldn't make out what they were saying.

Rose and Canasson came back. Rose was glowing pink and Canasson grinned when he saw me, and shook my hand.

"Some band, eh?" he said.

"Some band," I agreed.

"I feel like I've been through a *typhoon*," Rose said. "Are they this much every week? I can't imagine I'd survive it that much. I can only imagine how it wears on the musicians."

"Every week," said Canasson. He accepted a cigarette from me and when I offered the pack to Rose he took another and lit them both and handed one to her.

The dance floor was already clearing. Everyone had pressed forward into the bar. A couple of waiters in white aprons started sweeping up. One of them wore shiny black shoes and the other wore dull brown ones, and I wondered if the one in the shiny black shoes was going out after the bar closed, or whether they were his only shoes. They were walking back and forth across the floor, pushing broad brooms in front of them, weaving towards each other.

Down in the bar the two bartenders were moving up and down the line, slipping past each other. I watched one bartender take two bottles by their necks and crack them both open at once against the edge of the bar with the palm of his other hand. A little foam poured over and he let it spill onto the floor and then handed the bottles to a man. The other bartender was mixing drinks into two glasses, doing two things at once with both hands. I felt the tip of my cigarette burn down into between my fingers and I winced and pulled my hand away and my cigarette fell on the floor. I cursed and stooped and picked it back up.

"You all right?" asked Canasson.

"It's nothing," I said. "I'm just clumsy, that's all." Rose was pulling on my hand. She spread my fingers out.

"Ooh," she said, "that looks bad." She ducked inside the booth and came out a second later holding an ice cube in her cupped hand. "Here," she said, sandwiching my hand between hers, with the ice cube on top of the burn. "Is that any better?"

"I think so," I said. I couldn't feel the burn for the alcohol, but I let Rose keep holding my hand. Cold water ran down between my fingers and along my wrist and inside my shirt cuff. Then Rose squealed as the ice cube slipped from between our hands and fell to the floor. She let go of my hand and tried to catch it. "Don't worry about it," I said. "It feels fine." She stood back up. I was still holding my hand out to her. I looked down at it, and then let it fall to my side. Canasson dropped his cigarette and crushed it out under his toe. Rose had left hers inside the booth. We went back through the curtain and sat down.

"It's just something old, passed off as something new," Fritz was saying. "They can create a new demand for it by marketing it as something different. You can get people to do the same thing twice and not notice it. They think they're doing something for the first time." He turned to me. "Elliot," he said, "Beverly tells me you are quite the dancer."

"She's being kind," I said. "I was just trying to keep up."

"He's being modest," said Beverly. She gave me a smile behind her glass, then drank. Her husband saw her do it, and looked at me. Beverly rolled her eyes. "Oh Fritz," she said. "Don't get jealous. We were just having a little fun."

"I'm not jealous," said Fritz.

"Please," said Beverly, "you're positively green."

"I'm not jealous," Fritz said again. He looked at me, and shrugged. "I'm glad that Elliot is a good dancer. I'm glad you had a good time."

She scoffed. "Please darling," she said, "you know how unattractive it is when you lie." She laughed like it was a joke, but I didn't get it, and no one else seemed to think it was very funny either. Canasson offered me another cigarette. Rose's was still going and Tom and Fritz both declined. Beverly took one. "Elliot," she said to me, "would you light my cigarette for me?" I lit it from a book of matches someone had left on the table. "Thank you sweetness," she said, blowing smoke up to the ceiling. She leaned back into the cushions, folded one arm across her lap and propped the elbow of the other on the back of her wrist, the cigarette held high and smoking near her face. She watched her husband. I watched Fritz glance back at her without moving his head.

The waitress came back. "Ladies and gentlemen," she said, "the bar is closing. Can I get you anything else?" She carried her body like it was extra weight. She looked us over. Nobody said anything.

"Champagne," said Canasson. He looked around at us.

"That's really all right," I said. "You don't have to."

"I want to," he said. He turned to Rose. "Champagne, Rose?" he said.

"Mmm," she said. "I love champagne."

"It's settled then," he said. "Champagne it is." The waitress went away without saying anything.

"You really didn't have to do that," I said.

"Enough," said Canasson. "Besides, if I didn't want to I wouldn't have done it."

The waitress came back with the champagne and a half dozen glasses. She popped the cork and it shot off across the empty dance floor. She shook what fizzed over off of her hand and then poured it into the glasses. We passed them around. After the glasses were full there was not much left in the bottle, but Canasson sent the waitress for another glass and when she came back with it he filled it and handed it back to her. He set the empty bottle in the middle of the table.

"To new friends," he said, looking at me. "However we meet them. The world is too small to not share it with those who share it with you." He raised his glass. "And to the best waitress I've ever seen," he said. She laughed and looked at the floor. I could feel Beverly watching me so I watched Canasson. We all drank. The waitress took the glasses away. Then we put on our coats and left.

Outside Beverly wrapped herself in her coat and moved out in front, keeping her back to us. I watched her husband move up beside her and take her arm, but she pulled away and moved a step ahead. I hung back with Tom. Rose was between us. Canasson hung back and then came out a moment later and put his arm around Rose's shoulders. Then they dropped back a step, and Tom and I walked side by side, wrapped inside our coats with our collars up.

"I'm sorry," said Tom, "what did you say you did?"

"Newspaper," I said. "I'm a police reporter."

"Ah," he said. "So how did you say you met Arthur?"

"Somebody was interviewing him. Some business merger or something. I don't remember."

"Ah," said Tom.

"What's wrong with Beverly?" I asked, thrusting my chin in front of us, to where Fritz was walking a step behind her.

"Oh, who the hell knows," said Tom. It was cold and his words were coming in short bursts of breath as the cold air caught in our throats. The sidewalk was slick with ice. "She's just got a bug up her ass because you didn't fall all over her, I'm sure. She gets like this when she drinks too much. She picks some young guy, and if he doesn't go for her she starts feeling rejected and old and she gets moody like this. She's trying to make Fritz jealous."

"Why?"

"Why do women do anything?" he said. He shrugged. "I sure as hell don't know. She used to go on and on about how many people she could have married. Not like she didn't want to marry Fritz, or that she's unhappy or anything like that. Just that she had a lot of men after her. I think she misses it. Misses feeling wanted. Which... I don't know. I can understand."

"Yeah," I said. "Must be hell for Fritz, though."

Tom shrugged again. "I imagine he's used to it by now," he said. "She's been doing it for as long as I've known them." He shook his head. "The poor bastard. I think I'd go about six kinds of nuts, if I had to put up with that."

We walked down a couple of blocks and then Tom said this was where he turned and he gave me his card and we shook hands. Then he turned east and we continued on. Beverly and Fritz had not stopped when I had stopped to say goodbye to Tom, and I watched them moving together, far out in front of me. Fritz had his arm around Beverly's shoulders, and Beverly was tucked in against his ribs. I looked back and saw Canasson and Rose, stopped in the yellow glow from a window display. Canasson was pointing to something behind the glass, and Rose leaned in and kissed him on the cheek. I turned around and headed back towards them. Canasson stood up when he saw me coming.

"Well that's it then," I said. "Beverly and Fritz are too far out ahead, and Tom's headed home. I think I'll catch a taxi, if I can find one." I looked around, but the street was empty in both directions. The parked cars were covered with snow and the windshields were frosted with ice.

"Don't be ridiculous," said Canasson. He pointed down after Fritz and Beverly. "My apartment is only a couple of blocks from here. You're more than welcome to spend the night."

"I couldn't," I said.

"Then at least let me drive you home," he said. Rose laughed. "What," said Canasson. "I can drive. Honestly. I'm a very safe driver. My friend Jim the bartender told me so. He said, "Arthur, you have got to be one of the safest drivers I know. Every time you walk out of here I think you're never going to make it home, but you keep coming back!"" He laughed, but then he stopped. "Of course," he said, "I'm absolute hell on ice. All right, I'll make you a deal." He moved over to me and put his hand on my shoulder. "If you

see a taxi before we get to my building, I will let you take it.
I'll even pay your fare. But if you don't, you have to come
and stay at my place. All right? I won't take no for an
answer."

"What choice do I have?" I said. "Lead the way."

"Good man," he said. He moved over beside Rose.
Rose was leaning down, staring through the glass again. I
moved over beside her and looked as well. She was staring at
a thin silver bracelet on an off-white stand. Two small lights
shone on it, so that the silver caught the light and made it
sparkle as you moved around it.

"It's beautiful," Rose said.

"You like it?" said Canasson.

"I love it," Rose said.

"Well," said Canasson, "I'll buy it for you."

"Don't you dare," said Rose.

"But I will," he said. "First thing Monday morning."

"Don't you dare," she said again, but this time her voice
was pleading, yearning. "I would die if you did."

"Why can't I buy it for you?"

"Oh, I don't know," said Rose. "It. It's just. Well if I
put it on it'll be part of *me*, and I don't want it to be part of
me. I want it in there, behind the glass. I want to be able to
look at it as I go by, and see it in there where I can't touch it.
It's so much nicer that way." She was staring at the bracelet,
but then she broke off and turned to Canasson. "Please," she
said, "please don't buy it for me. Please I would die. Please I
couldn't stand it."

"All right," Canasson said, looking her full in the face.
"All right. All right I won't buy it." He kissed her on the
forehead. "You're wonderful," he said. "Don't ever change."

We continued down the street until Canasson stopped
beneath a broad green canopy covering a brass and glass and
dark wood door. He opened the door with a key and we went
into the lobby, where a doorman's desk stood empty, and
beyond where two pair of elevators faced each other. We rode

up to the eleventh floor. When the doors slid open we were inside a wide and open room, with a staircase going up one side. The room was dark and Canasson led us through it and up the steps. I could see the lights from the city outside a bank of windows behind the staircase. Upstairs three doors lead off the hallway to the left. Canasson led us down to the farthest one and opened it. Inside was a bed and a dresser. The far wall was a curtained window. The carpet and walls and dresser and the bed coverings and curtain were all white.

"Here you go," he said to me. He pointed down the hall. "The next one is the bathroom, and the one after is me. Knock if you need anything. I'll see you in the morning." Rose had her arms around his neck and was grinning up at him. "All right, all right," he said, smiling, without looking at her. "We're going." He looked at me again. "Really," he said. "Make yourself completely at home. If you're up before me there are eggs in the refrigerator, and you can call down to the front desk for anything you want that I don't have. The kitchen is in a little bit of disrepair lately." Rose tugged him and he fell back, slightly, catching himself on the doorframe. "All right," he said, laughing. "All right. We're going. Goodnight," he said to me.

"Goodnight," I said. "Thanks."

"Don't ever mention it," he said. "Just happy to have the company." He stood up straight, saluted, and then stumbled backwards laughing as Rose took his arm and dragged him down the hall. I heard his door open and close, and then I closed my own and got undressed. Standing in my underwear the room was cold and I felt drunk and tired. I got into the bed and curled down under the blankets. I could hear Rose laughing through the walls and, behind it, the lower stream of Canasson's voice rising and falling. I thought that if I could hear them I might have a hard time getting to sleep, but then I fell asleep.

I woke up in the morning feeling hung over and still a little drunk. I got dressed and went downstairs. Canasson's door was closed and the rest of the apartment was empty, so I kind of looked around. Both of the walls that made up the corner were mostly glass, and looked out over the city. I pressed right up against it and looked down, and watched the cars moving in the street and the black dots of people weaving between them. Looking down like that made me a feel a little bit sick to my stomach, though, so I stopped doing it after a minute. Then, after I stopped feeling sick, I started feeling hungry, and I went into the kitchen to make breakfast. I put the coffee on and while I was waiting for it to brew I went upstairs and took a shower. While I was in the shower I heard Canasson's door open and close, and when I went back down the coffee was ready and Canasson was downstairs.

"Good morning, Elliot," he said.

"Good morning Arthur," I said. "How are you feeling?"

"Not bad," he said. I sat down across from him. The table he was sitting at was set parallel to the glass. Canasson looked out, but I kind of looked around the apartment. I still felt kind of sick. Then, after a while, he said, "Diane, my wife, she left last night. Went to stay at her parents" place." I didn't say anything, but he wasn't looking at me, so it was easy to just keep my mouth shut. "A thing like this," he went on, "like her leaving – you see it coming for such a long time, but when it comes, you always think, or at least I always thought, with her, I always thought that it wouldn't come *yet*." He sighed.

"How long have you been married?" I said.

"Eight years," he said. "It was right out of school. Our parents have known each other forever."

"Jesus," I said. "I'm sorry."

"It's all right," He said. "Sorry to put it on you, anyway. I just. I don't have anyone else to tell." He winced, then looked up at me, and laughed. I laughed too, I guess because it seemed pretty funny at the time. I'm really not sure now what seemed funny about it.

Rose came down. She was wearing her dress from the

night before. She tugged it down around her knees as she came down the stairs. She smiled when she saw us watching her. She came over and put her arms around Canasson's neck, and kissed the side of his head.

"Good morning Rose," I said. "Would you like some coffee?"

"Please," said Rose.

I went to get it. When I came back Rose had her head down on the table. I set the coffee next to her and passed Canasson his. He took it and set it down without drinking. Rose rolled her head over towards him, and he stroked her hair back from her face and kissed her on the cheek. I sipped my coffee and stared out the window, out at the sun coming up over the buildings.

After I finished my coffee I said goodbye to them and then left. Outside the wind was blowing warm down the tunnel of the buildings and I walked a couple of blocks and then took a cab up to this diner I know. I ordered breakfast and then I went into the back and called the newspaper from the payphone. Finnerty was in, the secretary said, but he didn't answer when she transferred me through. I tried again and told her to transfer me down to the floor, but the guy who answered said he couldn't see Finnerty on the floor, and hadn't seen him all morning. From the phone I could see into the kitchen and I saw the cook slide my order through the slot, so I hung up and went and ate my eggs. After breakfast I felt better. I sat and read the paper and drank off a half dozen cups of coffee and then wandered down towards the newspaper. I got there just before noon. Finnerty was in the beat office.

"Jesus Christ," he said, "what happened to you last night?"

"Don't ask," I said.

He laughed. "You still got the same clothes on," he said. "That tall bastard you were with take you home and have his way with you?" He had a cigarette going, and he blew smoke out of the side of his mouth and looked up at me through it. He was bent over a sheet, arranging the pieces, just touching them with the tips of his fingers. "Easy shutting that door," he said as I reached for it. I closed it softly. He held his breath over the sheet, then let it out. I lit a cigarette, and pressed the heel of my hand between my eyes.

"I slept at his place," I said. "He's got this big goddamned apartment. Top floor. I watched the fucking sunrise over the city skyline, if you can believe that."

"No shit," said Finnerty. He marked the edges of the pieces against the sheet beneath, then lifted the sheet and slid the pieces into a pile. "What about the girl? Anything happen with her?"

"For him, not for me," I said.

"Aw," said Finnerty. "I would say nice guys finish last but hey, I know you." He stacked the pieces on top of the sheet in a pile, then leaned back against the wall and blew smoke up towards the ceiling. "You should've stayed out with us," he said. "We went over to Field's, and some chick when ape shit over Greene. He couldn't get her off of him." He laughed. "She danced with him the whole night. Every time the poor bastard tried to escape, she just held onto him tighter." He gestured out around him. "Huge fat woman," he said. "Bouncer told me she was in there every week, pulling the same thing. Picks some guy, and doesn't let him go all night." He laughed again. "We almost kicked Greene out of the cab, he smelled so bad. Broad wore enough perfume for three people. His wife must have given him hell when he got home."

"He should be used to it by now," I said.

"Yeah, sure," said Finnerty. "Hey, listen, you had lunch yet?"

"I just had breakfast," I said.

"I haven't eaten yet today," said Finnerty. "I got this Irish constitution, but I got the stomach of a goddamned syphilitic. No shit. I go out drinking like that, it's five, six hours the next day before I can eat. Hell," he said, gesturing in the air with his cigarette, "I almost threw up on the bus this morning. No shit. Riding along thinking, "oh no, here it comes," eyeing this lady's purse, thinking that if it does start to come I'm going to have to grab it just to contain the damage. With my luck, I probably would've gotten arrested for petty theft."

"I thought the Irish were supposed to be lucky," I said. "Maybe she would have felt bad for you. Taken you home, you know. Fed you chicken soup."

He shrugged. "I guess we'll never know," he said. "Thank God." He crushed out his cigarette, and flicked the butt out the window. "What are you doing in today, anyway," he said. "You aren't in until tomorrow."

"I just thought I'd stop in on my way home," I said.

He nodded. "Yeah," he said, "I know what you mean. I don't have shit going on at home either." He moved back to the desk, and began fishing around in the drawers. He came back with a folder and opened it out onto the desk. "Every night, same fucking thing. Go home, have a drink, order dinner, wait for it to get there, watch the news until I fall asleep. The only way I know the days are going by is sometimes my socks are dirty." He laughed. "Fucking ridiculous. There was one thing that happened. This one restaurant, Pancake Palace, that I ordered from sometimes closed down." He lit another cigarette, and talked with it in his mouth. "But that was, lets see that was almost a year ago. Since then it's been pretty much the same."

I laughed. "You used to order pancakes for dinner?"

"What's wrong with that?" he said. "I like pancakes. I like round foods. What? I like eggs, I like pizza, I like hamburgers, I like lots of things." He was counting them off on his fingers. "Whatever the fuck that means, I couldn't tell you. Probably that I like them because they look like tits or something. Or, no, that's good, that we make foods round because we think food ought to come out of tits. Like we're conditioned, from when we're little."

I was laughing harder. "What about waffles," I said. "Or toast?"

"Fuck waffles and toast," he said. "They don't mean shit. And besides, everybody knows the Germans invented the waffle, and the Germans are all soulless bastards. They're Germans. They like straight lines." He shrugged and turned back to sorting through the pieces from the file.

"You're nuts, Finny," I said. "You're fucking nuts. I'm going home."

"Don't let me keep you," he said.

"I knew you were going to say that," I said. He always said it when I was leaving.

"Toodle-fucking-loo," he said. "You know I was going to say that?"

"I think I could have guessed." I waited for him to say something else but he didn't, so I left and went home.

My apartment was a mess. I thought about cleaning it but thinking about it just made me tired because I didn't have anywhere to put anything and all the trash needed to be emptied already, I knew that after I cleaned up I would have to empty it again, and I couldn't get excited about anything I knew I was going to have to repeat right away. So instead I just sat around for a while, and then I fell asleep on the couch. I was still pretty hung over, even after breakfast and the coffee, and when I woke up I felt better but it was late and I knew all it meant was that I wouldn't be able to get to sleep later, when I wanted to. So I went for a walk.

I walked down to the end of the block, and then I ducked into the theater and caught the last ten minutes of a movie. I had seen the movie before, so I knew how it was going to end, but I kind of enjoyed watching it again. Then, as I was leaving, I thought I saw Rose crossing the street. I watched, trying to see if it was her, but the girl didn't turn around, and after a minute I followed her. I followed her for a couple of blocks, and then she stopped under a news kiosk and turned into the light and I saw that it wasn't her. I don't know what I would have said to her anyway. So I went home.

III.

The next day I went in to work, and there were a bunch of guys up in the lounge. Greene and Finnerty were there, and so were some of the guys from the floor. Ted Bradner was over in the corner, looking sort of stunned and like he was a million miles away from everything. Nobody was saying anything and so I walked through to the coffee maker and while I was pouring a cup Greene came over.

"Hi Ray," I said. "What's going on in here?"

"Bradner got called up," he said. "They're shipping the poor bastard out."

"Fuck me," I said. I leaned up against the counter. "Jesus," I said, louder to Bradner, "I'm sorry as hell, Ted." He smiled and waved me off. "Poor bastard," I said to Greene. "I think I'd rather do just about anything than go to Korea. I think I'd probably blow off a toe or something. Why the hell are they calling him up, anyway?"

"Reserves," said Greene. "They're calling up everybody."

"He's in the reserves?"

"It's how he paid for school."

"Be a hell of a waste if he gets killed," I said. "Life of the mind, death of the body. It's ironic. It's beautiful." Greene made a disgusted noise through his teeth and shook his head. "Well how the hell do you look at it," I said. "It's not as though there is really a good way to look at it that isn't dark in some way."

"He's serving his country," said Greene. "Making the world safe for freedom and democracy and all of that. You know. The big stuff." He held out his cup and I poured him more coffee. We both watched Bradner. He stood to shake hands with someone as they headed out. Then he sat back down. No one looked at him.

Bradner kept it together until everyone was gone, then he started to look like complete hell. His face got white and he kept his hand pressed to his mouth, like he was afraid of what he would say, like he was afraid to touch or do or say anything, because it might jinx him. It was just me and Greene and Bradner in the lounge, so I poured Bradner a cup of coffee and when I went over to give it to him I swung the door closed and sat down next to him.

"Hey," I said. "Here, drink this."

"Thanks," he said. He took it and blew off the steam. Then he drank some. The coffee was hot as hell. I had burned my tongue on it already. But Bradner didn't seem to notice. "I don't know how I'm going to tell my mother," he said. "Jesus Christ."

"Hey," I said, "cheer up. Maybe it'll make a man out of you."

"That's what my uncle said," he said. "I almost shot him."

"See?" I said. "You're ready to go."

He laughed and shook his head. He took another sip of coffee but this time he winced and then he leaned back in his chair. He looked at Greene and me, but Greene was looking at the floor.

"Look," he said, all of a sudden. "I don't know what's going to happen when I go. So. I just want. I just want to say now that I. I'm going to, you know. I'm going to miss you guys. I mean what I'm trying to say is that I just want you to know that the time we've. The time we've had together here, working here, together, it really, it has really meant a lot. You know. To me." He looked at us, I guess hoping that we would say something. But neither one of us did, so he looked at the floor and kept talking. "You know it's just. It's just you don't… get a lot of chances to really, to really take stock of what's important in life. I mean I guess, you know, I guess we don't take a lot of opportunities to do it. You know you just sort of go along and then somebody… somebody is gone and you realize that you never… you never took the time to tell them how you really feel about them."

"I tell people how I really feel all the time," I said. "I told a dozen people this week to go fuck themselves, and meant it for every one of them." I looked at Greene and Greene gave me a look that said that maybe it was a funny thing to say but that nobody was going to laugh at it. So I looked back at Bradner and I put my arm around his shoulder and said, "Look, most likely they're gonna give you some cushy job behind a desk somewhere and you're never even going to see combat. I mean, Christ, you've got *skills*. They don't just send guys with specialized skills to the front lines. They have the poor broke bastards who drop out of high school to do that. The sons of bitches who don't know any better, who think taking a bullet for the bastards in Washington is a high fucking honor." I slapped him on the back, hard. "Christ," I said, "you're going to be fine. I guarantee it. We're gonna laugh about this some day."

He smiled, but I could see that his heart wasn't really in it.

"You guys are good friends," he said. "I'm really going to miss this place." He looked at us. "Will you guys write to me? I can get letters and everything, and I can send the newspaper my address when I know where I'm going to be stationed. Do you think you could write me letters?"

"Sure," I said. "It'll give me something to do when I'm avoiding work around here."

"Sure," said Greene. "Sure we will, Ted. I'll even try and get Carol to send you some cookies or something. And you can write and tell us if there's anything you need over there, and we can try and send it."

"Tell you what," I said to Bradner. "Lets get out of here. I'll buy you lunch."

"Thanks," he said without looking at me. "But I don't feel very hungry."

"Come on," I said. "Do me a favor. You know this place drives me nuts if I stay in here for more than twenty minutes in a stretch. If I take you out to lunch everybody'll think I'm a good guy instead of a screw-off. It'll be good for my reputation." I looked at Greene. "Lunch?" I said. "I think I still owe you a hotdog. Come on. Hotdogs on me."

"I gotta get home," he said. "I promised Carol I'd take the kids shopping for spring clothes."

"What happened to their clothes from last spring?" I said.

"You know how it is with kids," said Greene, putting on his jacket. "They grow."

"What the hell are you even doing here?" I said. "You aren't in until Wednesday."

He was buttoning his collar. "I came to say goodbye to Ted," he said. "Vince called and said they were having a little send-off thing in the lounge, and that I should come by." He paused. "Didn't he call you, too?" he said.

"No," I said.

"Oh." He looked embarrassed, then said, "I guess he just figured you were in today anyway, and that you'd hear about it through the grapevine. I'm sure he just called the people who weren't coming in."

"Yeah sure," I said. "Come on," I said to Bradner. "Lets walk Ray out and then get some lunch, ok? It'll be good for you. Help you clear your head." I tugged at his arm.

"All right," he said, acting put upon but grinning. "All right, all right already, we'll go have lunch. Geez," he said to Greene, "how do you put up working with this guy?"

"They pay me extra," he said, "but you gotta take that to your grave." Beside me, I felt Bradner flinch. "You know, I mean," said Greene. "You know. Don't tell anyone."

"Come on," I said.

Greene said he was going home, but when we got him outside we changed his mind. I think it was the way Bradner looked that did it. Anyway, it was while we were at lunch that Bradner offered me his family's lake house for the summer. He had been quiet sitting at the table across from Greene while we ordered. He still wasn't talking after that, so I ordered him a drink. If he heard me he didn't act like it. Then, after the drink came, I clinked glasses with him and he looked up at me with a kind of frantic look in his face and offered me the house. I guess he felt like time was running out for him, before he had to go, and he had a lot of things to do, because he said it like he didn't have time to form the words, or wait for my answer.

"Sure," I said. It was strange, because he said it like me taking the place would be a favor to him. Like it would be one less thing for him to worry about. I didn't really have any plans for the summer anyway, and I wasn't really that in love with my apartment. For one thing, it was always about a hundred and fifty degrees in there from June until mid-September. The windows all opened onto an alley and you couldn't even get a breeze going through if you tried. I didn't really have any good reason to stay in the city, either, except for the job. What I mean is that I didn't have a girl or anything like that. Plus it seemed like it would mean a lot to Bradner.

"Oh thank God," he said. "Look there's a cat that comes to the back door and you have to feed it milk but if you leave the milk out overnight it will attract raccoons and other cats, so don't leave it out overnight, ok? And the front door sticks a little bit. And the third stair squeaks, but if you step on the outside edges it doesn't make any noise at all." He had his key ring out, but he was having a hard time getting the key off. He wasn't really shaking; it was more like he couldn't pay attention to what he was doing. "Here," he said, finally, handing me the ring. "It's that one." I took the key off and set it on the table between us. I gave the ring back to Bradner and he put it into his pocket and then put his hands in his lap.

"Drink up," I said. "For god's sake, you're making me nervous."

"And there's a trick to getting the basement door open," he went on, looking at the key, then off across the empty space of the restaurant. "You have to lift up on the handle. And local police and fire's numbers are all up on a note next to the telephone. And there's a rowboat underneath the back porch. You'll have to wash it off but it's." He couldn't think of the right word for a second. "Sea worthy," he said. "Ray," he said, "I have some suits that I think would fit you. Would you – would you like some of my suits?"

"Sure," said Greene. "You don't have to do that, though."

Bradner nodded, without looking at him. "I'm letting my apartment go," he said. "I've got to move everything up to my mother's anyway. It'll be one less thing to worry about."

"Do you need any help?" said Greene. "I don't get off work until probably five or six but after that-,"

Bradner shook his head. "It's ok," he said. "My brother's coming over, he's going to help me do it." Then his face got kind of calm, I guess because he was thinking about moving and it took his mind off being called up. He picked up his drink and sipped at it until it was gone, not really looking at it. I flagged a waiter down and ordered him another. He drank it down in one pull.

"Christ," I said to him, turning around to face into the room, looking for a waiter. "Maybe you should slow down, Ted." I put my hand up.

"No, that's all right," said Bradner. "I'm finished. Put your hand down. That's all. I feel a lot better now. Please. Really. Thank you for looking out for me but I don't need it. I'm all right now. Put your hand down."

I put my hand down. We all sat, looking down at the table. Our food came and we ate without saying much. Greene and I split the check and Bradner went to use the bathroom for about ten minutes. Greene and I waited at the bar. After about five minutes I ordered us two rum cocktails. Greene took his and held it, swirling the ice around, and I drank down half of mine.

"Bradner is sure having a hell of time of it," he said, finally. He looked over towards the bathroom. "Maybe they'll give him a psych evaluation, or something. Find him unfit for duty, on account of his nerves."

I shook my head. "It would never do," I said. "Everybody's like that before they go. I mean, they don't act the same way, but everybody feels the same way. Not everybody goes St. Anthony the Abbot."

"That's a hell of a thing to say," said Greene, wincing back the first swallow of his cocktail. "He gave you a fucking house. Free rent until fall." He looked over again at the bathroom. "The poor bastard is going to *war*," he said. "The fucking *war.*"

I shrugged. "He probably won't go to the front," I said, "even if he is sent overseas."

"That's not the point," Greene said.

We finished our drinks and I paid, and then Bradner came out of the bathroom, looking pale and with his hair wet down against his forehead, like he had washed his face a couple dozen times. Then we left and walked back towards the newspaper, but I left them when we got to my building. Bradner gave me directions to the lake house, and I asked Greene if I could borrow his car. He said he had to be at the paper all day, but if I came by the office he would give me the keys. I thanked Bradner and told Greene I'd see him tomorrow, and then I went upstairs and started packing. While I did that I called my landlord and told him I was moving out.

I finished packing by dinner time. I didn't have a hell of a lot of stuff to begin with, and when I had it all laid out and I saw how much of it I didn't really want to keep it seemed like a hell of a lot less. I had a couple of suits that had belonged to my father that I hadn't decided on, laying out over the back of the couch, and so I tried them on and when they fit pretty well I decided to keep them. We were about the same size. People always said that I looked like him, too, but I always figured that they thought it was a compliment and just said it to make me feel better. My father was a pretty

49

handsome guy, but the thing that made him seem really good-looking was the way he carried himself. He always stood up real straight, and he had his hair combed all the time, and he shaved every morning. That's one big difference between us, that made me think that they were lying when they said that I looked like him. I always look like hell, no matter what I do. Even when I shave and comb my hair and wear a suit and stand up straight. I just can't pull it off. When I got older and started to notice that it wasn't just normal kid bed hair, or the fact that I didn't stand up straight, that I actually just looked like hell most of the time, I told somebody that I didn't think I looked like my father at all. I explained about how he always looked great and how I never looked great. They told me it didn't matter, because there was something about me that just reminded them of him. They said I couldn't escape it, even if I tried. I think they thought that it was a compliment, but I don't know. Sometimes people can be pretty smart, but most of the time they don't make any sense at all.

After that I felt tired and so I lay down on the couch and tried to fall asleep, but I couldn't. I guess I was excited. So I read for a while. Then I started falling asleep without realizing it, and so I put the book down and just lay there and thought about Bradner going to war. I couldn't picture it, and the harder I tried the more awake I felt. I guess the problem was that I didn't know what to picture. I didn't really know what his uniform would look like, or what sort of setup they had over there. I didn't really know anything about it. So instead I started wondering what Canasson was up to. I thought about calling him, but then I figured that if he was at home he was probably asleep by now, and if he wasn't it meant that he was out and I wouldn't be able to find him.

It's weird, but thinking about Canasson made me sort of panic because I felt like I was missing something. This happens to me a lot. Suddenly, for no reason at all, I'll start thinking that everyone else in the world is out having the time of their lives, and I'm missing it. Like I could be there in five minutes, but there's no way I'm ever going to find out about it, and so I miss it. When I was a kid, one of my friend's parents showed me this test. He said you think of yourself in a white room, with no windows and doors, and then figure out how you feel about it. I told him I felt like I was missing everything, that the world was going by without me and that they didn't care that I wasn't there. He said that the test was to determine how you felt about being dead.

So after that I couldn't sleep, and I got up and walked around the apartment for a while. Then I decided what the hell and gave Canasson a call. He picked up after a couple of rings.

"Elliot," he said. "It's great to hear from you."

"Hi Arthur," I said. "How are you doing?"

"Better now that you called," he said. "I've been sitting here going crazy. What are you up to?"

"Nothing," I said. "I was hoping you were up to something."

"Nothing at the moment," he said. "But Christ, could I use a drink. Where are you?" I told him I was at home. "Look," he said. "What would you say to meeting me in a few minutes?" He named a bar a couple of blocks from my building. I said sure and then I hung up and got dressed. But after that I waited around for a few minutes. I didn't want to be the first one there. So I picked up the book I had been reading. I was right at a pretty interesting part, so I decided to finish the chapter and then go down to the bar. But the chapter was pretty long, and by the time I finished it had been almost twenty minutes. I hadn't noticed, and I got that panicked feeling again, and thought maybe he had gone and since I wasn't there he had left again. So I left my apartment and hoofed it down to the bar. But Canasson was inside, talking to the bartender. He waved at me when I came in.

"Jesus man," he said. "Did you run here?" I was breathing heavy, and I guess my face was red. He laughed. "Did you think I was going to leave?" I was going to say something, but I hadn't caught my breath yet. He laughed again and slapped me on the back. "My friend needs a drink," he said to the bartender.

"Whiskey and soda," I said.

"Make it two," said Canasson. He dropped a bill onto the counter and the bartender scooped it up.

"You're going to have to let me buy you a drink, one of these times," I said, climbing up on the barstool next to his. "I feel like a goddamned mooch."

"That's very decent to you," he said. "You get the next one." The bartender brought our drinks and Canasson sipped his and said, "so what are you doing up?"

"Packing," I said. "I've been packing all afternoon. A guy at the office got called up, and he's letting me use his house on the lake for the summer." I sipped my drink, but my stomach was knotted up from the running and so I set the drink down to wait it out. "I haven't been up there yet, but he says it's beautiful."

"Where is it?" he asked. I told him. "A lot of people have summer homes up there," he said. "A real seasonal kind of town. A lot of money, but only for half of the year. During the winter its pretty dead, except for the ice fishing. I've been up there a couple of times. Your friend is right, it is beautiful up there."

"You'll have to come visit," I said. "Show me the sights." My stomach felt better, so I took a longer drink. "So why are you up?" I said. "I was kind of worried that you'd be asleep."

"No, not asleep," he said. "Having a hell of a time getting to sleep lately." He laughed. "Ever since Diane left I just keep pacing around the apartment. I always convince myself that I'm going to fall asleep pretty soon, and so I never get dressed, I just walk around up there, thinking that it'll be too much work to go down to the street. But then I never end up falling asleep, and so I walk around for hours up there. God. It's like being trapped in someone else's head, up there.

All these pictures staring at me all the time and I don't have the heart to take them down or put them away."

"Do you think she's coming back?"

"I don't know," he said. "She's left before, for maybe a couple weeks at the most but this time was different. Usually it's because we had a fight or I did something that she's angry about. But this time there wasn't anything leading up to it. I just came home and she was gone. I mean I guess I know it had been coming for a while, but it had never come without that big, final fight that sent her off. It feels like - I don't know - like the wheel skipped a cog, or something, and now we're one step ahead of where we're supposed to be, and I haven't caught up. I don't know. Does that make any sense?"

"Sure," I said. "It makes sense."

Both of our glasses were empty and I called the bartender over and ordered two more, and while he went to get them I put the money on the counter before Canasson could do it, but he didn't seem to notice. He was facing me on his barstool, but he was staring at the ground. The bartender brought our fresh drinks and took the money.

"It's just that - ," Canasson said, taking his new drink. But then he stopped and looked at me and said, "I'm sorry, Elliot, I don't want to burden you with this."

"Please," I said. But I couldn't think of anything else to say, so I said, "you're not burdening me." That didn't sound right, I guess because he *was* burdening me, and we both knew it, and it was exactly *because* he was burdening me that I wanted him to continue. I guess I was feeling a little bit like a bad friend after my lunch with Bradner. I hadn't known what the hell to say to him, and when he said I could use the house it made it even more important that I said the exact right thing, to make him feel all right.

"Well," he said, "I guess it's just that. That usually she cries and yells and locks herself in our bedroom, and I wait downstairs sort of pacing around, and when she comes down I apologize, and she tells me that it's too late, you know, and I say give me another chance, and sooner or later we calm down. Or she leaves and goes to her father's house for a couple of days and when she comes back we patch things up. And it's kind of how we blow off steam when we need it, and in a way… in a way it's like we both understand how important the relationship is to us, because it makes us act crazy like that. Does that make any sense?"

"Sure," I said. I drained my glass and ordered another. Canasson saw me do it, drained off what was left in his and ordered the same. He dropped a bill on the counter without looking at it. He shook his head.

"But this time," he said, "and this is really throwing me for a loop, is that this time it just disappeared. It just evaporated like we left it out in the sun too long, or something."

"She's just upset," I said. "She'll come back."

"I know," he said. "I know, I know. It feels more permanent, this time. I mean I've called her father's house and I know she's there and all right and he says she doesn't want to talk to me and I understand that, because she never wants to talk to me when she leaves, but I don't usually have to call around to make sure she hasn't been kidnapped, or something like that. I mean I knew right where she would go, because it's where she always goes, but it really feels like this time she didn't want me to know. Like she didn't want me to find her."

"It sounds like you've been through this a hell of a lot of times," I said. I was feeling the booze and feeling very casual and friendly. Canasson looked sick in the face and I slapped him on the shoulder. He snapped out of it and smiled at me, but his eyes were blank. "Take it easy," I said. "She'll come back, no problem."

"I hope you're right," he said. "Or, Christ, I don't know. Maybe I hope you're wrong. I can't think straight about it. I'm all backwards lately. I don't even eat anymore. I don't know what to do when she's gone. I mean, not like I miss her. I mean I do miss her, but what I mean is that I don't know what to do with myself. There's no point in going home anymore."

He went on about it for a while. After a few more rounds we moved from the bar into a booth at the far side of the room. At some point I started talking, and I watched the people at the bar and the few people dancing around the jukebox and when I turned back to Canasson I found that I was still talking and I wondered what I had said. Then Canasson spoke for a while, but all I remember from it is the phrase, "like a rocking horse made of matchsticks" and the fact that Diane always only ate half of anything she got. Then, a while later, I noticed that he was crying. He did it with his head down on the table and cradled in his arms so that no one would notice. So I leaned back into the cushion and noticed how drunk I felt. The waitress came back and I ordered a couple of coffees and while she was getting them I excused myself and went to the bathroom. The light inside was pretty painful and for a minute I thought about peeing in the corner of the barroom, just so I wouldn't have to deal with it. But then my eyes adjusted, and I felt better. When I came out Canasson was sitting upright in the booth looking pale and sober, sipping his coffee. I took mine and took a sip and burned my tongue and cursed Christ and hell and everything in between and Canasson laughed.

"Look, Elliot," he said, leaning over the table towards me. "I want to thank you for making me go out tonight. I didn't really want to at first but now, now I'm glad that I did. I feel a lot better."

"I'm glad to hear it," I said. I stuck out my tongue and tried to look at it, but couldn't see it past my nose. "I'm glad you came out, too. I've had a hell of a good time." I lit two cigarettes and handed one to Canasson. It was a strange thing to do but I was drunk and anyway he didn't act like it was strange so I didn't worry about it. He took it carefully. He turned sideways in the booth, so that his back was against the side wall and his feet were up on the seat, and blew smoke up towards the ceiling. I watched him do it, then I did the same. I heard the bartender shout last call. The waitress came over with the bill. I closed my eyes and felt the room tilt, then right, then tilt and begin its slow, steady revolution.

"I think I need to go home," I said. "I'm drunk."

"Could be worse," he said. "You could be ugly." He was paying the bill. "All right," he said. "Lets go. Come on," he said, pulling on my legs. I slid down so that I was lying flat on my back on the bench seat. He pulled me farther, until my feet touched the ground. He helped me up, and put my arm over his shoulders and his arm around my ribs. One of the waiters came over but Canasson shook his head. The waiter backed off. We moved towards the door and then the door was opening and then we were out in the street and there was the loud noise of the door closing. I felt cold and I pulled my coat collar closed and held it there.

"This way," I said, beginning to walk, leaning on him. "This way is home. This. Way."

We made it two blocks, and then we stopped and had a cigarette, sitting on the front steps of a building I didn't recognize. Canasson didn't have a hat, and he huddled down inside of his coat, his body curled down over his knees. I went to piss behind some trash cans and when I came back he was walking around in circles to keep warm, and we walked to my building and went up the stairs.

"My place is kind of a fucking mess right now," I said. "But you – you can have the couch. I'm going to sleep in the bathtub." I got the key into the lock and pushed the door open. Then I stepped inside and tripped over one of the boxes I had left near the door. I heard Canasson feeling along the wall for the light. I rolled over on my back and stared up at the ceiling. The light came on and I closed my eyes and the world became a warm red glow. "Just leave me here," I said.

"I can't close the door with you here," said Canasson, "your feet are in the way."

"It's a safe neighborhood," I said. "Just put some. Hmm. Put some milk in a pan out there, to keep the cats away from me." I heard and felt his footsteps in close to my head, and then his hands were under my arms.

"Come on," he said, dragging me across the floor. His tie was hanging in my face and I swatted at it as we moved. "All right," he said. "All right. Ok." He let go of me and I heard the door close. "All right," he said again, but this time to me, "you want to go into the bedroom? Or up on the couch?"

"I've never been more comfortable," I said. "Just. You just. Just do what you have to do. Don't worry about me. I've never felt better. I got everything I need right here." I reached blindly around on the floor around me. "Everything I need," I said.

"You better be all right," he said, "because I'm going to leave you here."

"Hey," I said, "whatever you feel like you gotta do. Mi casa su casa."

"All right," he said. Then he didn't say anything for a while, but I heard him getting undressed. Then the lights went out, and the red glow stopped. I opened my eyes and looked around. I knew that I should get up, but I didn't want to. I heard Canasson moving around on the couch, but the couch's back was to me, and I couldn't see him. There was pain in my hip, I guess from when I fell, but it felt very far away. I pulled my coat closed around my throat and crossed my arms over my chest to keep it closed. Then I pulled my hat down over my eyes. I felt pretty comfortable. I lay falling asleep for a while. Then I started thinking about Diane, and wondering what I had said to him about her. I couldn't remember and I thought maybe that meant that he couldn't remember, either, and I felt a little better. Then I started wondering if maybe Diane wasn't coming back, since this time had been so different from all the other times. It seemed pretty easy to imagine, since I had never really spent any time with them together. I tried to imagine what it must be like for him, alone in that apartment, not used to just himself, the way I was, but I couldn't. I didn't know what to think of. So I gave up. I'm really no good at imagining couples. I've met a few people who have to be in a relationship all the time, and I think it's probably because they only understand people in couples. But I'm the opposite. I just see two people who sit in the same room a lot. That's what I saw when I thought of Arthur and Diane. So I went to sleep.

I woke up before him. I had already packed everything in my kitchen, and so I left and went down the street and bought a couple cups of coffee and a dozen donuts. When I got back to my apartment the couch was empty, and I heard the shower running. The paper was outside and so I sat down and ate three or four donuts while I read through it. While I was reading the paper Canasson got out of the shower and came out into the living room wearing only his pants. I looked up at him as he came in, and then I looked away again but I didn't want it to seem like I was looking away. So I looked back at him and tried to only look at his face. But that was no good because he kept moving. He just stood there in the living room, drying himself off. You could tell that he was the type that had a hard time keeping on weight. He looked like he probably ran the hundred meter or something in college, and his coach had sent him to the weight room. He had that kind of build. Real skinny, but thicker around the chest and shoulders than you would expect him to be. Anyway he stood there toweling off, and I sort of pretended not to notice. I finished the article I was reading and then folded up the paper and said, "There's coffee on the counter. I didn't know how you took it but there's cream in the refrigerator and a couple sugars in the bottom of the bag."

"No kidding?" he said. "Those guys were wrong about you, you're all right." He laughed and slapped me on the arm and went to get the coffee. I could tell that he was only joking because we both felt like absolute hell. It was like the way some people smile, even when they're in a lousy mood, and you can tell that they're not really happy even though you can see all of their teeth. It was like that, only with him it was joking. He mixed in the cream and the sugar, and then stirred the coffee with his finger. "Anything new in the world?" he said.

"Just the same old," I said. "Heads you win, tails I lose."

"Mmm," he said, nodding and sipping at the coffee. Then, "Christ, what time is it? I've got to be in to work." He checked his watch. "Damn," he said. "All right. Sorry to run out on you like this Elliot, but I really do have to go. Christ." He pressed his hand to his forehead. "I am so sorry to run out like this. Look, are you free this afternoon? Maybe we could have lunch."

"I'm moving all day," I said. "I don't know what time I'll be done."

"Right," he said. "Well look, give me a call when you get settled out there. We'll get together then."

"Sure," I said. He was moving towards the door with a donut in one hand and the coffee in the other. "Sure, I'll give you a call," I said. "You can come out to the lake." I opened the door for him and he stepped out backwards.

"I'm sorry to run out," he said again. Then, "thanks for the coffee. And for letting me stay here."

"Don't mention it," I said. He was moving across the landing, then turned towards the stairs and headed down. "I'll call you," I said.

He waved and then disappeared below the rise of the stairs leading up from my landing, and then listened to his footsteps as they moved farther and farther down. Standing in the doorway I started thinking about what I had to do and how to go about doing it. Then I went back inside and went into the kitchen I put my head under the faucet and drank a few mouthfuls of water. I woke up wearing my coat and hat, but took them off when I came back with breakfast. I put them back on and went out and down the street to the newspaper. I felt like I was skipping town under the radar, and I wanted to be in and out as fast as possible, before anyone saw me and asked what I was up to. It didn't make any sense, but that's how I felt. Sometimes it's easy to feel like that, when you feel lousy anyway. Sometimes it's easy to feel like the world is out to get you.

I found Greene up in the office. He was sitting at his desk, smoking in his undershirt. I looked him over and almost said something, but then didn't. He looked up at me, then turned back towards the desk and pushed out so he was facing me fully.

"Jeee-sus," he said. "You look like shit. What happened to you?"

"Canasson," I said.

"The slick from the bar the other night?"

"Yeah," I said. "I'm helping him work through some issues."

"Lucky him," said Greene. "He got you doing anything else you're unqualified for? He gonna have you circumcise his kid?" He laughed, then choked on his cigarette. His curled forward in the chair, coughing hard with his face down between his knees. The cigarette fell on the floor and rolled a little ways and got stuck between two planks. I leaned over and picked it up and dragged it all the way down to the filter, then flicked it over Greene's head out the open window. It was a pretty slick move, but Greene missed it because he was still coughing. So I said, "I need your car keys. You told me I could borrow your car today, remember?"

"Yeah yeah," he said, his voice all hoarse from coughing. He raised himself back up, then leaned back in his chair and fished around in his pants pocket. He came back out with the keys and tossed them to me. "Bring it back with a full tank, would ya?" he said.

"You know I won't," I said.

"I don't know why I associate with people like you," he

said, shaking his head.

"Please," I said. "You're married. You'd go crazy if you didn't have someone like me in your life. We'd find you in here one day hanging from the rafters in your undies with your fucking pants knotted around your neck. You'd die smelling your own ass." I held up the key. "Where is it?" I said.

"Back lot," he said. He was fishing in the pocket of his jacket, hanging on the wall. He came back with a fresh cigarette. "You're welcome," he said.

"Thanks," I said. He turned back to the desk.

I left the office and went outside and found Greene's car around back. He had this rusted-out Keller, and I figured I could haul most of my stuff in one trip, if I left my furniture on the curb. I didn't have the money or the energy to put my stuff in storage for the summer. So I drove back to my building. I hadn't driven in a while, and I felt really nervous going those few blocks. I knew I needed to get a car to go back and forth between the house and the city, but I wasn't sure if I should buy one there or look around here. I figured I had two more days until I had to be in to work, and I could probably find a car out by the lake. While I was thinking this out I loaded up my stuff. Then I dragged my couch and my bed down the stairs and leaned them up against a telephone pole. Then I said goodbye to my apartment and locked the door. One the way out I put the key under the landlord's door.

Then I left the city. Outside the limits the buildings gave way to farms. The day was clear and there was a dusting of snow on the ground that was melted along the ridges of the ruts out in the fields.

The main route to Bradner's house ran south of the lake and then turned north, and then turned off and onto the road that looped the lake. Turning right the loop took you down along the south shore, and then past the north end of Main street. Past that you went up a hill past the facades of a couple dozen houses and then the bay ended, and the road went along the shore south until you came around heading due east again, and the lake wide enough you can't see the far shore. Turning left onto the loop the road cut in to run along the beach and the carnival gates. Past that the road went around with the shore to take you east, along past small summer homes and waterfront cabins. Then, beyond that, before the bay opened up into the lake on the north side, the first few condominiums showed, with their aluminum docks all bobbing on pontoons.

I got to Bradner's house around noon. It was just south of the turn-off. It was a pretty nice-looking house. I looked around for a minute, then I started unloading my things into the yard and then carrying them into the house. Lifting all of that stuff, I sort of sweated out a lot of the booze. Then I started unpacking, but the house was freezing and I couldn't figure out how to turn on the heat. So instead I left and went into town. I had lunch in a diner on Main street. It was two o'clock, and I knew Greene needed his car back by five and it would take me an hour to get back to the city, so I ate pretty fast and then went back to the house and unpacked my gloves and a sweater and put them on and then unpacked the rest of my stuff. It took a couple of hours. Then I locked up and drove back to the city. I would have made it in time, but I got caught in traffic downtown and had to wait for half an hour to get through. By the time I got to the newspaper it was five-thirty, and Greene was standing on the sidewalk outside, huddled down in his coat. He looked up when he saw me coming, but he didn't move. There were no parking spaces, so I had to pull into the lot. Greene came running over.

"Where the hell have you been?" he said when I got out. He sounded more anxious than upset. "Christ, I even tried to call Bradner to get the number to the lake house."

"I was stuck in traffic," I said. It was true, but I felt lousy about saying it, like I was giving him a bad excuse, like I didn't respect his intelligence to come up with anything better. So I said, "honest. It was ridiculous coming through downtown. A total pain in the ass. When you go home, you may want to skirt the city."

He was moving around the car, over towards me, but looking at the car and moving for the driver's seat. "All right," he said. "Ok. Thanks." He got in and started the engine. I swore under my breath because I had forgotten to fill the tank. I had meant to, I had just forgotten in the rush to get back in time. So I just laughed.

"God, this looks awful," I said. "I meant to fill it up, honest I did. I just was rushing to get back here so I wouldn't make you late. Look, I can give you some cash for it pretty soon. I don't have any on me right now. I'll leave it on your desk next time I'm in."

"All right," said Greene. He looked miserable.

"Look I'm really sorry," I said. But that didn't seem to help, so I said, "what? What is it?"

"Look Elliot," he said, looking right up at me through the open window. "You ask to borrow my car to move your stuff, that's fine. That's what friends are for. You bring it back late, with an empty tank, not so fine, but not a huge deal. But you act like a prick all the time, Elliot, and it makes me not want to put up with this shit. Ok?"

I nodded. "Yeah, ok," I said. "I know. What can I say? I'm sorry. I really am."

"I know you are," he said, nodding and looking straight out through the windshield. "I know. I. I don't know. I gotta go. I'm late for supper." He started rolling up his window.

"I'm sorry," I said again. "I'm really sorry, Ray. I'll give you some money. I'll leave it on your desk." He waved, but he didn't look at me or stop rolling up the window, and by the time I said "your desk" the window was already closed. I leaned back from the car and he pulled away and made a loop around the parking lot, then waved as he pulled past me and out into the street. I waved back and then stood watching him drive away. I felt pretty lousy about the whole thing, and felt like just going back to my apartment and pretending it didn't happen, but then I remember that I didn't have an apartment, and so I went inside. The beat office was empty and I sat down at my desk and smoked a cigarette. I kept feeling worse and worse while I was sitting there. By the time my cigarette was finished I felt like I could barely move. One of those times where you feel so lousy that you can't think of a good reason to do anything. Even simple things, like lifting your arms. And the other thing was, my hangover started to come back. I couldn't believe it.

Anyway I thought about calling Canasson for a ride back out to the lake, but it was a big favor to ask and I worried that I would be bothering him. I tried to imagine him sitting in his apartment, the way he told me he did, not doing anything, just wishing that somebody would call, and I tried to think that maybe he would be glad to take a ride and get out of his own head for a while. Then I thought maybe he was with Rose or somebody, and that he probably didn't want to be bothered. Then I thought that maybe he did. I went back and forth with it for a while. I finally decided it would be weird and so I didn't call. It was stupid, I guess, but for some reason it didn't feel right. So I tried to think of who else I could ask. I couldn't ask Greene, not after showing up late with his car, and Finnerty didn't have a car. Ranks had a car, but I didn't feel like putting up with him for an hour, and I didn't want to owe him any favors. Ranks was the kind of guy you didn't want to owe favors to. He was the kind who would as likely take his favor as you having dinner with him, or something like that. Like he just appreciated your company, and you were supposed to be all flattered that he considered you spending time with him enough return on a favor. The truth was that the bastard just wanted someone to sound smart to. He had already driven so many people away with his goddamned pontificating that now he had to do people favors to get them to spend time with him. It would have been hilarious if it weren't so sad. I actually kind of started feeling bad for him, and I thought maybe I'd give him a call. But in the end I just called a taxi. I had to write the cabbie a goddamned check. I didn't feel like talking to anyone.

I got back out to the house a little after seven, but it was already dark. The sky was clear, and away from the city you could a hell of a lot of stars. After the cab left I kind of stood in the driveway just staring up at them. I had only seen stars like that once, when I was a kid, and I stood out there looking and looking before I realized that I was freezing cold and I went inside. The house was even colder than it had been that afternoon, and I fumbled around, trying to find a thermostat. Finally I ended up sitting in the kitchen with the door closed and the oven door open. I knew I couldn't sit like that for very long without suffocating, but I didn't care because I was so cold. But after a little while I thought it would be a good idea to leave. So I turned off the oven and while I was still warm I ran upstairs and got into bed with all my clothes on. But I cooled off pretty fast and I lay there shivering until I fell asleep.

I woke up pretty early the next morning. From my bed I could see sunlight shining straight in through the window at the top of the staircase. The window was all lit up around the edges. I didn't want to get out of bed. I could see my breath hanging in a fat cloud around my head. That's how cold the house was. But pretty soon I started to get hungry. So after a while I sort of dove out of bed and grabbed my keys and my wallet and my coat and shoes and got bundled up and left and started walking towards town. I figured if I hurried I'd probably stay pretty warm. But I was wrong. The second I got out of bed I was freezing. A thing like that never works the way you hope.

I went down to the diner I had eaten lunch at the day before. I didn't have a clock in my room at the house, but it must have been pretty early because it looked like the place was just opening. I sat down at the counter and the waitress brought me coffee without me ordering it. I guess she could tell that I was cold. She was this very cute blonde. She was only about four and a half feet tall, but she was one of those people who could have been anywhere between twenty-five and forty. You know, like she had a real classic look to her, if that makes any sense. Anyway I thought that she was the only one working, but then another waitress came in red-faced and shoved a half-empty pack of cigarettes under the cash register. I could hear the cook moving around in the kitchen, but couldn't see him from where I was sitting.

Anyway I sat there drinking coffee, kind of planning out my day while I looked over the menu. What I thought I'd do was once I ordered I would find a newspaper and look through the classifieds and try and see if there were any cars for sale. Then I'd call around and see if I could take a look at any of them. I knew I had to have one in the next couple of days and besides that, I wanted one. In the city I didn't need one, but ever since Bradner offered me the house I sort of had been imagining myself with one. I had this image of myself cruising around the lake, being able to kind of move around when I wanted to. It felt right for summer. It's a bad way to go into looking for something like a car, though, because you know most people who are selling them are ready to unload them for less than they're asking, but if you're too eager even a chump will figure he can take you for the whole cost. But sometimes, when you're eager, you can't do anything about it. It just shows through, no matter how detached you're trying to be. I don't really know, but my old man used to talk about it when I was a kid. He was a real stickler for getting a good deal. Whoever was selling would give him the price and he'd stand there staring at the thing, running over how much money we had, how much we could afford to spend, how much we would probably need to fix up whatever it was that he was buying, and then finally what else in our house he could throw in to sweeten the deal. That was part of it, too. He was always figuring what the other person wanted or needed. The point is he had this elaborate system of trade and barter and marketing strategy, all worked out in his head. He tried to pass it on to me, but I was a total failure at it. I think part of it was that he, my old man, was pretty quiet and pretty hard to read, and so people were never really sure if he wanted what they were selling. Me, you can always tell what I want. That's the bastard of it. That's why I don't buy very much. People are always trying to fleece me, because they think I'll pay. I will, too, is the bitch of it. I just don't know the difference.

So anyway I figured that I would try to buy a car. I had some money saved up, and I figured I could spend more and justify it because I wasn't going to be paying rent for a while. Then I thought maybe I'd buy an electric heater if I couldn't find the thermostat. I started thinking that if I found a store with a good, thirty-day return policy, I could probably buy one and use it and then return it when it got warmer. It was late March, then, and I figured by mid-April, even if the nights were cold, the cold would be pretty manageable. Anyway I figured I'd either buy a heater or not, and then if the day got warm enough that I could move around the house without my coat on I'd try to unpack. I felt better with the day planned out. I ordered breakfast and then told the waitress I would be right back and went to get a paper.

But nothing else on the block was open, and I had to go down a couple of blocks to a gas station. It was this sort of brown wooden shack with two pumps out front and a dock hooking out into the lake, with two more pumps on the end of it. I bought a paper and a pack of cigarettes and smoked as I walked back. When I got back to the diner my breakfast was sitting there, waiting for me. I ate it pretty fast. I hadn't realized it before, but I was really hungry. I guess it was from being cold all night. Anyway while I was eating I looked through the classifieds. There were a couple of cars that sounded all right, so I had the waitress change a dollar and then I went back and used the payphone to call the numbers for the cars. But while the phone was ringing on the first one I realized that it might be too early to call, so I hung up. It was eight-thirty, and I figured that it would be all right to call after nine, so I went back and sat down and read the paper and drank two or three more cups of coffee. I don't know how much I had because the waitress kept refilling it when it was half-empty. I thought that she was some waitress, but then I remembered that I was the only one there, and that to take care of one customer wasn't a hell of a hard thing to do. After that I didn't think so much of her. I didn't think less of her, I just didn't think as much. I couldn't help it. That's the way I am, though. I think about a thing until I've ruined it.

At nine o'clock I started making calls. There were six cars that sounded all right, but two of them didn't answer and one of them was too far away for me to walk, and the guy on the other end said he couldn't give me a ride. He got really suspicious when I asked for one, like I was really just going to let him pick me up and then take him hostage, or something. I told him if I had a car and could get to his house then I wouldn't be talking to him, but he said he had to be somewhere in an hour anyway, and driving me around would eat up half of that.

"Call me back tomorrow," he said. "We can probably work it out."

"Sure," I said, then I hung up. I was started to get a little frustrated with the whole thing, but then I got three in a row that said I could come take a look, and I felt better. Then, once I hung up with the last one, I started feeling worse, because I knew it would be a bitch to decide between three, especially when you're standing there with the guy looking at you. That's my problem, is I'm always worried that I'm going to hurt somebody's goddamned feelings or something, if I try to negotiate. Like they're going to be insulted. I'll be going along, getting pitched at by some schmuck, having no problem telling him I don't want whatever it is he's selling, when all of a sudden from out of nowhere I'll get this sudden pang of guilt, like I'm really a bad guy, because I don't appreciate the effort this guy is putting into this spiel. Like there's this social ritual that's playing out, and I'm not holding up my end of it.

Or I'll suddenly start thinking that his salesman is really a good guy, that he's got this deep reserve of hidden feeling that is going to be mortally wounded if I don't go along with what he's asking. Not that I usually end up buying whatever it is, but I always end up feeling bad as hell, having to tell anyone in that position no to their face. And I can't do a goddamned thing about it, is the other thing. I'm a sucker born, if ever there was one.

Anyway I asked the waitress where each of the houses was and she drew me a map on the back of a paper placemat. I folded the map inside the newspaper and thanked her and left. Outside it was warmer than it had been when I left the house, but it was still that kind of bright cold you get when there are no clouds but the ground is still frozen in the shade. By the time I got to the first house I couldn't feel my toes, and I stood kicking them against the concrete step leading up to the front door until the owner came out.

The car was a "41 Nash with rusted panels. The foot wells were filled with pine needles but when I turned the key the engine started up, and I drove it around the block without any trouble. I drove it back and told the man I'd think about it, but he said if I took it right away he'd give it to me for a hundred less than he was asking in the paper. I figured that meant something was wrong with it so I turned him down, and he offered me another fifty off. So I bought it. That's another reason I'm not a good haggler. Buying anything from someone makes me so uncomfortable that even if a have to pay more to get what I want right away and not bargain them down, I consider it money well spent, because it gets me out of dealing with them. But this time I felt like he would have gone lower if I had just told him I was going to go check out the other two cars, and then call him later. It didn't matter that I had already gotten the car for less than he was asking, because I immediately started thinking that I could have gotten it for less than that. I guess you can't win.

But driving back towards the house I started feeling

better. The car ran fine, and it was a good day for driving. The sun was out and the roads were clean, but the air was cold and there was no wind coming off the lake. I drove back through town and then instead of turning left onto the road I turned right, and drove up the hill past the big houses and then down to where the bay ended up. I stopped where the bay broke around a rocky outcrop and got out of the car and looked along the far shoreline until I lost it in the distance. Then I just looked out at the water for a while. It was flat and gray and silver where the sun hit it in a long streak that shimmered and rippled around the edges. Nobody came by in either direction on the Loop road, and I sat down on the hood of my car and smoked a couple of cigarettes, kind of staring out and not thinking about anything. Then I got in and turned the car around and drove home. I thought about unpacking, but I ended up reading a book, hunkered down in the kitchen with the door closed and the oven on, until it got dark. Then I went out for dinner. While I was out I thought about calling Canasson, but by the time I got back to the house it was almost nine o'clock, and I figured he wouldn't want to make the drive now, to come see the house, and I didn't really feel like trying to set something up for sometime later in the week. Plus I couldn't invite him up until I figured out how to turn on the heat. And besides, I'm awful on the phone. I hate it. So instead I just read some more and then I went to bed. It was still cold, but it was warmer than it had been the night before. Or maybe I was just expecting it, and it didn't seem as bad. Anyway, I fell asleep.

I was going to call Canasson the next day and then, when that didn't happen, the next. Someone told me that when you live by water it's easy to forget time and I guess that's true, because it was almost three weeks from when I moved to the lake to when I saw Canasson again. The longer I waited, the harder it became to call, and the easier it got to imagine that by now he was too busy to come out. It was early April before I called, and he didn't answer.

But about a week later I ran into him in a restaurant. I hadn't worked that day, but Greene and Finnerty had invited me out for dinner. It was something they did every year, before the end of tax season. We always went out and ran up a huge bill, and then wrote it off as a business expense. Finnerty thought it was funny as hell and Greene didn't feel right about it and I couldn't have given a shit if you paid me to. But the dinner was always a good time. I liked those guys. But anyway I drove down from the lake and met them for dinner. It was pretty warm out, so I had the windows down and the radio up pretty loud. I got to the restaurant early and I picked a table over near the bar, back tucked away in a corner, away from the door. Greene showed up first, then Finnerty. He was stuck late at the office working on a story we had all heard about, a robbery that went bad.

"He robs the register," said Finnerty, "but the clerk presses the silent alarm. It's all in the statements. He does it real fast, while the gunman is looking away for a second. So the gunman says, you know, "what was that? What the fuck was that?" And he's got the gun up in the clerk's face." He held his thumb and forefinger up like a gun and pointed it ahead of him. "So the clerk starts babbling about it wasn't anything, I swear to God, you know, on and on, and what does the gunman do but jumps over the counter and starts clubbing the clerk with the gun. The clerk goes down and then the fucking gunman, he shoots the clerk. Right in face, while he's just lying there on the floor. Yeah, fucked up. Then he opens up the register and starts taking out the money, but the dumb bastard doesn't even think to put it into a bag. He just keeps stuffing it into his pockets and it keeps falling out. But he gets most of it in and he's about to jump back over the counter, you know, to get the fuck out of there, and who shows up but the goddamn cops, responding to the silent alarm. So this guy, he slinks back against the wall, and the cops give him the old "come out with your hands up, we've got the place surrounded." So he knows he's fucked. And he kinds of stands there holding his dick for a minute, and then he puts the gun to his head and blows his brains all over the register." He laughed and lit a cigarette. "Made the most fucking incredible mess," he said. But the funny thing is, the gunman, he sort of toppled over on the ground the opposite direction of the clerk. You know, like their feet are almost touching. And they're both bleeding from the head. It's like a mirror image. It's fucking nuts. God couldn't have planned it better. I've never seen anything like it."

"It's a strange way to handle the robbery," said Greene.

"The whole fucking thing was strange," said Finnerty. "I mean, the guy comes in with no mask, no bag to put the money into, and he shoots the fucking clerk for no good reason. Then he's got no escape plan, and he kills himself. I mean, the son of a bitch had to see it coming. It was a kamikaze run, or something."

I was listening to Finnerty's story when the door opened and Canasson and Diane came in. I recognized her from the pictures in Canasson's apartment. Neither of them was smiling, but they weren't really frowning, either. They just sort of stood, not looking at each other. The headwaiter led them to a table across the room from us. After he went away Canasson said something to Diane, but Diane didn't respond. She just kind of turned away and looked at the menu. Canasson sagged back away from her and looked at his own menu. Neither of them did anything for a while. Finnerty went on talking, but I wasn't listening.

We ordered dinner. I had been watching Canasson and Diane, and as far as I could tell they still hadn't spoken. Then I saw Canasson say something, and Diane turn to him, her mouth moving big and fast and her face turning red. Canasson had his hands up and was pushing them, palms down, towards the tabletop, I guess he was trying to quiet her. Then he sagged back again, and Diane threw her menu down on the table. It slid and knocked her glass over and Canasson stood with his napkin in his hand to try to stop it from spilling onto the floor. Diane stood, too, and headed for the door. I saw Canasson call to her and when she didn't stop he left the napkin and ran after her. But a waiter called after him, holding up his coat. He turned to the waiter, and when he turned back he saw me. He just stood there for a second, looking at me, holding the coat with both hands. Then he seemed to remember what he was doing and he hurried after Diane. She was already outside, and Canasson glanced back at me before he pushed through the door.

I ate dinner without saying much and then I said goodnight and went home. It started to rain halfway to the lake, and the wiper blades left streaks where the rubber had pulled away from the glass. I felt lousy and sober and over-full. When dinner arrived I thought that it was too big to eat, but the next thing I knew it was gone. I guess I had been thinking about something else. The rain was coming down pretty hard, and when I pulled up in front of the house I felt the car sink in the muddy driveway. I slipped on the grass on the way to the front door and went down to my knees. I knew that the pants were ruined, but I had a hard time caring much.

It was warm inside, and I changed clothes and had a couple of drinks standing by the back door, watching the rain hit the porch and the lawn and the dock and the lake. I watched a puddle form down in the depression where the slope of the lawn met the retaining wall, and then I watched it grow until the whole front of the lawn was under water. It was some rainstorm, but it didn't feel like anything. I couldn't see the far side of the bay and it seemed impossible that something could be that big that it would make the far side disappear, and so it didn't feel like anything. And anyway I knew that in the morning the storm would be gone, and most of the water would have drained back into the lake.

I fell asleep on the couch, and so when my alarm went off upstairs I didn't hear it and I slept until almost one. Then I got dressed and went into town for lunch. It was warm out and the bay was dull and metallic from all the runoff. The sky was flat and pale and looked as washed out as the bay. The streets and the sidewalks and all the buildings were still wet, but they didn't look clean because the sky looked dirty.

After lunch I took a walk, and when I got back to the house the phone was ringing. I heard it from outside and I figured that whoever it was would hang up by the time I got to it, so I didn't rush. But when I got inside it was still ringing, so I picked it up and said hello.

"Elliot?" It was Canasson.

"Arthur," I said. I was pretty surprised to hear from him.

"Jesus, Elliot," he said. "It's been such hell."

IV.

He came up on Friday afternoon, looking like his clothes didn't fit him. He had a suitcase and an overnight bag, and after the cabbie drove off he stood in my front yard staring up at the house. I watched him from the window, expecting him to move, to come down the front walk and knock on the door. But he didn't, so I went out.

"Come inside and have a drink," I said.

We crossed the lawn and went up the steps and went inside. I told Canasson where his room was and he thanked me and went up the stairs. I went into the kitchen and made a pitcher of pisco sours. I could hear Canasson moving around upstairs and I took the pitcher and a pair of glasses and went out onto the back porch. The sun was almost down, and the bay and the far shore were lit up pink and gray and I leaned against the railing and drank some of the pisco. I could hear the horns from the band playing at the fairgrounds. Then the door open behind me, and I poured the second glass without looking at him. But when he didn't come over I turned around. He was standing just outside the open doorway with his hands in his pockets. He had taken off his jacket and his tie and his shirt collar was open. He didn't look at me, but he didn't seem to be looking at anything else, either. I moved beside him and handed him his drink and he took it in both hands.

"What time does the fair start?" he said.

"It's started already," I said. "It goes all summer. Have a seat, we have time."

We sat down in a pair of wooden deck chairs. I lit two cigarettes and handed one to Canasson, but after he took it he seemed to forget it was there. It was pretty obvious that he was in bad shape and hadn't really been sleeping. For one thing, his shirt was rumpled and it looked like he had worn it and maybe slept in it for a few days. It was hard to notice when he was wearing the tie and jacket, but once it was off it

75

was obvious.

"I'm sorry, Elliot," he said after a while. "I think maybe I just need another drink and I'll be all right."

"All right," I said. I filled his glass from the pitcher.

"I knew this would happen," he said. "Somehow that doesn't make it any easier." Then he didn't say anything for a while We finished our drinks and I refilled our glasses. The pitcher was almost empty. After a while he said, "I do feel a lot better. Just being away from the city. Lets go down and see the band."

"All right," I said. "There's a bar down that way. We can stop in and get a drink, and sit out on the back porch and listen to them."

We each took half of what was left in the pitcher and drank it and then we went inside. Inside it was dark and I fumbled for the light switch along the wall. I was feeling very warm and like I didn't care very much what happened. I was pretty happy to see him, I guess, but I wasn't sure what to say to him because he looked so broken up. I put the pitcher and the glasses into the sink and then waited while Canasson went upstairs. He came back down wearing a fresh shirt. We went out and behind the houses and along the waterfront towards the fair.

We got down where the houses started to end, and we went across a field and over in front of the bar. The bar wasn't very crowded at all, and we got a table on the back porch and I ordered two Knickerbockers. Our waitress came back with the gin and vermouth and mixed them with cracked ice, and then strained it out into two short glasses. The glasses were frosted and when she poured the drink in the liquid cut the frost and left a wavering pattern of white around the lip. She dropped in the twists and handed them across and I took mine and drank and for a minute couldn't taste anything, the drink was so cold. Then the gin and vermouth and the lemon rose from behind the cold. I leaned back in my chair, tasting it and watching the Ferris wheel. I watched a car go up and then as it reached the top I took another drink and when I looked back I could not tell which car I had been watching, so I looked out across the water instead.

"How do you like this bar?" I said.

"It's a good bar," said Canasson.

"You know, a few weeks ago you'd be lucky to get any kind of cocktail. They only had one bartender, and he only knew how to make rum and cokes. I had to tell him what a screwdriver was. He said he would remember for me, but there wasn't much point in learning how to make drinks, since most people only ordered beer. Then, a week ago, I came in and there are all these new waitresses, and every one of them knows how to make every goddamned drink I can think of." I laughed. "I asked the old bartender about it. He said they do this every year, hiring up people to work there for the summer. He said his back was killing him from unloading all the crates of booze the manager ordered up for all the swells who would be coming in. He said that every year he thinks there's no way any number of people will ever go through all the liquor the manager orders up, but come September, he says, every drop of it is gone, and a heck of a lot more ordered since, too. I said if they ordered as much as it sounds like, it would take a hundred people drinking for seven or eight hours every day to go through that much. He said I wasn't far from it. This summer is going to be a hell of a time." I took a drink. The chill had gone out of the booze so that I could taste it, now, and I winced and then let the flavor work over before I swallowed.

Canasson drank, too. "I appreciate you having me up," he said.

"Don't worry about it," I said. But Canasson didn't look any better after that, so I said, "look, I know what it's like. You're just stuck in a rut is all." Then I gave up talking, because what I was trying to say wasn't coming out right. I guess I wasn't really sure what I was trying to say. I wasn't really sure why I had invited Canasson up in the first place, except that I knew that when I saw him I was glad he was there. So I said, "drink up, already. I'm going to need to be drunker if we're going to be this heavy all night."

"All right," said Canasson. He was grinning now, but into his drink, not at me. "All right. I won't be heavy. I'm having a good time." He drained off the rest of his drink and waved the waitress over, and then he looked at me and I understood and drained off the rest of mine, as well. "Two more, by God," he said. "Two more for the table, then two for the lake, then two for the fair, then two for the road."

"Christ," I said, "If we drink all those and you can order two more for my wake. Just dump mine on top of my damned casket. Right there on top of the flowers and everything."

He laughed. "You know what the Irish say," he said. He turned to the waitress. I tried to tell her something, but I was laughing too hard and by the time I was finished I had forgotten what I was going to say. "We'll have two more of the same," said Canasson. Then, when the waitress went away, he turned to me and said, "you're *drunk*."

"What are you?" I wasn't really that drunk, but it felt better to be drunk and to agree that we were drunk than figure out what the hell to say to each other.

"I'm drunk too, then, I guess," he said. "Funny how I don't really feel it yet. I guess we've had plenty to drink. Let's finish this one and then go over to the carnival," Canasson said. The band started playing *You're a Grand Old Flag*. The horns belched noise and the big bass drum kept time. I could feel it, even across the water.

"All right," I said. "I'd like to see this band, before they finish. They sound like a hell of a band."

The waitress brought our drinks, and we drank them and Canasson overpaid and then we left. We walked through the parking lot and then down further around and then to the entrance. Canasson bought two tickets at the booth from a flushed fat woman and we went in through a row of turnstiles. On the other side we gave our tickets to an old man. He was wearing the uniform shirt of the carnival, but it was too big for him. It sort of hung around his chest and arms. He didn't say anything, and so we walked past him and into the fair.

The fair was crowded. Barkers were yelling at the people and at each other across and along the main aisle. There was a low kind of groan going all the time from the voices and the machines. I could hear the band playing somewhere up ahead and I moved forward into the crowd and someone shoved me and I fell back into Canasson. He helped me back onto my feet and I looked around for who had done it, but the people made a flat, moving wall, and there was no way to see who it was.

"Did you see who just pushed me?" I yelled to Canasson.

"No," he said. "Besides, they probably were getting pushed themselves."

Up above and ahead, the Ferris wheel lurched to a stop, then changed directions. The heavy blasting horns and the bass drum overrode the record soundtrack from the merry-go-round, but you could hear it in the breaks.

"Mother of Christ," I said, "we're never going to get through this."

"I think it bottlenecks near the entrance," he said. "If we get down a little farther, maybe it won't be so bad." We pushed our way down the aisle and then it sort of opened up by the main tent and we went inside. The band was up in front, and there were six or seven people seated around the room, watching them. I was sweating pretty heavy from being pressed up against the crowd and I unbuttoned my collar. The band members were wearing matching white suits and hats. They looked miserable and hot. Their faces were red and when it was their turn to play their faces got redder as they blew into their instruments. The limp sheet music on the stands fluttered in the blast from the horns. There was a kind of buzz from the music on the heavy tent vinyl. We took seats near the back and Canasson offered me a cigarette and I took it and we sat smoking, listening to the band play *The Gallant Seventh.* When they were finished we clapped, but they didn't look at us. I guess they were too hot to care if we liked it.

We stayed for a few songs. Then the band took a break, and we left and walked down towards the point.

We went under the Ferris Wheel and then past the merry-go-round. The horses went up and down and forward, and then came around. I watched a girl riding, hugging the horse's neck, and then I watched a boy who held onto the pole with one hand and leaned far in, reaching for the brass ring. I watched him go around three times, and on the third time he touched it and let out a cry as he almost fell. When he came around the next time he looked at the ring but didn't reach for it, and then I turned away because Canasson had moved off, and I hurried to catch up with him.

Down at the end you walked down a narrow brick pathway to the stone steps leading up to a gazebo. At some point the land ended and the fairgrounds continued on a pier, and so at the end you were pretty far out into the lake. There were a half dozen people inside the gazebo, but I couldn't see anybody's face because the shadows inside were so heavy. I watched Canasson disappear into shadow as he sat down then I went in and I sat down, too. Someone lit a cigarette, and their face glowed orange for a second before it went dark again.

"But I didn't see any reason for it," someone was saying. "It seems like an awful waste. It's an institution of the region, after all. It holds certain intangible qualities that can't be measured monetarily. What could possibly inspire a move like that?"

"Some vision of the future, I guess," someone else said.

"It doesn't make a damn bit of sense," the other said. "Why now?"

"It was bound to happen sooner or later," the second replied.

Then these two fell silent. I started feeling more tired

than drunk, and I wondered how Canasson felt. Behind us the band started playing again, only now the sound was behind the grating of the Ferris Wheel and the merry-go-round. I leaned my head back against the railing. The water sounded very close and the air that blew off the lake was already cold, even though the sun had not been down for very long.

"Excuse me," said a woman's voice. I opened my eyes. She was standing right in front of me, almost between my legs. "Do you have another cigarette?" she said. I fished one out of my pocket and handed it to her, then held out a match. As she leaned into the flame I saw pale skin and dark red hair and a full, red mouth. She watched the cigarette and watched it begin to glow, and then she leaned away and looked at me. Her eyes were big and in the pale orange light they flashed blue and green and grey. Then the match started to burn my fingers, so I shook it out and turned to flip it over the railing, and when I turned back her face was dark.

"Thanks," she said.

"Sure," I said. I wanted to say something else, but I couldn't think of anything. Beautiful women always do that to me. If I say the right thing, it's usually just luck. She turned and moved away from me, across the gazebo, and as she crossed the entrance she stepped through a square of light thrown from the carnival that illuminated one white arm and one hip, and then she disappeared across it and was in the shadows again. She sat down across from me, and I watched her blow dark smoke against the lighter gray of the sky behind.

"Of course," said the man who had been speaking earlier, "there's this summer, and probably part of next. They can't do it all in one year."

"Of course not," agreed the other. "There's plenty of time yet."

"Do you live around here?" I said.

"Up on the hill," said the woman with my cigarette. "Not far."

"All year round?"

"In the summers. The rest of the year I live in the city."

I said, "do you ever read the paper? I write for the paper."

"Oh?" she said. "Would I have read anything you wrote? I mean, do you write a column or anything?"

"No," I said. "I write for the police beat. I mean I report on police investigations and things like that."

"That sounds interesting," she said.

"It's pretty interesting," I said.

"Elliot's a great reporter," said Canasson, sliding down the bench towards me. "You should see him at work. He's like a human bloodhound. He's a photographer, too."

"A photographer?" she said. "An artist then, too."

"Not an artist," I said. "Just a newspaper photographer. Pictures of crime scenes and things like that."

"He's being modest," said Canasson. "I've seen what he can do with a crime scene. He can take the grizzliest scene you can imagine and make you want to hang it in your living room."

"He's exaggerating it," I said. I could feel her looking at us, and I could feel everyone else in the gazebo looking at us as well. I crushed out what was left of my cigarette, then lit my last one. The woman flipped hers over the railing. Canasson took out his pack and offered her one. She accepted. I reached for a match but Canasson beat me to it. I took one of his cigarettes.

"Elliot and I were about to go for a drink," he said. "Would you like to join us?"

"I'd love to," she said, "I really would, but I've got to be getting home."

"Maybe we could walk with you to the gate," Canasson asked.

"Thanks anyway," she said, "but I think I'd like to walk alone." She stood up and gathered her coat from the bench. It was a thick green coat with large buttons up the front and she left it open and left the cigarette hanging out of the corner of her mouth as she put it on. Then she took it out and blew a long plume of smoke up at the ceiling. "It was nice meeting you both," she said. "Maybe I'll see you around."

"I hope so," said Canasson.

"Goodbye," I said. "It was nice meeting you." She stepped into the square of light that fell through the entryway, but then turned to go down the stairs and she kept her back to us down the steps and I lost her in the crowd around the base of the Ferris wheel. Then my cigarette burned my fingers and I cursed and dropped it and it rolled under the bench, and I had to get up and crouch down to find it.

"Beautiful girl," said Canasson. He sat back down, and I sat down next to him. "Hey, any of you guys know that girl's name?"

"That's June Hautdesert," somebody said. "Bernard Hautdesert, the sculptor, is her husband. You know that white house up on the hill? That's where they live. They come up every summer."

"Do you know them well?" said Canasson.

"Oh, pretty well," said the man. "I've been to parties at their house. They have at least one every year. Sometimes more. Nice folks. Big in the arts community, back in the city. He is, anyway. She's not an artist."

"Oh, no?" said Canasson.

"No," said the man. "She's a hell of a tennis player, though. You see her at the courts. She was an athlete in college. Water polo or something. Still very athletic. Her husband is a hell of a guy, too. Beautiful artwork. He always has a show at the end of the summer, before everyone leaves. Everything he's been working on. Cleans up, too. He once told me that some years he does as much business in the one summer show as he does the rest of the year back in the city."

"I've seen some of his work," said Canasson. "He's very good."

They all agreed. Then they started talking about

something else, and Canasson turned back so that he and I were facing the same direction. The band had stopped, and the only sound coming from the carnival was the turning of the wheel and the music from the merry-go-round. I felt sober but happy and did not feel as though I needed to be anywhere else. I guess Canasson felt the same way, because we sat there for a long time not saying anything, just staring out at the water. Then the music from the merry-go-round cut off. It was pretty late, I guess. Pretty soon the others got up and started out, and we stood and fell in step behind them. The booths were all closed up, and the main aisle was almost empty. The old man was gone from the gate. We stepped around the turnstiles and out onto the sidewalk.

"Well," I said, after the others moved off, "what do you want to do now?"

"Lets take a drive around the lake," he said. "Can you drive?"

"Sure," I said.

We walked back around the lake along the street. The moon was half full and hung above the horizon just ahead of us. I felt pretty sharp and not at all tired, but I knew that if I lay down I would fall asleep almost instantly. It was a kind of feeling I didn't get very often and still don't get very often, and it was nice to know it was there but to not need it. But anyway we walked back to the house and got in the car. Canasson switched the radio on. We caught the beginning of the midnight jazz hour, and I pulled out onto the loop road and headed south along the bay. We rolled the windows down. Up at the top of the hill I slowed down. There were lights on in the windows of the big white house, but it was set far back off the road behind a row of trees, and I couldn't see much. Canasson leaned in close to me to look out my window as well, but when he leaned back I stepped on the gas and we shot up and over and then I slipped the car into neutral as we coasted down, the engine running quiet and the tires humming beneath us and the water black and calm beside us.

AURIC ADAMS

We ran out of momentum just before the road turned south, and I put the car in gear. Canasson had been telling a joke, and as he got to the punch line I put the car into gear and stepped on the gas and the car lurched, and I missed it and he had to say it again. We headed south, along the wooded section of the lake where there were no houses yet. As the road curved back east a few houses began to break up the woods, and then pretty soon we were out of the woods entirely and into the next town over. The road became the main street of town and we drove past dark shops and then were out the other side again. The radio station cut to commercials, and we listened to ads hocking mattresses and used cars for a while, and then the music came back on again. We didn't talk much, but between the radio and the wind noise we didn't have to. I felt tired but like I could keep driving for a while. We went through another wooded section and then another town and then more woods. Then the road started to curve north and Canasson asked me if I wanted him to drive and I told him sure and pulled over and we switched. The radio went to a commercial again, and I spun the dial until I found more music. The reception was lousy, though. We were both laughing at nothing. It was late enough that things seemed funnier than they were. Or maybe we were just tired enough to notice that they were funny. I guess it doesn't matter.

We headed north for what felt like a long time and with the woods I couldn't tell if the lake was still there, and I started to think that maybe we had left the lake and were heading north along another road. We rode for a while longer and then I said I thought maybe we had gotten off the road, but he said he hadn't taken any turns, and this could only be the right road. We went for a little while longer, then Canasson said that if we didn't start to come around pretty soon he would go back and see if we took a turn somewhere that we hadn't noticed. That maybe the road had turned left, and in among the trees we had mistaken it for a driveway or something. But then pretty soon the road started to come around. We headed back along the north shore driving west, ducking in towards the lake and then coasting back out among the trees.

About halfway around, Canasson stopped the car. There was a gravel pullout bordered in by long chunks of railroad tie, and then a narrow strip of sand leading down to the water. I was tuning the radio and so I didn't see the sign. Canasson pulled over and cut the lights, and we left the radio on and got out. We looked across the lake and smoked the last of his cigarettes. Canasson said something, but I couldn't hear him over the radio, and when I asked him to repeat it he said that it was nothing and I let it drop.

You know it's true, I always knew, I knew right from the start, sang the radio jazz singer. *When I shook her hand, said howdy ma'am, I always knew she'd break my heart.*

After a while the music ended and some more commercials came on. It was cold out by the lake in the middle of the night, and I said so and Canasson agreed and we got back into the car and headed west for a while. Then Canasson said he felt tired and would I mind driving, and I told him that I didn't, and so he stopped on the road and we switched. He leaned his head against the door and fell asleep. I didn't mind. It was nice driving along with the radio turned down low. It was almost like being asleep. The road stayed straight and the headlights showed the same thing on and on and you felt nothing but the vibration of the engine through the wheel. With the dark and knowing that everyone else was asleep it sort of felt like me and Canasson were the only people on earth. I thought about it for a while. I figured that it would be hell for a little while, and then we'd get into a pretty good routine. It's be like being on a ship or something. People can go for a long time through anything awful if there's a routine to it. I figured we'd hardly even notice after a while that we were the only people left.

Then the road curved sharp left, and we drove down along the north coast of the bay, along past the new condominiums and the bobbing aluminum docks and past the summer cabins. Then into the north part of the real town, and past the carnival, and then down towards the dark downtown, and I pulled into my driveway before we got to Main Street. The engine kicked a little when I shut it off, and that woke up Canasson, and so when the car was still he gave me a real groggy look. Then we got out and went inside. We went upstairs without saying anything, and then said goodnight at the top of the stairs. I closed my door and I heard him close his, and then I leaned against the door and heard him moving around. I heard his footsteps and then I heard them stop and then I heard him get into bed. Then after that I didn't hear anything but I knew he was there. So I got undressed and got into bed. I was real tired but I wasn't very sleepy, if that makes any sense, so I lay awake and thought about how I felt like the last person on earth except for Canasson, who I knew was across the hall, and I wondered what he had said when we were looking at the lake, when he said it was nothing. I realized there was no way to know. So I forgot about it. After that I thought about the fair for a while, and then about the woman in the gazebo, and then I tried to think of things to do the next day. I couldn't think of anything. I thought about hauling the boat out from under the porch. Then, even though I hadn't noticed it before, I realized I was starting to fall asleep. So I fell asleep, and I had this dream where I was the only one riding the Ferris Wheel, and Canasson was standing under it, and I kept going down towards him, and then watching him disappear as I went backwards and up and around and he got farther away and then closer and then farther away again. I kept calling to him to get on, but the Ferris Wheel kept going around, and Canasson never got on. I could hear the music from the merry-go-round, but it wasn't the high fluting circus melody it had played all night. Instead, it was the jazz singer from the radio, singing, *You know it's true, I always knew, I knew right from the start. When I shook her hand, said howdy ma'am, I always knew she'd break my heart.* Then pretty soon that dream ended, and I dreamed about something else.

Then the dreaming ended and I was awake. It was still dark out, so I tried to fall back asleep, but I couldn't. I lay there for a while, thinking that I would fall asleep pretty soon. But when I didn't I got up and walked around the floor for a little bit. I thought about going across the hall to see if Canasson was awake, too, but instead I just went downstairs and read for a while. I thought I was hungry and so I ate something, but after I did that I didn't feel any better, so I looked around for a cigarette, because I thought that might be it. But then I remembered that I had given my last one to the woman in the gazebo, and we had smoked the last of Canasson's when we were parked on the shore. I thought maybe he had another pack in his luggage, and so I went upstairs to ask him. But when I was up the stairs and outside his door I felt better, so I just went into my room and read in bed for a while. After that I started to feel tired again, so I turned off the light and waited to fall asleep. I did pretty soon. I didn't wake up any more after that. I probably dreamed some more, but I don't remember what it was.

V.

The next morning I woke up pretty early. My window faced east is why. But also, I didn't feel very tired. I thought maybe Canasson got woken up early by the sun, too, because his room also had an east-facing window, but when I opened my door I saw that his was still closed. I thought maybe he had just closed it when he went downstairs, but he wasn't downstairs and the car was still in the driveway. I thought maybe he had gone for a walk or something, but I moved around pretty quiet downstairs because I wasn't sure if he was still asleep. But when I went to make coffee I banged my knee into the corner of the cabinets and I cursed loud before I remembered to be quiet. A little while after that I heard him moving around upstairs. I went out on the back porch while the coffee was brewing and a little while later Canasson came out with two coffee mugs and handed one to me. We stood looking out at the lake for a while. The sun was still low over it, and for a while you almost couldn't see at all because of the glare. Then it got higher and the angle changed, and you could look out at it without squinting, if you weren't looking right at the reflection.

"I feel pretty good," I said. "I think I sobered up enough while I was still awake that most of it was gone when I went to sleep." I did feel pretty good, but with the coffee I felt even better. Canasson laughed when I said it, though.

"That was still a hell of a drive to undertake in our condition," he said. "We wouldn't have stood a chance if we had been pulled over."

"It was good, though," I said. "I've been wanting to drive around the lake since I got here, I just never got the chance to. I mean I just never did it before now. Anyway I'm glad we did it."

"Yeah, me too," said Canasson. Then he squinted out at something in the water. I looked in the direction he was. Out around, far down the south shore of the bay, something was

89

moving in the water. I watched it until I could see arms and kicking feet, and then I looked towards the dock where the swimmer had gone in. It was at the bottom of a long, sloping lawn. These two cone-shaped trees made a sort of gate to the dock, down near the water where the ground evened out. Off to the side of the lawn, connected to the house by a long stone staircase, was a small, stone boathouse. The house was white and had a deck stretching along what must have been the first floor, and a brick patio underneath, extending off where the ground cut away and the lower part of the house was exposed. It took me a minute to recognize that it was the house we had stopped in front of the night before. I had never noticed it before, and I might not have recognized it except that it was the highest house along that side of the shore.

Out in the water, the swimmer had reached a platform that I hadn't noticed and climbed up onto it. I watched her shake the water out of her hair. She was wearing a white bathing suit and with her pale skin she almost melted into the reflection of the clouds on the water behind her. Then she balanced on the edge, waited for the float to tilt and rise, and then made a short, perfect dive, using the momentum of the rising edge of the float to push her forward and in so that she sliced in and the water closed over her almost without a splash. She came up a dozen or so feet away, then began an even stroke back to shore.

"It's June Hautdesert," Canasson said. And then, "I'm going to swim out to meet her."

"You'll never make it in time," I said. "She's almost to shore. You can't possibly swim that fast."

"I could try," he said, watching her. "I could catch her up on the lawn."

"Too late," I said. "She's almost in."

But when she reached the dock she turned and headed out to the raft again. I watched her for a moment and then he next thing I knew Canasson was going down the steps towards the water, pulling off his shirt. He looked sort of ridiculous running down the dock in his shorts and I laughed and then he dove off and came up ten or so feet out and began swimming. I watched him, and then I looked out and I saw her, too, bobbing out of the water, moving towards the raft. She was moving at a good pace, but Canasson was moving twice as fast as her, pin-wheeling his arms and kicking hard with his feet. I walked down the steps and down the lawn and out the dock and I picked up his shirt where he had dropped it and put it over my shoulder. She reached the float when he was still about ten yards from her and pulled herself up onto it and sat facing him as he closed the distance. When he reached her he pulled himself up onto the float and stood over her. She looked up at him, and then he sat down across from her and she seemed to relax. I don't know if she really relaxed, but she leaned back on her arms and put her legs out straight in front of her. I didn't know what to do, so I just stood watching them. Then Canasson looked up and waved to me, and she turned around and waved as well. I waved back and then turned around and went up the dock and the lawn to the porch and went inside and I watched them through the kitchen window. Pretty soon they both stood up, and he followed her into the water and then they both swam towards her dock. Then they got out and went up the lawn and I couldn't see them anymore. A little while later the phone rang and it was Canasson.

"Elliot," he said.

"Arthur," I said, "where in the hell did you go?"

"Didn't you see?" he said.

"No," I said, "I stopped watching after you waved. I figured it was none of my business."

"She invited me over for breakfast," he said. "She invited us both over."

"Oh," I said. "All right. I'll be over in a minute."

"Bring me a change of clothes, would you?" he said. "I'm standing in her kitchen in a towel. I feel like some sort of displaced Roman."

91

"All right," I said again. "I'll see you in a minute."

I collected some of his clothes. I felt sort of strange standing in his room and going through his things. But then I drove up the hill and past the row of trees and pulled into the courtyard. The door was open and I went inside, carrying his clothes.

"Hello?" I said.

"We're out here," said Canasson. I followed the sound of his voice down a hall and into a broad room at the rear of the house. There was a bank of glass doors that ran the length of the room and looked out onto the porch. The room was divided in half by a black and white marble countertop. Behind the counter, to the left, was the kitchen, and on the other side there was a long table and, against the far wall, two couches and two chairs set around a glass coffee table. There were two doorways on either side of the one I came through, and one had a staircase going up and the other had one going down. I could see Canasson and June out on the porch, and Canasson was wearing a rumpled pair of pants that were too short for him and a faded shirt. He was barefoot and his hair was wet and dark and hanging across his forehead. She was wearing a bathrobe.

"Good man," said Canasson, when he saw me with the clothes.

"It looks like you don't need them," I said. Then, turning to her, I switched the pile of clothes from my right hand to my left and said, "I don't think we've actually met. Elliot Poulain."

She shook my hand. "June Hautdesert," she said.

In the light out on the porch, standing face to face, I got a better look at her. She was older than I thought she was at first. Not old, but older. Her skin was lined around her mouth, and up around her eyes, across the tops of her cheeks. Not in a bad way, but in that healthy Irish way, and aside from looking right for her complexion it also looked good on her. With her makeup off I could see that her eyebrows were thin and light, almost blond, and it made her eyes seem even darker than they already were, which was pretty dark. She was a really good-looking woman, if you want to know the truth.

"What's for breakfast?" I said.

"Whatever Arthur makes," she said, turning to him and touching him on the arm.

"I can't cook worth a damn," said Arthur,

"It's true," I said. "He really can't."

"Elliot can cook, though," said Canasson.

"I guess I can try," I said. "I mean, I can cook eggs, at least."

"All right, then," June said, "I'll leave you boys to it." She went through the glass doors, and I watched her go up the stairs. I guess because the man at the gazebo had said that she was an athlete, I watched the way she moved. She moved really forcefully, but it wasn't awkward. It was actually kind of graceful, but I don't think anyone would ever call it that. It was more like the way cats are graceful in that way that comes from knowing that in a second it can be moving faster than you can do anything about. And on top of that she had these really solid but slender ankles. I don't know if that makes any sense, but it's the only way to describe them. She was pretty great to watch move. So I watched her go up the stairs and then when she was gone I turned around and gave Canasson a look.

"What?" he said.

"Take your clothes, already," I said. "What are those, her husband's?"

He shrugged, taking the pile of clothes, and looking down at the ones he was wearing. "Yeah, I guess so," he said. "He must be kind of a little guy. This was the biggest shirt I could find, and these pants barely fit me." He moved the pile of clothes so that he could look down at his ankles, below where the pants he was wearing ended.

We went into the kitchen and started cooking breakfast. A few minutes later I heard the shower running, and then a few minutes after that June came back down. We all went out on the porch to eat. June and Canasson talked about places in the city, and then they talked about things around the lake, and what happened for the rest of the summer. June said that her husband usually put his work on display in a gallery in town at the end of the summer, but the owner had sold off the gallery over the winter and now they were thinking of having the display in the house, and having people over for dinner.

"We usually have one or two big parties up here during the summer," she said. "I guess this year the show will just be one of them. You're both invited, of course. Write down your address before you leave. I'll put you on the list for an invitation. Do either of you play tennis?"

"I do," said Canasson. "At least, I used to."

"That's good," she said. "No one around here will play with me, and Bernard is too busy with his work. We'll have to play some time."

I watched them for an hour. After a while Canasson turned in his chair. Not a lot, just enough so that he was facing more towards June than he was towards me, or to the lake. I didn't really care. It gave me an excuse to look out at the lake. It was Saturday, and there were a lot of boats out on the water. I assumed that people were picnicking on the islands, because boats kept going out beyond the bay, and then coming back from there. The reason I thought that is that I heard someone talking about having a picnic on the islands when I was having breakfast in the diner once. They said, "maybe we should wrap this up and go to one of the island," and then the other said that the boat wasn't fixed, and that finished it. I sat and wondered what the islands were like, and whether they were very big, and what they looked like on Saturdays, when all the families went there to picnic. I sort of imagined it as something between Seurat's *Sunday on the Island of La Grande Jatte* and the carnival, with kids running around and a lot of noise, and the sound of motorboats out on the water.

For a while I thought about nothing but the island. I thought about what I would bring, and how long I would want to stay, and how I would get there. It's something I did when I was a little kid, in bed at night. Back then I thought that it helped but it also seemed to make everything worse, because when you imagine something that clearly, like you're almost already there, and then remember that you're not, it makes wherever you are seem like absolute hell. It's like wanting anything. All it does is make what you've got now seem worthless and bad. But it was all right this time because I didn't care about the island and didn't want very badly to go to it, I was only thinking of it because I was bored and because Canasson had turned his chair away from me.

Canasson and June talked for a while. They talked about tennis and about players they both admired, and then about when would be a good time to play. I could see that the conversation was coming to an end, and so I finished my coffee and turned my chair back to face the lake. Pretty soon Canasson said that we should be going, and June walked us to the door. We all shook hands. Canasson wrote down our address on the back of a business card he pulled from the pocket of the pants I had brought him. He was still wearing June's husband's clothes. Then we went out and got into the car. June stood in the doorway and waved to us as we left. Canasson turned around in his seat to wave back, and then watched her until we were through the stand of trees and the house was hidden behind them. Then he turned around to face front again. He was grinning and kept adjusting and readjusting the pile of clothes in his lap.

"You seem awfully up," I said.

"Tell me," he said, " what did you think of her?"

"She's great," I said. Then I added, "and married."

Canasson scoffed. "Married," he said, not looking at me, but out the window. "For Christ's sake, *I'm* married." Then he didn't say anything, and I thought that he was angry at me for bringing it up. I decided I didn't care because I was angry at him for dragging me all the way over there to bring him clothes and then ignoring me after I cooked them breakfast. But I guess it kind of bothered me that he might be upset with me. So, as we pulled into the driveway, I said, "did you meet her husband before I got there?"

"No," he said. "He was out in his studio. You know, that little boathouse? He had it converted into a studio. They don't even have a boat. I suppose we'll meet him tonight."

"Tonight?" I started up the walk behind him.

"Yeah," he said. "They're coming over for drinks at five, and then we're going to go out for dinner. Where were you? We made the plans while you were sitting right there."

"I guess I wasn't paying attention," I said.

We went inside. Canasson went upstairs and then came back down wearing his own clothes. While he was doing that I checked the freezer. I had a little bit of pisco left. Aside from that I had a bottle of bourbon that I hadn't opened, and two fifths of gin, each about half full. I didn't have a hell of a lot to mix with any of it. I'm actually pretty awful at shopping. I tend not to buy anything I have to eat right away, and so my kitchen usually ends up full of crackers and canned vegetables.

"I think we need to go shopping," I said.

"So what do you think of her?" he said again. "Really, I mean."

"I like her," I said. I had to admit that. That's the thing about charming, beautiful women. You have to like them, even if you don't want to. And that's the other thing. While we were sitting there she had said some pretty funny things. I had kind of enjoyed being around her. So it didn't really have anything to do with wanting to like her or not wanting to like her because I did like her, before I even noticed it, and I understood what Canasson meant. It was pretty easy to see that she was a hell of a girl. But then pretty soon I realized that it didn't matter about all that, because she was a hell of a girl and I was going to live here and it was nice to know someone else. So I said, "I like her. I don't know her very well." I said it like he was the one making a big deal out of it, even though I knew it was me who was making it into something bigger than it was. But Canasson didn't argue with me about it.

"All right," he said, like he was making too big a deal out of it. "All right, you're right, it's not a big deal. Let's just have a good time. It doesn't matter and if we have a good time that's good and if we have a bad time then we don't need them."

"All right," I said. "What do you want to drink?"

"Now?"

"Tonight."

"Tom Collins."

"We'll have to go buy lemons," I said.

We went to buy lemons. By the time we got back it was mid-afternoon and hot. We had a Tom Collins each, to test the lemons, and then we went swimming. The water was cold but felt good against the heat. We swam out a ways, and Canasson looked around and said he loved it here, and I said why don't you stay another couple days, and he said all right. I had to go into the city on Wednesday, and Canasson said he would ride in with me, and that way he could pick up some things from his office. It sounded pretty good and so we didn't talk any more about it, I guess so we wouldn't spoil it. Then Canasson said it must be getting on towards four and that we had better swim back and get cleaned up. So we did that. We went side-by-side halfway, and then Canasson put on steam and pulled out ahead. I tried to catch up but after a minute later I gave up and treaded water and watched him beat a line back to the dock. Then, when he was a ways in, I started in after him, going half-speed. I didn't really feel like racing in the first place.

When I got to the house Canasson was already in the shower. I stood in the kitchen and listened to the water running, and then I realized I was dripping all over the floor so

I went back out on the porch and stood, looking out at the lake and drying off, until I heard the bathroom door open and heard him going up the stairs. By then I was pretty well dry so I didn't worry about dripping and I went down the hall to the bathroom and got in the shower. But the hot water ran out pretty fast, and I had to get out before I had washed my hair. I figured that it didn't matter because my hair was pretty clean before I went in the lake, and I had rinsed it in the shower. Still it kind of annoyed me that Canasson had used up all the hot water. But then, while I was brushing my teeth, I forgot about it.

I went upstairs and got dressed. When I came back down Canasson was in the kitchen mixing up a batch of Tom Collinses. One of the gin bottles was out and empty and he had a half dozen squeezed lemon halves on the counter next to him, and another dozen or so uncut lemons beside those. He was squeezing the lemons into the pitcher but standing far away from it so that none of it would get on his clean shirt.

"Here Elliot," he said, "help me squeeze these lemons." He said it looking over his shoulder at me, and before he was finished saying it he had already turned back to watch what he was doing. He seemed nervous. Or maybe I was nervous. I went over and cut a lemon and squeezed one half and then the other into the pitcher. While I was doing that Canasson got the club soda out of the refrigerator and poured it in, a little at a time. It fizzed in the lemon juice. I cut another lemon and squeezed it in. I threw the crushed peels onto the pile.

"What should we do with all these peels?" he said.

"I don't know," I said. "Throw them away, or something. What do people do with them out here? Compost them?"

"I don't know," said Canasson, but he said it like he wasn't thinking about the peels anymore, so I didn't say anything else about them. He took a glass down from the shelf and poured it a quarter full. Then he made a face. "God, that's awful," he said.

"You didn't add the sugar," I said.

He got the sugar down and stirred it, then tried the drink again. Then he poured in more sugar. "Easy," I said. I took his glass and tried it. It was too sweet and I cut and squeezed in two more lemons. While I did this Canasson went outside and smoked a cigarette. I guess he was pretty nervous. I was pretty surprised to see him that way, but I guess it was just because I didn't know him very well.

About twenty minutes later June arrived. She came around back and came up on the deck. There was another woman with her, who June introduced as Rene, the goddess of Eros, which made them both laugh. They seemed to have been drinking already but they both seemed very happy.

"I'm sorry about Bernard," June said as they came inside. "He wanted very much to meet you both. But then when the time came to leave he just wasn't ready to be finished yet. He was firing some things and if he leaves them in too long, you know, it ruins them."

"That's fine," I said. "Would you like a drink?"

"I'd love one," said Rene. She took the cup I handed her in both hands and then made a deep pleasure moan in her throat as she drank. "What is that?" she said, in a loud voice, "what is that?"

"Jesus Christ," I said.

"It's lemons," Canasson said. He put his arm around my shoulder. "Elliot here squeezed them himself."

"Did you?" she said. "Mmmm."

"June," I said, "why did you say your husband couldn't be here tonight?" I felt Canasson's grip tighten for a second on my shoulder, then release. June waved a hand around in the air.

"He was going to come," she said. "But then Rene came over, and we called him up to the house to have a drink with us, and he had to be quick, because you know how clay dries, but we made him have two, but by the time he was finished the second one he said it was too late for him to finish what he was working on and get cleaned up in time to come over. So he said we should go instead. And so we did. Aren't we enough for you?" She made a face, and Rene laughed and almost spit her drink all over the kitchen. It was pretty easy to see that they were up and a little drunk and having fun and when you are around women like that you can only play along or go somewhere else, and since I couldn't go anywhere else I kept my mouth shut and drank off about three-quarters of what was in my glass.

"We were just looking forward to meeting him," said Canasson, although it was pretty easy to tell that he was lying and didn't give a good goddamn about her husband and would just as soon never meet him. I mean, he said it so that everybody could tell. It was a way of letting June know that she didn't have a husband as far as he was concerned. It seemed pretty harmless, though.

"I just love this shirt," said Rene, rubbing my shoulder. She put her arm through mine, and put her head on my shoulder. "Mmm," she said. Not at me, but just kind of in general. She wasn't a bad-looking girl. In fact, she wasn't bad-looking at all. She was short and her legs were a little thicker than they looked like they ought to be for the size of her body, but you could hardly tell. I mean, you could tell if you studied her ankles, but that was about it. She was wearing a sleeveless dress, like the one June was wearing when we met her that first night, but hers was dark blue and was tied around the waist with a sash. What I mean is, with what she was wearing, you could really tell that her body was pretty good. But you could also tell that it wasn't one of those bodies that was naturally good, it was more like one she had to work on a lot, and the way she carried it you could tell that there were a lot of things she still wanted to change about it. It was the kind of thing I might not have noticed, except that when she was around June you could tell because June carried herself so well, and you could tell that June was proud of everything her body could do, and wasn't concerned with the way it looked, because of the way it felt. Still, Rene wasn't a bad-looking girl. She had a very square chin and a small mouth that she held tight and a little puckered and that made it look smaller still. It was a good mouth, but it did not feel like you could kiss it because it did not look like it could move. Like I said, she wasn't bad-looking, but that is different from saying that she was beautiful.

"Lets go out onto the porch," said Canasson. "We can have a drink out there and decided where we're going for dinner."

He took the pitcher and his glass and I opened the door for him. He went out and June followed him and then Rene unwrapped herself from my arm and went after. I drained off the rest of my drink and then I mixed another for myself. It was hard to tell how much gin to use and I ended up making it very strong. Then the lemon squirted when I tried to squeeze it into the glass, and I got lemon juice on my sleeve. I knew they were waiting for me out on the porch and I didn't have any good reason for staying inside and I felt the way you feel when someone else's child is hanging on your leg, kind of anxious and also like you wish the whole thing wasn't happening. But once my drink was finished and I added the sugar I took a sip and felt a little better, and I walked out onto the porch with my drink in my hand, feeling like I didn't have to explain myself, anyway.

The girls were sitting in the chairs, facing the lake, and Canasson was leaning against the railing, facing them. I went over and stood beside him, then leaned back against the railing as well. The sun was just behind the peak of the roof and the sky behind the house was washed out yellow and white. There was a warm breeze blowing in off the lake. I felt fine and like there was nowhere else I would rather be.

"It was an absolute nightmare," June was saying. "Here I am, coming into the museum, and I'm just absolutely soaking wet. And I'm thinking to myself, "is it going to be worse to show up looking like this, or to not show up at all?"

I don't think I ever made a decision on that, either. But I hadn't come to a decision, at least, by the time I reached the door, and so I went in. Naturally, right. And who is standing inside the doorway but Jimmy Stewart. I swear to God. And he looks me over, and here I am, this sixteen year old girl, and I'm soaking wet, and he looks at me and he said, I'll never forget this, he said, "I see they've reopened the fountain." Oh my goodness. And then he gave me his handkerchief and I made an absolute mess of it in the bathroom, and I was so embarrassed about it – it was smeared with mascara and everything, that I just kept it, and I avoided him all the rest of the time I was there." She laughed and hid her face in her hands, and I could see the muscles form up under the skin of her bare arms. "I still have it, somewhere," she said. "The handkerchief, that is."

"That's an incredible story," said Canasson. "My god." He took a drink.

"So Rene," I said, "do you live around here?"

"Oh no," she said. "I live in the city. I just come up here sometimes during the summer. My mother lives up here and so I come up and stay with her. Most of the year I live at my father's apartment in the city. He travels for business so he's barely ever there. It works out very well. When ever I get sick of one, I just go to stay with the other!" She laughed. Then, when none of us laughed, she went on like she hadn't laughed. "That's how I met June, though." She touched June's arm. "I came up here because my father was home and we were on the outs, I guess you'd say, and my mother and I weren't getting along very well either and I...," she sighed, and then turned the sigh into words, so that the sound fell from high to low. "I was just sitting in that bar over down the street and June came in and bought me a drink because she said I looked sad, and she asked me what was wrong, and I told her, and pretty soon she was insisting that I come and stay with her at her house, until I got things worked out with my parents." She looked at June that kind of over-acted affection in her eyes, like you could tell she was thinking of someone describing her giving June an affectionate look. "We've been friends ever since. She saved my life that night."

I choked on my drink when she said that and then, because she looked upset at me I made an apologetic face and turned away to cough into my hands. But I really almost died laughing. It just about killed me not to. The image of Rene in her navy blue dress drinking a martini and thinking of a poetic way to off herself to get back at her parents made me want to bust a gut. But pretty soon I got back under control and I tried to look as serious as Rene was acting about the whole thing.

"I tell you what," I said. I picked up the pitcher and refilled everyone's glasses, and that killed the pitcher. "Arthur, you want to help me squeeze the lemons?"

"Ooh," said Rene. "I want to!"

"All right," I said. I walked around the chairs with the pitcher in one hand and my glass in the other, and I waited for Rene to catch up so she could open the door. Then we went inside. Through the kitchen window I watched Canasson take Rene's chair, and then I got busy laying out the ingredients and I stopped watching them. I guess I was pretty annoyed at Canasson, but only because I was stuck with Rene in the kitchen. I should have been annoyed at Rene, but it didn't make much sense to be annoyed at her. It was like being annoyed at someone's dog. It seemed like you kind of had to forgive her for the way she was.

So while I poured in the gin and then added the ice cubes Rene cut the lemons and then started squeezing them. She did it by putting the lemon half in between both hands with her fingers intertwined and then pushing her palms together, with her elbows up. She looked pretty ridiculous and so I took the lemon half from her and squeezed out the rest of the juice with one hand. She must have thought I was trying to impress her, because she looked at me like it was some kind of something that I could get more juice out of it that she could.

"You've got really strong hands," she said. "Here, let me see." She took my hand and held it up, then pressed her palm against mine and examined the lengths and widths of our fingers. "Wow," she said. "You've got really big hands."

"Thanks," I said. I pulled my hand away from hers and started squeezing lemons again. She didn't move, and I could feel what she was about to do before she did it. So I watched out the window. But all I could see was the tops of their heads over the high wooden backs of the chairs. Then, she did it. I just kind of let it happen. First she leaned over so that her hip was resting against the counter. Then she slid down the counter to where I was standing. She put her glass down on the counter next to the lemons and then reached up and turned my face towards her. Her fingers were sticky from the lemons against my cheek and tasted bitter and citric against my lips. Her eyes were half-closed and it was pretty easy to see that she was drunk. She took a small step forward, and slipped her hand around the back of my neck and pulled me down towards her. I let her. Her lips tasted sweet from the gin and the sugar and when she pulled away the taste turned sour with the aftertaste of lemons. She smiled up at me like she knew something, now. Then she turned around and went back out onto the porch. She looked at me from the doorway, still smiling, then turned and went out. I guess she thought she was being seductive. I went to get the club soda.

I finished mixing the drinks and then I went back out onto the porch. Canasson had given Rene back her seat and I didn't look at her until I was back around beside Canasson, against the front railing. Rene looked at me over the top of her glass. She seemed like she had moved into that slow, down kind of drunk that comes on sometimes when you have been drinking for a few hours and your mind and body have readjusted. But then, a minute later, she was up again, chatting with June. June seemed interested, but not excitable. Canasson was watching her. I watched him watch her, and then I just watched my drink because they all seemed like a horrible pain in the ass and for a minute I thought maybe I would excuse myself and go up to bed and not deal with any of them anymore. But then they started talking about dinner, and I realized that I was hungry, and with realizing that I was hungry I realized that I was drunk, and that when I am drunk it is always easy to feel this way, and that perhaps they were not all so bad after all. So I decided to stay. If nothing else, this way I would have dinner.

So they talked about where to go for a while. June listed off all of the restaurants that she knew well around the lake, and then listed off the ones she had heard of that she had not been to. Then Canasson refilled everyone's glass, and we toasted new friends and the sunset. Then June said that she loved to swim at sunset, that the water felt warm because the air had gone cold, and Canasson agreed and Rene suggested that we all go for a swim before dinner. It sounded like a hell of a lot of trouble to me, but everyone else seemed pretty keen on it. Canasson went to get a pair of undershirts for the girls to wear, and then the girls went inside to take off their dresses, and Canasson and I walked down to the dock.

"This is so stupid," I said, pulling off my shirt.

"Why?" said Canasson. "What's stupid about it?" He was not angry, but he was very up. He unbuttoned his shirt, then untucked it, then took it off. "I think it sounds like fun."

"We just got out of the damn lake," I said. "We just got cleaned up. We're going to have to do it all over again." I took off my shoes and socks and stepped out of my pants. I crossed my arms across my stomach and stood shivering in my shorts. It wasn't very cold, though, and so I guess I must have been shivering about something else.

"We won't have to do it all over again," Canasson said. "And besides, what's it matter?" He was drunk and I could see that nothing mattered to him. I tried to think of a reason why it mattered, but I couldn't. I was thinking that maybe I could be an indifferent drunk, too, when the girls came down from the house. In the dusk their legs and arms and faces were the most visible and then as they got closer I could see the rest of them. They moved quickly across the grass, with their arms crossed across their chests and Canasson's shirts hanging down to their thighs. You could really see how thick Rene's legs were, then.

"Gentlemen," June said, and they giggled, and I could see why she hung around with Rene.

"Ladies," said Canasson, very serious, "after you."

"Oh no," said June.

"Oh yes," said Canasson, making a move at her. She shrieked and pulled away but she let him catch her around the waist and he lifted her and carried her to the end of the dock. He tried to drop her off, but she clung around his neck and they both toppled forward and hit the water. They came up laughing. Rene looked at me like she expected me to drop her in, too, but instead I just reached my hand back to her and she took it and we ran off the end of the dock together.

In the water everybody was happy and then expectant and then tentative and then quiet. It all went straight down. No one knew what to do once we were in. We all treaded water around each other for a minute, and then when no one really said or did anything I pulled my legs together and my arms to my sides and sank, and then paddled my arms upwards until I hit the bottom. The water turned much colder a few feet below the surface and turned black. The bottom was a little less that five feet below where the water turned cold, and I felt the line of cold close up around my stomach and then around my chest, and then my feet touched the muddy bottom and I came up. Rene shrieked when I did, but it was only because there was nothing else to do or say. She splashed me like I had done something awful to her, but when she stopped paddling with one hand to splash me she began to sink, and so she only splashed me once.

"You're positively wicked!" she said. I splashed her a little to show her that I was, or that I was game, or maybe just because I didn't want to talk. She squealed and covered her face with her hands and started to sink and then began paddling again, bobbing up out of the water a little with each stroke. She was really a pretty weak swimmer.

"Is it very far to the float?" said June. She and Canasson had swum further out. I could just see them as dark shapes on the water.

"Not too far," said Canasson.

"Let's race," said June.

"All right," said Canasson, "Elliot, you count us off."

"Ooh, I love races," said Rene.

I counted them off and then they both took off at once. I watched them out to a distance of five or eight yards, and then they melted into the darkness. I listened to the sound fading.

"I saw a bicycle race, once," said Rene. "We got seats right up on the curve of this hill, and when the bikers came around it they ducked down really close to the street, and one of them, he fell, and another of the bikers ran him over. We had to move to let the ambulance get through. It was all very exciting." She was speaking in time with her strokes, emphasizing every third or fourth word as she kicked down and pushed out with her arms. It's a funny way to hear someone talk. I think it would make anything sound better.

"You know what they ought to do," I said, "they ought to have big vats of water that the news anchors tread water in while they're reading off the news. It wouldn't be that different, it would just be a tank of water with a head coming out of it, instead of a suit. None of the bad news would seem that bad, I bet. It would be hard to be scared of something said like that."

She got what I was saying, but slowly. She didn't say anything when she got it, but it was pretty easy to tell. Or maybe she didn't get it, and she just didn't know what to say. It's certainly possible. A girl like Rene, it's usually that she doesn't know what to say. I swam out a little ways and listened for Canasson and June. I heard them pretty soon.

Then, I saw them. June was out ahead. They came in fast and I told Rene to move but instead she just made a sound like she was being menaced and so I ducked under the water and let them pass over me. Their kicking was loud underwater and when I came up I could hear Canasson's heavy breathing and so I swam over towards it. He was hanging on the dock with one arm. June was there beside him, but when I swam over she dove and then a minute later I heard her talking to Rene, but I couldn't hear what they were saying. They moved far enough off so that we wouldn't hear. I figured they were talking about me, and about what an ass I was being, and I didn't really mind except that it was going to make dinner awfully unpleasant.

"So she beat you," I said.

"Damn it, Elliot," he said.

"It's all right," I said, "a lot of men get beat by women. It probably doesn't mean anything." I was ribbing him and he knew it, but he wasn't enjoying it. "Maybe," I said, "if you bring anything back from the city next time, she can help you unpack. You know. Carry the heavy stuff." He launched at me, and caught me on the shoulders, and we went under, and I swam out from beneath him and pushed him down with my feet. He started to come up and then I surfaced and couldn't see him anymore, and a second later he came up beside me. He came up facing away from me and as he turned to me I ducked under and went for his legs. I heard him call out before I pulled him under. He came down even with me and shoved me back, and then paddled for the surface. I stayed under a little longer, knowing that he was upset at being beaten and by my ribbing him, and that with him mad and Rene convinced that I was an ass it would be uncomfortable on the surface, but that below the water it was peaceful and still. I normally don't like being underwater for very long, but now it seemed nicer than what I thought was waiting for me on the surface. But then I needed air so I went up.

Canasson was back hanging on the dock, and June and

Rene were next to him. I swam up and grabbed onto the dock on the other side of Canasson, away from the girls. He was still breathing heavy, but he was trying not to show it. It was pretty easy to tell, though. The dock made a hollow slapping sound with the water moving around inside the boards. You could hear it from up top, but down next to it that sound was all you could hear. After a minute I pulled myself out and turned around to sit on the end of the dock, facing out. The lake was a different black from the shore and the sky. The sky was paler, almost gray, and you could see all of the stars. Which is to say you could see a hell of a lot more of the stars than you could see in the city. The water was close to the sky color but it was darker. The shore was pure black except where there were yellow squares of lit windows. There was a fire out on one of the islands, far out outside of the bay. Nothing made very much sense and I felt drunk and very calm, and like I was dead and a ghost and detached and only watching. That's a pretty stupid thing to say, but that's how I felt. Sometimes when I'm drunk I get like that. Everything is distant and nothing matters very much.

I fished a cigarette out of Canasson's pants pocket and lit it and sat smoking and felt better. I could hear June and Rene and Canasson down in the water. They were talking about races, and then Canasson changed the subject. I guess he was pretty upset about being beaten by June. Or maybe something had happened that I hadn't seen. Either way he took my kidding him pretty hard. Then Canasson came over and hung on the dock near me and took a drag on my cigarette. The girls stayed out in the water. I could hear them talking and then a little while later I could hear them singing. They sang an old song that I knew and I thought about joining them but then I decided against it. Then, a little later, the girls swam over and we all got out. The girls stood with their arms crossed. Canasson and I picked up our clothes and we all went up to the house. Going up the steps to the porch Rene slipped and caught herself with her arms, and when she stood up I could see her nipples standing out through her shirt, and the shape of her breasts, and I thought again that she really wasn't such a bad-looking girl.

We went inside, and went upstairs. The girls went into Canasson's room and Canasson brought a change of clothes and we went into mine. We stood facing away from each other as we changed and then I faced away from him for a lot longer than I needed to because he didn't tell me that he was finished. Then he said, "Rene thinks you're mad at her," and I turned around.

"I'm not mad at her," I said. "I think she's goddamned insane, but I'm not mad at her."

He sat down on the bed and buttoned his cuffs. "Look," he said. "The way to a woman's heart is through her friends. You not getting along with Rene makes a problem for June which makes a problem for me." He was all business, now. You could tell it just by looking at him. "You don't have to marry the girl," he went on, "but do me the courtesy of being civil with her for the evening, all right?"

"All right," I said, like he was making a bigger deal out of it than he needed to. He was, too, but I felt like an ass and wanted to have a good time more than I wanted to be right. "She's not bad," I said, trying to make everything all right again. "She's pretty good-looking, and you can tell that she means well, even if she says the wrong thing." But that didn't seem to change anything, so I said, "how did the race go? I mean, when you guys reached the raft and all? I lost sight of you after about twenty feet."

"It went fine," he said, not looking at me.

"Don't be like that," I said.

He looked surprised. "Be like what?" he said.

The door to Canasson's room was still closed, and we went downstairs to have a drink and to wait for the girls. Halfway through our second the girls came down. By then I was starting to feel pretty good again and like I didn't give a damn one way or another about anything. When Rene came down I was actually glad to see her. She looked pretty relieved when she saw me smiling at her.

"Hello girls," said Canasson. "Would you both care for another drink before we go out?"

"Oh, just a little one," said Rene. She came over and put her arm through mine. "Just make me a little one."

"I'll have another," I said. I felt drunk and warm and happy enough to have Rene on my arm. Then Canasson and June went into the kitchen to make the drinks, and I sat down on the living room couch with Rene. She folded her head against my chest as we sat down and then leaned up and kissed me. I held her there and kissed her back and for what felt like a long time we didn't move very much. I could hear Canasson and June in the other room, but I couldn't hear what they were saying. There was the sound of ice in glasses. I thought at first that there might not be enough ice and then I remembered that there was, and then I tried to think of what was in the freezer and what was in the refrigerator, and what they could make, and whether Canasson knew how to make certain drinks that I thought of, and then I remembered that Rene was kissing me. So I kissed her back and then kissed her neck and touched her and she seemed to melt a little into me. What I mean is she softened into me the way clay gets soft and forms around whatever you press against it.

But then I figured Canasson and June would be coming back, so I backed off of her. Not enough to make her ask what was wrong, but just a little, like I was teasing her. I *was* teasing her, I guess. But pretty soon Canasson and June came in, and I was glad that I had backed off. You could tell that Rene was, too. She was a lush, but you could tell that she didn't want people to know it. She pulled her skirt down over her knees and touched up the edges of her mouth. It was pretty easy to tell what we had been doing, though. It's not like it was a secret. Canasson winked at me when he put our drinks down on the table. Rene smiled up at him.

"What are we going to drink to this time?"

"Let's drink to finding a good restaurant," said Canasson.

"No, no," said Rene, over June's laughter. "It has to be something important. It has to be something like a baby or a *hunt* or something." She was looking at June, and when June giggled Rene lost her composure for a second. She got it back, though. "I mean it," she said, slapping her palm into the empty fold of cloth between her parted knees. "It's got to be something. You know, *something*." She pressed her hand to her forehead and smiled, weakly. "I don't know. Elliot, you understand, don't you?"

"Sure," I said. "I understand." But I couldn't think of anything to toast to, either, so after a minute I just raised my glass and said "to the eternal and wholehearted propagation of that which is not and which we wish was." I thought that sounded pretty good, so I left it at that. I guess everybody else thought it sounded pretty good, too, because they lifted their glasses and we all drank.

"That was very nice," said Rene.

"Rene, dear," said June, "do you even know what he said?"

"Of course I know what he said," said Rene. "He said, may we always not have everything that we want, so that we always have something to want. Right, Elliot?"

"Sure," I said. I put my arm around her shoulders. "Sure, that's what it meant."

She smiled, then took a drink, then coughed and said, "you didn't make this one weaker at all, did you?" Canasson laughed. "You fink," she said, swatting towards him in the air. "You are an absolute fink."

"There's no getting out easy," said Canasson.

"That's a rotten thing to do," said June, but you could tell she didn't mean it. Then, to Rene, "you don't have to drink it, sweetie, if you don't want to."

"It's all right," said Rene. "It just surprised me is all. I'm all right." She took another drink to show us that she was all right. We all drank with her. She coughed a little, but she didn't say anything about it, and none of us did, either. But you knew she didn't want to drink it but that she was going to and that nobody was going to stop her and it was awful, in a way, to watch. So we all drank our drinks and pretended not to notice.

When we finished our drinks we all went out to the car. Canasson said he could drive. He could, too. He handled booze better than anyone else I've ever met. Rene was a mess. I helped her to the car. She was stumbling over her shoes in the grass. The heels kept sticking in the ground. It wasn't her fault, really, about the heels and the ground being soft. She would have looked clumsy anyway.

We got going and then June picked a restaurant and so instead of just going we were going there, and it made everyone feel better. I was in the backseat with Rene. She had her head on my shoulder and then she slid down and curled up with her head in my lap, and kicked off her shoes. I asked June how long it would take to get to the restaurant and she said twenty minutes and probably thirty because we wanted to take it slow and not get pulled over because the police did not understand a thing like Canasson being able to drive very well when he had already had a few and was going to have a few more before the night was over. I figured that Rene would sober up some in half an hour and that everything would be fine again if we could keep her from drinking anything or too much with dinner. It seemed like a good plan, and it kept me from getting anxious, and so that made it seem like a much better plan than it actually was. It was not a very bad plan, but necessity made it seem better. Anyway I tried to relax now that I had a plan and have a conversation with June and Canasson. But they were already talking together, and they did not let up until the restaurant was in sight. I listened for a little while, but when I realized that I was not going to be able to add anything I gave up and stopped listening. There didn't seem to be much point.

HERE GROAN THE DEAD

When we got to the restaurant I shook Rene and she woke up. She seemed very much like she did not want to get up, but that she understood that she had to, without me saying anything. Canasson opened her door and she swung her legs out and then put on her shoes sitting sideways on the seat. I got out the other side and opened June's door for her. She gave me her hand and I helped her stand. She was very stable and when she was up I let go of her hand without worrying about it. She and Canasson were some pair.

Rene hung on my arm while we went inside. We got a booth in a far corner and I let Rene get in first. A minute later she was passed out against the wall. It was pretty embarrassing, but then I remembered that it was none of my damned business if she wanted to get drunk and fall asleep in a restaurant. Not that I respected her decision, but that it had nothing to do with me, and to hell with the wait staff. So once she was out I kind of relaxed and got a chance to look around.

The place was more or less a pub. A big loop of bar stood in the center of the room and around it there were maybe two dozen men and women. Around them were tables, most of them empty, except for the few people who had taken their drinks from the bar to talk away from the noise, and then the booths. Up in front there was a small dance floor and jukebox was playing music. I could see people dancing through the crowd at the bar. Not very well, though. The place was pretty dark.

"I feel like I could eat for a goddamned week," I said. It was true, too. I hadn't eaten anything since breakfast, and the booze and the lemon and the sugar were all churning in my stomach. But nobody seemed to hear me. Canasson and June were talking, and I couldn't hear what they were saying. So I gave up trying to talk and just looked at my menu.

The waiter came, and we ordered. Then, while we were waiting for our food, Canasson said that he and June were going to go dance, and they slid out of the booth. June was excited and you could tell Canasson was excited, too, even though he tried not to show it. After they were gone I called the waiter over and ordered a couple of coffees. When he brought them I woke Rene up and made her drink some of the coffee. She didn't want to but I was bored and feeling pretty antagonistic and pretty soon I got her to drink a fair bit of it, by adding in cream and sugar until it wasn't really like drinking coffee at all. After that, though, she went back to sleep. I was too drunk to really have the energy to feel much of anything, but I remember being pretty annoyed that they had left me with Rene like that. I guess I was marked for it when I kissed her, but I didn't give a good goddamn about her and I gave less of one after every drink. I would have left, too, if it hadn't been for Canasson's speech about Rene and June and how it would be bad for him if I did anything like that. I don't know. Maybe there were other reasons.

So I drank my coffee and watched the crowd on the dance floor. There were actually only about six or eight couples, but the floor was so small that it looked like there were more. Every once in a while I caught a glimpse of June and Canasson. They danced big on the up songs. You could see them from a mile away. Canasson really was a hell of a dancer, and it looked like June was, too, but maybe she was just good at following. It's hard to tell, sometimes. But then I caught sight of them on one song, and it was pretty obvious that June could hold her own. Then a slow song came on and they danced close together, and I saw Canasson lean down to kiss her, and her pull away. She pulled away, but she never stopped dancing. And the other thing was, she didn't pull away like she didn't want him to kiss her. She knew it was coming and she waited until he got in close and then she pulled back. You could tell how it was because Canasson came up grinning. Then they went behind another couple, and then another couple came in front, too, and I couldn't see them. I leaned out to try and see, but I couldn't, and so I decided I didn't care and I woke Rene up and made her drink some more coffee.

HERE GROAN THE DEAD

Our food came, and then a little while later June and Canasson came back. Canasson was in front, and he was holding June's hand. I don't want to say that June was holding his hand, because I don't know. But if she wasn't holding his hand, she was doing a hell of a job of looking happy about it. It was the kind of excitement over innocent flirtation you see in people who know they will go home to their spouses. I guess she knew that Canasson wouldn't be, though. Still, somehow, it looked pretty harmless.

So we ate, and about halfway through Rene woke up and said she was hungry and I gave her the rest of my dinner. I wasn't really hungry anymore, anyway. It's funny how that happens, sometimes. How you can be hungry and then wait too long and then it disappears. I mean, you think it disappears, but it always comes back. But right then it was gone and so I didn't mind giving it to her. Besides, it seemed to sober her up, and that meant that I wouldn't have to carry her up to the house. Canasson kicked me a couple times through dinner, but I don't think it was my foot he was going for.

After that we decided we were pretty tired, so we drove June and Rene back to June's house. I was going to help carry Rene in, but Rene said she could do it herself, and goodnight, and since Canasson was already out of the car he gave her his arm and walked her up. June walked out ahead of them. I watched them from the back seat, and then I got out and got in the front seat, where June had been sitting. Then the front door closed behind them, and I turned on the radio and found some light jazz and I put my head back and tried to fall asleep. But when the song on the radio ended Canasson wasn't back yet, and when the next song ended I got sick of waiting and got out and headed up to the house. But when I was halfway up the walk the front door opened and Canasson came out. I stopped and he walked down to me. He had his hands in his pockets and he was grinning and when he reached me he didn't stop. He went straight to the car and got in. I ran around and got in the passenger side.

"What happened?" I said. "Did something happen?"

He shrugged. "Whatever could have happened?" he said. "She's a married woman."

"So what the hell are you grinning about?"

He shrugged again. "A gentleman never kisses and tells," he said.

"You son of a bitch," I said. "I don't think anything happened."

"You are, of course, entitled to your opinion."

"Come on," I said. "Tell me what happened."

"Nothing," he said, still grinning. "Nothing at all." Then he pulled out of the driveway, and I didn't talk to him anymore because he was focusing hard on the driving, and when we got going he was still focused on driving and didn't look at me. "What are we doing tomorrow?" he said.

"I've got some work I need to do," I said. "And I was thinking of pulling the boat out from under the house, and see how it looks. You're really not going to tell me?"

"Tell you what?"

"Fine," I said. "Fine."

"You seemed to be getting along pretty well with Rene," he said. He only said it because he knew I didn't give a rat's ass about Rene, and what we both wanted him to talk about wasn't going to get talked about. You could just see how much he was loving doing it. That was the thing about Canasson. He could be a real son-of-a-bitch sometimes, if he wanted to be. He was generous as hell, but he also had this malicious streak that knew how to torture someone if they wanted something he had. I only saw it later, though. Then I thought he was just getting me back for what I said to him about June beating him in the swimming race.

"Oh, yeah," I said. "Rene. She's a doll, Arthur. A regular peach. It's just that I got a little tired of worrying about her throwing up on my shoes. Other than that though she's perfect for me."

HERE GROAN THE DEAD

"June wanted me to apologize to you for her," he said. He said it in this way where you could just tell that he was proud as hell that he could say it like he and June had a private conversation about it. "She said that Rene usually doesn't get like this," he went on, "but that things have been a little hard for her at home lately. June says that Rene is going to be sorry as hell in the morning, and will probably call and try to make it up to you. She says that's the way Rene is. That whenever she does this she always tries to make it right." He knew it was killing me to hear him say "June says" and not hear the rest of what she said, or what happened, while I was in the car. But I didn't want to give him the satisfaction, so I just looked out the window.

But then, pretty soon, I forgot about it. I started thinking about something else. But pretty soon I remembered and I wanted to know even worse than I had before. That's the thing about it. You can't just ignore it, because that only makes it worse.

We got home and went inside and went upstairs without saying anything more about it. Then I got undressed and got into bed and lay awake for a while. But it was pretty late and I was tired. I knew I wasn't going to have any trouble falling asleep when I wanted to, so I didn't really mind laying there, awake. I wondered some more about Canasson and June. Probably nothing had happened, I thought, and his whole act coming outside and in the car had been just to make me crazy. But then, since I was awake already, I started to think about maybe it wasn't just an act, maybe something did happen, and I thought about the things that could have happened, and how it might have happened. The weird thing was, though, that it didn't make me crazy, the way him not telling me had. It was kind of exciting. I thought about it for a while, and then I thought that probably nothing had happened, and I closed my eyes and went to sleep.

VI.

The next morning the phone rang but I stayed in bed and fell back asleep and then when I woke up I saw that I had slept through the sunrise. I got dressed and went downstairs. Canasson wasn't on the porch, but there was a pile of clothes out on the dock and I followed a line straight out until I saw him. He was far out and for a while I couldn't tell if he was going away or coming closer. But then, a while later, I saw that he was coming closer. He was still a ways out, though, and so I went back inside. I thought about making breakfast, but then I decided against it. I didn't feel too well. I hadn't eaten much the day before and all the lemon and sugar and gin had worked my stomach over. So instead I washed the glasses and the pitcher and I threw away the lemon rinds. Then Canasson came in and helped me finish cleaning up. There wasn't really much to do. Then we made some coffee and went out on the back porch.

"So did you see her?" I asked.

"No," he said. "I guess I missed her. I wasn't really going out there to see her anyway. I just sort of wanted to see how far I could swim."

"I saw you. You were a ways out there."

"I thought I might be able to make it out of the bay, but then I got too tired."

"That would be a hell of a swim," I said. "What are you doing today?"

"I have some work I need to get done," he said. "Some things I need to do for the divorce to go through."

"Things are moving forward?"

"Yes?"

"Is it getting easier?"

"No."

"I've got to say," I said, "it seems like you're taking it pretty well."

He shrugged. "I guess I don't know how to act about

it."

"Do you want me to leave you alone about it?"

"I guess so," he said, "though I don't feel right about telling you what to do in your house."

"It's fine," I said, standing. "I'll leave you alone while you're working." I was pretty happy to be leaving, anyway. I didn't really know what to say to him. "Come find me when you're finished."

"All right," he said.

I went inside and went upstairs. After a little while I heard Canasson come in and come up the stairs and go into his room and then go back down again. I pulled a chair up to the window and sat there reading for a while. I could see Canasson down on the porch. He had a pile of papers in his lap that he was shuffling through and signing. Then the phone rang and I went to answer it. It was Greene.

"If you want to keep your job," he said, "you had better get down here. They just found her and Hinks wants to send Finnerty because he thinks you're MIA. I told him I'd give you a call and try to get you to come. He's not happy with you."

"What?" I said. It's a hell of a thing to hear out of the blue. "All right, all right," I said. "I'll be there in an hour."

"Gonna have to be here sooner," he said. "They're probably gonna have it closed up in an hour. We didn't get the call until after they'd started. See how fast you can get here."

"All right," I said. Greene gave me the address. Then I hung up and put on my suit jacket and got my camera and notebook and went downstairs. Canasson was still out on the porch, and I called out to him that I had to run into the city and would be back later. He waved over his shoulder, but didn't turn around. I went out and got into the car and headed back to the city. It was Sunday and traffic was pretty light, and I made good time all the way to the outskirts. But then the speed limit dropped and the road got clogged going through the city. I got through but I lost the time I made going between the lake and the limits.

They had the alley blocked off. She was laying on her back. The blood had pooled beneath her and glued her clothes to the pavement. There was a line across her neck where the necklace had been ripped off. But the necklace had broken, and there were pearls all over the ground. The cops were picking them up when I got there. She was older than she looked from far away. With her makeup you could hardly tell, though. You could tell by her hands. Her hands were old. The cop I talked to said whoever had done it probably got scared and ran off when they shot her. Her purse was still clutched tight in her fist.

I was going to go right back to the house, but instead I went to the newspaper to see if Greene was still around. I found him up in the beat room. He looked good. I hadn't seen him for a while. The sun always made him break out in freckles, and it made him look about ten years younger. When I walked in he stopped what he was doing and came over and hugged me.

"How'd it go?" he said. "How have you been?"

"It went fine," I said. "I've been good."

"Listen," he said, moving around me and shutting the door behind me. "Hinks is not happy with you. I heard him talking to Finnerty about it. The whole arrangement with you at the lake house. He says your work has gone to complete hell since you moved out there. He says you've "lost your calculated edge."" He made quote marks in the air with his fingers, then shrugged. "I don't know what that means," he said, "but it doesn't sound good. Are you all right?"

"I'm fine," I said. "Never better."

"I don't want to tell you your business," he said, "but you had better make good on this story."

"You worry too much," I said. "How's your wife?"

"She's fine," he said. Then, "all right, I get it. I'll mind my own business. Just giving fair warning."

"I appreciate it," I said, "but I'll be fine." I checked my watch. It was almost five o'clock. "What are you doing now?" I said. "Want to get a drink?" I felt like having a drink. I was actually a little shaken up by the scene in the alley. Usually those things don't bother me, but this time for some reason it did. The truth is that the way she looked when I first saw her, she kind of looked like a girl I used to know. Even after I saw that it wasn't her, I still felt like hell about it. I figured I'd be better after a drink. But Greene said he couldn't.

"I've got to get home," he said. "The wife's got dinner waiting."

"All right," I said, "maybe I'll catch you some other time."

"Sure," said Greene. He was putting on his jacket. "Sure, next time. Just tonight is no good. You understand."

"Sure, I understand," I said. "Hey thanks for the call, by the way."

"Of course," he said. "I know you'd do the same for me."

"Yeah," I said, although I couldn't think of any reason why he would know that. "Yeah, I'd do the same for you."

"All right," he said. "Good night, Elliot."

"Good night, Ray," I said. "Thanks again."

He went out and I watched him walk down the stairs and cross the floor and then go out through the main hallway. Then I sat down at my desk. I sat there for a while. I didn't really feel up to the drive back to the lake, but I figured I ought to go pretty soon, because Canasson was probably wondering where I was. So I left and started back, but after a few miles I started feeling lousy and I pulled off at one of the exits on the outskirts and had a drink. The bar was pretty awful, and since it was Sunday it was almost empty. The bartender just sat in the corner not really looking at anything and no one had put on any music. A couple of guys were playing pool in the corner, and every time the balls hit each other I jumped a little. I thought that I would feel better, but after a beer I just felt worse and like I felt lousy and wasn't doing anything good about it, and so I paid and headed home. On the way home I turned on the radio, but I turned it off when this one song came on. The reason I turned it off was because I started listening to the words, and pretty soon I was crying. I didn't know what to do about it, so I turned the radio off. After that I felt a little bit better. It really was a hell of a thing. But after the radio was off I didn't think about it any more.

When I walked into the house I could hear Canasson moving around upstairs, and when I closed the door he came to the top of the stairs.

"Jesus," he said, "where have you been? I called the newspaper, but they said that you left an hour and a half ago. We're going to be late." He was really excited and seeing him excited made me forget about everything.

"Late for what?" I said.

"Dinner," he said. "We're having dinner with June and Bernard tonight. June called right after you left and invited us over. Bernard wanted to make up for missing last night."

"All right," I said, "just give me a minute to get changed."

I went upstairs to get changed. When I came down Canasson was in the kitchen having a drink. There was another one sitting on the counter and when I walked in he handed it to me. We touched glasses then bolted them down, and then I followed him out the back door and down the steps and across the lawn. Canasson walked fast, with his hands in his pockets, and I almost had to jog to keep up with him. Around the southern curve of the bay the ground started to rise and we moved out onto the side of the road as we climbed. It was still pretty hot from the day and I could feel myself sweating through my undershirt.

We got to the house and walked between the trees and up the driveway. Across the bay the sun was setting behind

Bradner's house. The sky was pink around the edges and then pale blue-gray above and everything was still very clear. Canasson knocked on the door and June answered. She was wearing white and it made her skin look pink.

"Come in," she said. "Bernard is just getting cleaned up."

We went inside. June offered us a drink. We each made one and then we all went out on the porch to drink them. While we were toasting Bernard came down. He was small and wore a white dress shirt open at the collar and rolled to his elbows. His arms and the "v" of chest above his collar were covered in black hair but his face and neck were shaved clean and the hair on his head was cropped close and had just begun to pull away from his forehead above his temples. Despite that, he looked older than any of us. The wrinkles in his face were deep and obvious and ran out on long falling arcs from the corners of his eyes. He came down and then came across the kitchen and out onto the porch, and June rose and he held her shoulders as he kissed her cheek. Then we shook hands. Canasson stood and I stood and June said everyone's name. Then we all sat down. Bernard had to pull up a chair. Canasson offered us his cigarettes and we each took one.

"Have you been working a lot since you've been up here?" Canasson said.

"Oh yes," said Bernard.

"How is Rene?" I asked June. "Have you talked to her?"

"That poor girl," said June. "She was so embarrassed about last night. I invited her to come over for dinner, but she declined. I think she just didn't want to face you after the way she acted. She really doesn't drink that much, usually, and I think she wanted a little bit to impress you."

"Impress me," I said.

"Yes," she said. "She thought you were very charming. She's going back to the city tomorrow, though, and I don't know when she'll be back out. I think she and her mother had a bit of a fight about her coming in so late. She called me in tears this afternoon, poor doll. She wouldn't say what the matter was, but I think that's what it was. She and her mother don't really get along."

"Well tell her I had a great time with her, when you talk to her again," I said.

"That's very sweet of you," she said. "I will."

Bernard checked his watch. "Dinner must be ready by now," he said. "Lets go inside."

We all went in and took our seats around the table. Bernard brought the food over and we ate. I don't remember what it was. During dinner we had a few more drinks and I felt a whole lot better, even though I knew it was the kind of high that wasn't built on anything and was bound to collapse at any moment. And besides that, since it wasn't built on anything that had happened or anything that was said, I knew that nobody else felt quite the same way I did and so I kept my mouth shut. That way I got through dinner and then after June made coffee and I had two cups and felt that I was coming down and was relieved. It's easier to come down from a high like that than it is to maintain it. So after the coffee I felt sober and like I was part of the world again and pretty comfortable being around Canasson and June and Bernard.

During and after dinner Bernard let June talk and kept pretty quiet. I watched him watch her and then later I watched him watch Canasson. I looked at Canasson and saw the way he looked at June, and the way that June looked at him, and could see why. Still, you could tell that June was doing it because it was part of the act, part of her charm.

We had another drink after the coffee, and then somebody suggested we go over to the fair. Bernard said he could use a break and June said she would love to. I guess Canasson suggested it. Bernard got on the phone and then led us all downstairs and out across the patio and the lawn to the next lawn over and down the dock to a boat that was tied up there. He got in and told Canasson to man the lines and

Canasson made a mess of untying us. Then Bernard started the motor and Canasson pushed us a little off and then balked and then jumped and only made it halfway into the boat and June and I pulled him onboard. He was laughing when he stood up and June was laughing too and I didn't see what was so damned funny about it all but then Bernard gunned the motor and we all lurched and then adjusted to the speed and the chop of the waves against the hull and Canasson yelled over the roar and pulse of the spray that this was certainly a nice boat and Bernard said yes it is isn't it my neighbor lets me borrow it when he's not using it. After that nobody tried to talk and we just leaned against the railings and tried to stay out of the spray.

Bernard cut the motor as we pulled up along the pier, and Canasson climbed a ladder on the side of the pier with the rope in his hand and tied us off. Then June got out and climbed the ladder and Canasson helped her the last step up and Bernard and I climbed up on our own. Bernard waited for me and when I got up June and Canasson were already moving off towards the fair and June had her arm through Canasson's. I looked at Bernard to see how he would take it, but he just looked at them and then looked back at me as if was all about the same to him.

"I'm worried that the fair is going to be crowded tonight," he said. "The first weekend is always crowded."

"It was pretty crowded on Friday night," I agreed.

"All the new summer people are arriving," he said. "There are getting to be so many of us, I can hardly keep track."

For some reason I started feeling lousy again as soon as we left the boat and started up along the booths towards the gate. For one thing we were in the dark, and there was a lot of noise from the fair, but the booths made a wall and you couldn't really see in. On top of that, between June and Canasson, and Bernard, and the woman in the alley, everything felt awfully goddamned heavy. Bernard seemed like a nice enough guy, but he was the kind of a guy you couldn't spend too much time around, if you know what I mean. It was like there was an awful lot of him hanging in the air around him all the time. You could tell he tried not to do it in a bad way, that he was trying to do it in a way that would let people know that he was a serious artist while still being on their level. But that only made it worse, because then you felt like you were part of it, too. What I mean is, he made everyone else around him pretentious, without necessarily meaning to do it. It's just that whatever way you were around him became an act because you ended up looking at it too much.

June did that a little bit, too, but beautiful women always do that and so it didn't seem so strange with her. And besides, she handled it better than Bernard did. She did the same thing, but it was tempered with indifference. A lot of beautiful women act like that. But that's better than someone who acts like every goddamned thing you do or say is the most important thing ever said. Like everything you say is the goddamned sermon on the mount. A beautiful woman makes you wonder if she cares the whole goddamned time you're talking to her, so you never get a chance to pay any attention to yourself, because you're paying too much to her. Usually it drives me nuts, but with June it was kind of charming. She didn't make much of a big deal about it. She let you make the big deal, so that in the end when you felt like hell you could only look back at what you had said and done, while she stayed pretty much untouched.

But pretty soon I was tired of the whole damned thing. Canasson paid for everybody and we walked down past the booths, and Bernard knocked down a half-dozen wooden pins with a baseball for a buck, and then he bought us all tickets and we rode the merry-go-round. Under the big tent you couldn't hear anything except the metallic echo of the record and I took a horse a couple back from the rest of them and leaned against the pole so I could close my eyes while we went around. It's funny, but I kind of started to miss my old apartment and the way we all used to hang around the beat office. I guess it was the way that I caught Greene right when he was on his way out, and the way he couldn't go get a drink with me. It was a pretty stupid thing to think about, I guess, because I knew even when I was thinking about it how nice it was at Bradner's house, and how glad I was that Canasson had come out to stay with me, and what I thought of June. For a minute it just seemed like a hell of a lot of work to keep it all going.

I figured I was just tired, so after the ride stopped I said goodbye to everyone and I walked back to the house. We had left it dark and it was nice to know that there was nobody there to talk to. So I went in and didn't turn the lights on when I went up to my room. I could see the moon through the window at the top of the stairs, and I kind of stopped and looked at it for a while. It was almost full and it was right over the lake. It was a pretty nice scene, and right away I wanted Canasson or Rene or somebody to be there so I could show it to them. But after that, after wanting somebody to show the moon to, and there being nobody there, I started feeling pretty lonely again, so I just got into bed. I started to fall asleep, but then I realized I was falling asleep, and that woke me right the hell up.

About an hour later I heard a boat engine on the water, and then Canasson came in. I thought about getting up, but he came upstairs and went into his room and shut the door. I listened to him moving around, getting ready for bed, and for some reason that made me feel better. I guess maybe the thing with the moon bothered me more than I thought it had. Pretty soon I started thinking that the moon was probably still up right over the lake, and that maybe what I should do is get up and go get Canasson, and show it to him. He'd probably think that he woke me up when he came in, and then I'd have to tell him that he didn't. But then I figured that, since the window was right at the top of the stairs, he would have seen it already on his way up, if it was still there to see. I don't know. I guess it felt pretty important at the time is all. But pretty soon he stopped moving, and I didn't want to get him up if he was already in bed, so I just forgot about it. It's funny how sometimes things feel important when you're awake at night. I guess it's easy to forget that they aren't.

The next morning, when I came down to breakfast, Canasson was already up.

"I need to borrow the car," he said.

"Sure," I said. "What for?"

"I have to run into the city," he said. "Some things with the lawyers."

"Will you be back in time for lunch?"

"It's going to be tough," he said. "I'll call once I know. Better just have it without me, though."

"All right," I said. "The keys are by the door."

After he was gone I ate breakfast. Then I got my notebook out of my coat pocket and started writing up the story about the woman in the alley. It all made sense when I wrote it out. It seemed almost inevitable, actually. I guess it was because I already knew how it would turn out, but I was writing it from the beginning. But while I was doing that the phone rang. I figured it was Canasson, and since it was still so early he was calling to tell me that he couldn't make lunch. But it wasn't Canasson, it was June.

"Hi, Elliot," she said. "Is Arthur there?"

"No," I said. "He just left for the city an hour ago. I don't think he's going to be back until after lunch. How was the fair?"

"It was wonderful," she said. And then, without saying anything else about it, she said, "look, I was hoping to get together with Arthur for tennis this afternoon. There isn't any chance that he will be back by about two, is there?"

"I really don't know, but I don't think so," I said. And then, for I don't know the hell why, I said, "I could play."

"You play?" She sounded surprised. "Well, that would

be all right."

"I don't have a racket," I said.

"That's fine," she said. "You can use Bernard's. He never wants to play. He never uses it." Then she told me how to get to the court. It was on the north shore, around behind the new cabins, but I guess it had been there for a lot longer than them. Then she said, "I'll see you at two, then."

"Sure," I said. "Goodbye."

After I hung up I wondered why I did it. I didn't really feel much like playing tennis. I finished typing up the story and then I walked into town and mailed it off to the newspaper. By then it was mid-morning and I had a few hours to kill before meeting June. So I walked around town until I found a hardware store, and then I bought a couple sheets of heavy grit sandpaper and some paint. What I figured I would do was work on the boat for a while, and then take a swim and then get cleaned up. But when I got back to the house I couldn't find any brushes, and so I had to go back to the store and buy some. By then it was almost noon, and it felt like I wouldn't be able to get that much done. The boat wasn't really in such bad shape, but if I was going to paint the bottom I figured I would have to take all of the old paint off, like on a house. So I sanded down the bottom for a while. Then it started to get pretty hot, so I took off my shirt. Pretty soon I could feel myself burning, and so I went inside and changed into my trunks and jumped into the lake. I swam out a ways, then turned back around and went back to the house. It's funny. Swimming always sounds pretty good, but there isn't much point in doing it for very long if there's no one with you. So I got out, and then I went inside and took my time about getting cleaned up. But I actually took too much time, because by the time I came down to leave it was a quarter to two, and I still had to walk to the court.

The area around the courts was pretty crowded. You walked in through a squat brick building and past the locker rooms and out along a fenced-in swimming pool, along to a row of brown clay courts beneath a stand of trees. The courts were all in a row together and the leaves from the trees from last fall were blown into the corners and up against the fence. I walked along behind the near side of the fence until I saw June down at the end. She was kind of hard to spot. The courts were crowded and she was wearing a white visor and white skirt and sleeveless shirt and looked like a lot of the other women. The way I could tell it was her was by her hair. You could see it clear across the courts. So I went in and walked out across from her. She was hitting balls into the net, but she stopped when she saw me.

"Hello Elliot," she said. She didn't check her watch.

"Sorry I'm late," I said. "It's a longer walk than I thought it was." We were walking towards each other. Then she veered right and went over to the end, picked up Bernard's racket and came back and handed it to me. It was a pretty nice racket, and it didn't look used. "Thanks," I said.

"You serve," she said. She bent and picked up three balls at her feet, up against the net, and handed them to me.

"Sure," I said. In that skirt you could really see just how good her legs were. I caught myself looking at them, and so I said, "I'm sorry Arthur couldn't make it. I know how much he's been looking forward to playing against you. I guess next time." And then I said, "what," because she had laughed and when I said his name.   "Oh, nothing," she said. "Just. Ah. Just Arthur, that's all. He's just a character, that's all." She smacked a ball sitting at her feet, and then dribbled it up. "Come on," she said. "Let's play."

We played for an hour, and June won every match. I started off poor and then got better and then got rapidly worse. The other thing was, my wind was terrible. It's funny how you don't notice a thing like that going until it's already gone. But for a while after the game I couldn't even talk. I sort of walked around the court with my hands on my hips, sucking air and trying to look all right. June was sweating but she didn't look too tired.

"Come on," she said, "come have a drink with me."

I followed her past the pool and back through the building. We went out through a side door and then around the corner to a small patio bordered by a high wooden fence and covered with big umbrellas over the tables. There were trees beyond the umbrellas, and the light through them came in spots and shafts and the bar was cool and dark and I felt like I could finally breathe the air. The bar was built out of the side of the building and we sat down at it and June ordered our drinks. When they came we moved to one of the tables. I felt the sweat on my shirt starting to cool and stick and pretty soon I felt much better.

"It's too bad you couldn't have stayed last night," said June. "It wasn't as much fun after you left."

"Oh no?" I said. "Arthur seemed to be doing all right for the two of you." Then I added, "I had a pretty long day yesterday, and I wasn't feeling like very much fun. I was a little worried that if I stayed any longer I'd start feeling bad for myself."

"Did you end up feeling bad for yourself?"

"A little bit," I said. "But when I got home I went upstairs and – you know that window at the top of the stairs? – the moon was shining right through that, right over the lake, and after I saw that it was pretty hard to feel bad. I guess that's a stupid reason to be happy."

"No," she said. "I don't think so. It sounds nice." But I guess she didn't really think so, or didn't have anything else to say about it, because after that she just stirred her drink and looked down at her knees. I looked at them, too. She had one leg crossed over the other and the skin over her kneecaps was lined and the skin above and below on her thighs and calves was smooth and pale. "Bernard is going to be leaving soon," she said, all of a sudden. "He's going back to the city for a week or so, to set up things with galleries for the winter shows. After that we're having some friends out, a couple of Bernard's artist friends from the city. We'll have a dinner.

Will you both come?"

"Sure," I said. I was getting pretty cold in the shade. All the sweat that was soaked into my shirt had cooled and was sticking to me and up under my arms. I took a big drink and felt it warm down my ribs and then felt it cool just as fast and I felt colder than before.

She gave me a ride back to the house. The ride wasn't very long and we didn't talk. I got out and didn't turn around to look back as I walked up the lawn and up the steps and went inside. I went into the kitchen and made a drink and then went out on the back porch to drink it. The boat was still sitting in the middle of the yard with the paint cans next to it, but the sandpaper had blown away. I saw one sheet over on the far end of the lawn, but I couldn't see the other one anywhere. Out on the pier the Ferris Wheel was standing still, but the music from the merry-go-round was still going.

And then, pretty soon, Canasson came back. He looked like hell. He came out onto the porch and sat down in the chair next to mine without saying anything. I didn't say anything, either. We sort of watched the lake for a while. It must have been about four or five o'clock. I watched a boat go in a broad circle around the bay and then turn around and go back the opposite way.

After a while Canasson said, "what did you do all day?"

"I played tennis with June," I said.

"Who won?"

"She did, naturally."

"Is she very good?"

"It might just be that I'm pretty awful, but I imagine she would be good, anyway."

"I imagine she would be, too."

"She invited us to a dinner they're having in a couple of weeks. I told her I'd have to find out if you were free that weekend."

"When?"

"I'm not sure," I said. "Bernard's going back to the city

for a week or so, and it'll be the weekend after. He's going back to set things up with the galleries for the winter shows. I don't know when he's leaving. She said he was leaving pretty soon." Then I said, "what did you do in town?"

"I had to pack up some things," he said. "I guess Diane's father told her that I was staying out here, and she moved back into the apartment. She's got her lawyers saying that it's hers now. So I went back and packed up a few things." Then he looked at me and said, "is it all right if I stay here until I find a new place? It shouldn't take very long. I've got my assistant out looking for one, but it may take a week or two. Is that all right?"

"Sure," I said. "Feel free to stay as long as you want."

Then we both kind of sank into our chairs and didn't say anything for a while. A little later Canasson got up to make himself a drink, and he asked me if I wanted one, and I told him sure. So we had a drink and didn't say much. I was feeling pretty hungry. I hadn't eaten since before I went to play tennis with June, and the booze was going to my head. So I decided to sit very still and not say anything. Then the sun started going down. It went straight down in front of the house, and the house made a long shadow across the yard and along the dock and on the water in front of us. The trees around us turned gold and the waves turned white. We finished our drinks and then had another and by the time we were finished the sun was down and the world was dusty pink and gray and the light from the kitchen window showed yellow across the deck. Canasson asked what I wanted to do for dinner. I said I didn't care.

We got into the car. I had to move some of his things off the seat to get in. The backseat was loaded up, too. We headed north along the lake and then took the road back to the city for a couple of miles until we got to a restaurant I had driven past but never really looked at. They put us in a booth and Canasson ordered us a couple more drinks and we talked about tennis. Canasson talked, mostly. After a while we ordered some food and when it came we ate without talking and afterwards we had another drink and then coffee and I felt tired and that the car and home were very far away. I wanted to fall asleep in the goddamned booth. But pretty soon Canasson paid the check and I didn't argue with him about it, and we headed back. We said goodnight at the top of the stairs and then I closed my door and listened to him moving around while I got undressed and got into bed.

VII.

For the rest of that week I wrote copy or did things around the house and Canasson talked on the phone to lawyers and made trips to his office and his apartment. He brought back boxes and made a long line of them in his room, running the length of the exterior wall, dipping down around the window in the middle so that by midmorning his room was cut by a narrow shaft of light that shone horizontal through the dust that rose from the floor. He didn't say anything about it except that he didn't need my help carrying anything upstairs. In the afternoon, when the house shadow stretched almost to the retaining wall, we met in the kitchen to make drinks and then moved out onto the back porch to have them. On Tuesday I painted the boat and on Wednesday I put it in the water, and so for half of the week it was there to watch, drifting in a slow orbit around the post where it was tied.

On Friday evening we rowed over to the Hautdesert's. We kept close to shore and switched off rowing. Once we almost tipped and Canasson dove into the bottom of the boat and got dirt on the knees of his pants and I laughed. He had taken off his shirt and tie and bundled them beneath the seat, and I watched the pink growing on his shoulders. Then he took the oars and I moved into the stern and lit a cigarette and held it to his mouth on a forward stroke, and I laughed as he took it with his lips and then took it away as he pulled and then brought it back and I took it and leaned against the side. The oars churned up mud and weeds in the shallows and I watched them rise and then crest and then fall in supple motions and the mud rolling into clouds and then washing out to flat brown. Then he pulled hard left as we came around and out across flat water to the end of the dock, and I jumped out with the bow line and secured it and Canasson threw the one from the stern. He threw up the bundle and then reached up and we took each other by the wrists and I pulled him onto the dock beside me.

"Are you sure you don't want to come?" he asked, putting on his shirt. "I'm sure it wouldn't be a problem. Maybe we could call one of June's friend. Maybe Rene or somebody. We could get a group going." He didn't say it to be funny or anything. He said it like he really thought it would be nice if I went out with them.

"No," I said. I was climbing back down into the boat. "Maybe we can all have dinner tomorrow or something."

"Sure," said Canasson. He was putting on his tie without watching himself do it. Then he said, "I'll call you if I don't see you. I mean. You know what I mean."

"Sure," I said. "Untie me."

After I was untied I pushed off and caught my balance as the boat rocked and moved out a little into the bay. I sat down and gave two strokes and I was out away from the dock. Arthur waved and then turned and walked towards the house. I watched him leave the dock and climb the lawn, and I saw June standing on the balcony above him, with the yellow light from the kitchen behind her. Then I dug in and gave a dozen hard pulls, and when I looked up again she was gone, and Arthur was gone, and the house was smaller in the distance.

I tied off at Bradner's dock and went up the lawn and inside and made myself a drink. Then I took it out on the porch and sat watching the boat bobbing in the bay. But that was hard because I kept looking over at the lights from the Hautdesert's. I couldn't see anything from the porch. The house was just a few squares of light in a row along the rear glass doors leading out onto the deck. I sat and looked at the house lights for a while.

After a while it was really dark and I made myself another drink and started feeling pretty bad for myself. I tried to keep it off, but the harder I tried, the worse it got. By the time I was finished with my second drink I was feeling pretty bad. But then I got up and went inside, and took a shower even though I didn't feel like it, and after my shower I felt better and decided to go out. So I went upstairs and got dressed. Then I left and I walked north along the lake, around past the restaurants to the shops and bars and restaurants that ringed the entrance to the fair.

The fair was running full tilt. You could hear the music from the band from my back porch but up close it was loud and there was no break, with the sound from the machines and the children and the barkers and the merry-go-round record filling in the gaps. I thought about going in, but I decided I needed another drink first, and so I went into a bar across the street from the gate. The place was pretty packed. I shouldered my way up to the bar and waved the bartender down, but the bartender was busy and called for me to hang on a second. While I was waiting I heard somebody call my name, but when I turned around I couldn't see anybody I recognized. When I turned back around I heard my name again, but the bartender was coming over and so I ordered my drink and while I was doing that somebody grabbed my shoulder and then fell out of the crowd against me. He pulled himself up with a hand on the bar and a hand on my shoulder.

"Elliot!" he said.

"Nick," I said, "how the hell are you?" I was pretty surprised to see him. Nick was a mechanic in town. I had him give the car a once-over after I bought it. He had told me that the car was in pretty rough shape, and that the best we could hope for was as much as I could get out of it, and nothing else. "It's going to run until it dies," he said. "I can't tell you any better than that." That would have been the end of it, but Nick asked me what I did, and when I told him he said that he had read my articles. "I always read the police beat," he said. "It keeps me one step ahead." He had a very long face and the skin was stretched tight over his cheekbones, and when he laughed the skin over his cheeks got red and mottled.

"Bartender," he yelled, "another of whatever Mr. Poulain ordered." He pulled a wad of bills from his pocket and slapped them onto the bar. The bar was so loud that I wasn't sure that the bartender had heard him, but a minute later he came back with two whiskey sours and Nick paid him and held up his glass. "The car still running?" he yelled.

"Hell yes," I said, raising my glass.

"To your car then," he said. "And to all other lost causes, automotive and otherwise. To the car!"

"To the car!" I said, and we drank off half of our drinks.

"What have you got on tonight?" he yelled, holding my shoulder and pulling my ear close down to his mouth. "Do you have any plans?"

"No," I said. "I was thinking of going to the fair in a bit, to walk around."

"So were we," he yelled. "We were gonna get some beers and then go throw rocks at the construction site first, though. You want to come?"

"Sure," I said. "When are you leaving?"

"Finish your drink," he said. "I'll go get the guys."

I finished my drink and then Nick came back and we walked outside. There were three other guys standing outside. Nick introduced me around. Then we all piled into Nick's car. We sat three across in the back and I faced towards the window to make room. We pulled out onto the road heading south, and then down along Main Street and off along the smaller residential streets. Everyone in the car was talking all at once and then someone said "that one" and Nick cut the lights and stopped in front of a house with no lights on and I heard the trunk pop and then the passenger door opened and Gill who was sitting there got out and moved up the yard in a low crouch and around the side of the garage and gave one look back as he ducked inside and then nobody said anything as we waited and it felt like he was taking a long time and then like he was taking a very long time and then he came out of the dark into the glow from the streetlights running in the same low crouch with a case of beer held close to his chest and he threw it into the trunk and then hopped in the passenger door as the lights upstairs in the house came on and Nick hit the gas and laughed loud and Gill laughed too, and the two guys beside me yelled and we picked up speed and then Nick cut it hard and we skidded around the corner and I felt the back end start to go and then catch and then Nick flipped on the lights and we were cruising north and around and safe and gone.

"Oh hell," said Gill, laughing, "oh hell."

"Well done Gilly," said Nick.

"Well done," said the guy beside me.

"You should have got more," said the man on the other side of the backseat. "That'll never last us."

"You get another one, then."

"I will," he said. "You bet your ass I will. Pull over, Nick."

"Here?"

"Up there, by that one."

Nick cut the lights again, and we coasted in close to the curb. "All right," he said, turning around to look at John. "Make us proud, Johnny boy."

John ducked out and sprinted across the yard. He was out a second later clutching his coat tight closed around him. He jumped in and said, "go, for Christ's sake, go!" and Nick hit the gas and we took off and John unwrapped his arms from around his middle and held his right one up. There was blood running down from his knuckles and the guy between us lurched towards me.

"Jesus Christ," said Gill. "What happened?"

"The door was locked," said John. "I had to bust out the window."

"With your bare skin?" said Gill. "You're a fucking idiot."

"Oh yeah?" said John. He went down into the inside pocket of his coat and came back with a bottle of something clear. The glass was frosty white and showed dark wet lines where John's fingers touched it. "Huh? What do you think now?" he said.

"I think you're on your own with that stuff," said Gill.

"That shot's *poison*."

"I think you better stop bleeding on my seat," said Nick. "Here." He threw a handful of paper napkins back at us and John picked up a couple and pressed them to the spot. Gill opened the bottle and took a long pull, and then passed it to Nick who did the same. Nick passed it back to Gill and Gill passed it to John and John passed it to the guy in the middle who passed it to me.

The road began to curve back east, and a minute later it put us back onto the loop. We followed the loop around, past the tennis courts, and then down past the rental cabins and on to where the row of dark condominiums and the black rectangular crater stood behind a chain link fence. Nick stopped the car in front of the gate and we all got out, and the guy whose name I didn't know told Nick to pop the trunk so he could get the beer. Nick did, and the guy took out the case and some plastic mesh bags and we all walked down to the water.

"Who's got the beer?" said John.

"Bill has it," said Nick. "You have the bottle?"

"I've got it," I said. We walked down in front of the condominiums, and then across the dirt and onto the floating docks. The water clanked against the aluminum, and the dock swayed slightly with our steps. John was holding a napkin against his fist. I took a pull of the vodka, then handed it to Gill, who drank and handed it to Nick, who drank. Bill put the beer into the mesh sacks and sunk them in the water, hanging them off the dock. Then he set the empty case on fire. Nick spit vodka onto it in a spray that lit everyone's squinting face for one fast moment and then was gone and left us all blinking. John said his fist had stopped bleeding. Gill took a beer from the water and Nick asked for another, and John and Bill, another each, and one got handed to me. We all drank them and dropped the empties into the lake and I watched mine sink. Then someone handed me another one. The empty cardboard burned down flat against the aluminum and John toed it over the edge and it hit the water with a hiss and then sank. Bill filled his mouth with vodka and then blew a fireball with his lighter, and the air filled with the smell of singed hair, and we all laughed. John finished another beer and threw the can out into the lake. The rest of us sipped at ours. Bill and John and Gill began talking about a girl I did not know, and Nick moved and sat down next to me.

"So where's your friend tonight?" he asked.

"My friend?" I said.

"The guy who's been staying with you," said Nick.

"How did you know somebody's been staying with me?" I said.

"It's a small town, once you sort out who lives here and who just stays here some of the time," said Nick. "It's the sort of thing people know. Actually," he said, "Rene told Bill, and Bill told me. Rene and Bill used to go around together in the summers, when they were in high school. Back before Rene decided she was high class. Bill always said that they were in love, and going to get married, but I think Rene just did it to piss off her parents." He laughed. "Poor Bill was pretty broken up about it for a while," he said.

"He's out with June Hautdesert," I said.

Nick nodded. But, then he didn't say anything. I had the feeling that he wanted to say something, but he didn't. Then, all of a sudden, John stood up and ran towards shore, and the dock starting shaking like crazy. The tin sound of his footsteps echoed up off the water. Gill and Nick and Bill and I watched him. Nick fished up the beer and handed me one, then took one himself. John yelled from the shore. Gill yelled back, a long wordless yell that echoed back off the condominiums. Then there was the sound of busting glass, and Bill and Nick yelled, too, and then Gill got up and took off running towards the sound. Bill stood up and I stood up, too, and the dock swayed under us and I felt drunk and happy as Bill handed me the bottle and took off running after them.

"I'm going to go see what those guys are into," said

Nick. "You coming?"

"I'm gonna stay out here for a minute and finish my beer," I said.

"Sure," said Nick. "Bring the rest of it in when you come in, would you?" He reached down and fished up another, then set the sack on the dock.

"Sure," I said.

He took the bottle and moved off down the dock. I watched him go, and then I sat down and finished my beer, then opened another one. I started thinking about Canasson and June, and where they were, and what they were doing. But then someone yelled for me from shore, and so I went in. The four of them were inside the crater behind the fence. They called me and I climbed over the fence and stood beside them. I had the beers, and they each took one and then the sack was empty and I threw it away. We were standing around a long pile of two-by-fours, and Bill took the vodka and uncorked it and dumped it in a long line down the length of them. Then John took out his lighter and lit it. The booze caught and then the boards started to catch, and Bill threw the bottle down on them so that the glass shattered and the rest of it splattered out into a broad flaming circle in the center of the pile. Then we all ran back to the fence and climbed over, and we piled in the car and Nick took off down the loop with the headlights off and then down along the first side street, along past dark houses until we were away and turned a corner and Nick turned on the lights.

"Oh Christ," said Gill. "Jesus Christ, it's been too long."

Nick laughed. "You feel better now?" he said.

"Hell yes," said Gill. "I've been waiting to do that for months."

"We're out of booze," said John.

"Forget it," said Nick.

"Let Elliot get it," said Gill. "How's your hand, John?"

"It's started bleeding again."

"The booze, the booze!" said Bill.

"Forget it," Nick said again. He pulled off the side street and back out onto the loop, heading south around the bay towards the fair. "It hasn't even hit you yet. In a minute you're going to be too blind to see. Just give it a second to work into your system." I felt the car accelerate and I knew that Nick was trying to get there before it hit him, too. "Besides, if we sober up too much, we can go across the street and Elliot'll buy us all a drink, right Elliot?"

"Sure," I said.

"See?" said Nick. "No worries."

We pulled onto the broader stretch surrounding the entrance to the fair, and Nick pulled us onto a side street and parked at a bad angle to the sidewalk and we all fell out laughing about it. John had his hurt hand tucked up in his armpit with a napkin held to his knuckles and Gill took a full beer from his pocket and cracked it open. He passed it to me and I drank and passed it to Nick who drank and passed it on. John killed it and then crushed the can in his good hand and tossed it over his shoulder. We lurched out of the dark and into the light from the gate and the bars and the streetlights. The noise was huge and the wheel at the end never stopped and blurred into a continuous burning loop. We slapped bills onto the chrome and the old man waved us through and I slid down to my hands and knees and John tripped and caught his balance and then kicked me in the haunch and I stood and swung at him laughing hysterically and John too laughing and we fell into the small space between the end of the booths and the fence where leaves and junk had collected and the smell of dust and old wood and then hands grabbing and pulling and John's laughter and my laughter loud and Gill and Nick and Bill laughing, too, but hushing us as they brushed us off, and the ugly red stain of John's blood across the front of my shirt.

"Get moving," someone said. "Get moving, will you?" and then shoved roughly into the crowd, regaining our balance as a group and hanging on each other's shoulders as the people melted around us and we were inside of it then, flowing with it with the moon of the Ferris Wheel spinning above and the earth below and the water all around.

"Where to?"

"To the wheel!"

"To the tent!"

"Go to see the strong man, make him lift us up over his head."

"Go to win the goldfish."

"A drink, I need another drink."

"You're drunk enough," and all the time laughing and yelling and not hearing and then repeating and laughing more as the faces moved in jarring stutter-speed like images through a fan-blade and the people all wreathed in drunk-haze and shadow and their light touch a shadow's touch.

The door to the strongman was locked. We stumbled across the hay-covered causeway to the tent and went inside. Inside the tent was hot and dim and glowed many colors with the light filtered in through the colored vinyl of the roof and sides. A steady chatter rose from a group of a dozen or so women, seated near the front. They had pulled the folding chairs into a close circle. We went over to them. They looked at us as we approached and then looked away as we neared.

"You've got something on your shirt," one of them said to me.

"It's blood," I said. "But don't worry. It's not mine." I pointed to John. "It's his."

"He's just kidding," said Nick. "It's catsup. He was a little clumsy with his French fries."

She warmed to that, but only a little. The light was poor and when she turned even slightly away her face was in shadow. The other women's faces were upturned and glowed pale and many-colored. They were watching me, watching us.

"Would you like to dance?" Bill asked one of them.

"To what?" she asked.

"You don't hear that?" he said. "You don't hear the

music? I could dance all night to this music. You don't hear this music? Can't you hear it?"

"You're crazy," she said.

"Forget it," he said, turning away. "Damn broads think I'm crazy because they can't hear the music."

"What did he say?" said the one who asked about the blood. "What did your friend just say?"

"He didn't say anything," I said. "Say, how would you like to go around with us?"

"I don't think that's a good idea," she said. "Maybe some other night."

"Is it because you can't hear the music?" I said. "Don't feel bad. To tell you the truth, sometimes I can't hear the music either. But if you just go along with it, nobody knows the difference. Really, it's not a problem if you can't hear the music. Is it because you can't hear the music?"

"You mean that horrible music from the merry-go-round?"

"No!" said Bill, turning fast around, falling forward, catching himself against the backs of the chairs in front of him. "The music! The music!" He fell forward, catching the chair back across his middle, and then pushed himself up.

"I think maybe you should take your friend home," said the one by me.

"To hell with you," said Bill, waving one menacing finger in the air. "To hell with all of you. To hell with all women and most men, too." He started singing, waving his arms in the air. "We are the damned the damned we are, we are the damned lets find a bar, and drink a pint to our souls' health, and pray the devil can't find our wealth." He sang hugely, loud into the empty tent above him, waving his arms and moving in a marching circle between the chairs, running into them and knocking them over. One of the women screamed and I laughed and Gill and Nick and John laughed too as he sang, "we are the damned, the damned are we, so build a ship and go to sea, and keep our quarters neat and prim, and pray the devil cannot swim!" Then he fell over into the chairs and more chairs came down on top of him and the three of us went wild with laughter and the women stood and ducked out while our backs were turned. We helped Bill up.

"Damn fine song you've got there, Bill," said John. "Did wonders for you with the ladies."

"To hell with the ladies," said Bill, lying on his back, not attempting to move. He closed his eyes. "My grandmother used to sing that song to me. Grandpa was a navy man, you know. Never understood that part about the devil finding the wealth. The navy men were all broke as stones."

We hauled him to his feet and went out through the flap and down the causeway between the merry-go-round and the Ferris Wheel, down to the gazebo at the end of the pier. It was empty except for one man sitting in the shadows at the far end, and he left as we entered, sidestepping down the stairs beside us, turned away so that I did not see his face. Nick and I sat down at the far end, and John sat to our right and Bill and Gill, to our left. Nobody said anything. Bill had his head down between his knees and was moaning, slightly. Gill patted him on the back, and Bill winced. John took out his pocket knife and began carving a hole in the bench seat beside him. Across the water I could see red lights flashing and I tapped Nick and pointed, and Nick laughed, and John looked up and laughed too. Gill saw and told Bill, but Bill didn't lift his head. Then Nick stopped laughing, and shook his head, and John stopped laughing too, and the scrape and bore of John's knife returned with gusto over the sound of Bill's heavy breathing.

"Won't matter!" Bill yelled, suddenly, into the stone floor. "Won't matter. To hell with the women and the contractors. It won't change anything."

Nobody argued with him. John stopped boring and put his knife away. He peeled the napkin from his knuckles and held his hand over the hole with his fingers hanging down. I watched the blood seep from the gash between his knuckles and then run down along his middle finger and then drip.

"What does he mean?" I said. "What does he mean it won't change anything?"

"The construction," Nick said. "He means it's not going to stop the construction."

"It might," I said. "At least for a while, it could."

"They have insurance for things like that. If they show up Monday and the boards are gone, or the glass is broken, they can have them replaced by Wednesday night. It's not going to stop anything. It's just more of a way to blow off steam. But it doesn't work as well when you know nothing you do is going to have an effect."

"I guess everything changes," I said.

Nobody said anything to that. Bill gave another small moan, and Gill patted his back. Nick leaned back against the wood of the bench back and I leaned forward with my elbows on my knees, tracing the lines between the stones in the floor. After a while I looked up and watched the Ferris Wheel, then looked at each of them. Nick had his head back and was staring at the ceiling. John was looking at his hand. I watched John's blood drip and heard it hit the tiny pool already formed inside the hollowed out place.

After a while I said goodnight to them and I started back towards home. I was drunk as hell and I walked carefully out through the gates and turned left along the loop. The lights were off along the street and I went across an empty lawn to be down by the lake. I walked along the retaining wall and then I walked on it, balancing with my arms up and moving forward with fast steps. While I walked I thought about Canasson and about June, and I wondered if Canasson was home, and what had happened, and I wanted very much to tell him about what I had done. Thinking about him, I lost my balance and almost fell.

I walked upstairs in the dark and when I reached the top I did not look to see if Canasson's door was open or closed, and didn't listen as I passed by, to see if I could hear him breathing inside. I got undressed and lay awake in the dark, until the room began to spin and I closed my eyes and tried to make it stop. In the dark the whole world was spinning, too. It spun faster and faster and I thought that I was going to get sick but after a while the spinning subsided and I fell asleep. In the morning I woke up covered in a cold sweat and sick to my stomach. My mouth tasted like copper and I had that feeling that everything I had ever done was wrong, that I had wasted every moment of my life.

Canasson was downstairs, having breakfast. I poured myself a cup of coffee and took the paper and went out onto the porch. The sun was bright and high up over the bay. I turned my back to it and read in the shade of my body. The war was still going on. I wondered where Bradner was, and what he was doing, and if anyone had heard from him. Someone must have heard. I made a note to ask Greene and then I read a few other stories. There wasn't much in it besides the war, and none of it seemed very important.

While I was sitting out on the porch I heard Canasson moving around in the kitchen, and a little while later he came out with a plate of eggs and toast and held them down to me.

"What's this?" I said.

"It's breakfast," he said. "You want some more coffee?"

I took the plate. "Sure," I said.

He went back inside and brought the pot and filled my cup and then threw the little that was left over the railing and set the pot down and pulled the other chair over next to me, but still facing the lake. I folded the newspaper and set it on the deck and then turned my chair around, too.

"Thanks," I said.

"You looked hungry," he said. "What did you end up doing last night?"

"I went out with some of the guys," I said. "We had a few and walked around the fair. What did you end up doing?"

"June showed me some of her paintings," he said. "She

149

paints, you know. Not professionally, or anything. But she's very good. I mean, better than a lot that I've seen. I told her that she ought to try to have a show, or to sell them or something. She could do it, especially with the connections she has through Bernard. But she said it was just a hobby, you know, and that she knew too many artists, and that she didn't want to become one of them. But anyway she showed me her paintings and then after a while she had me sit for a portrait. Just a sketch, you know. So I did and then afterwards it was late and with the drive we decided that it wasn't worth it to go out to dance, and so we went for a swim."

"How did the portrait turn out?" He was talking too much and too fast and I kind of wanted him to leave me alone. But it was pretty obvious he wanted to talk about what happened with June and anyway he had just made me breakfast and I didn't want to be rude and I didn't want to miss my chance to talk to him, even though I felt like hell. I guess I was kind of worried that with Bernard gone I wouldn't see much of him, if that makes any sense. So I just pretended I felt fine and sat listening.

"It's a good likeness," he said. "I mean, very close, in a lot of ways. I asked to keep it, but she said she needed to work on it more. I'm sure she'd show it to you, if you ask her to. She may ask you to sit for one. She said she might. You should see her sketches. All portraits. And she does them all in the same way. I mean, the faces and the poses are different, but there's something that's very much the same in all of them. I can't quite place it. There's some way that they're all the same, you know that they're all the same to her, in one small way."

"That's funny," I said. "That's very funny."

"Why is it funny?"

"I don't know," I said. "I thought you were telling me because you thought that it was funny." He didn't say anything, so I said, "it's funny, you know? A portrait is supposed to be very specific, is supposed to be this intense study in what makes one person different from everybody else. It's funny that they end up all looking the same." "I suppose that is funny," said Canasson. "I hadn't thought of it like that."

"Did your portrait look the same?" I said. "I mean, did you feel that way about the picture she drew of you?"

"It's awfully hard to know," he said. "And besides, she didn't let me look at it for very long."

I finished the eggs and bread and washed it down with coffee. The coffee was burned and bitter and I choked down a mouthful and then leaned and threw the rest over the railing. I set the plate on top of the newspaper and the mug on top of the plate and then I leaned back in the chair and closed my eyes.

"How old do you think she is?" I said.

"Hell if I know," said Canasson. "Younger than Bernard, I imagine."

"I was going to say older."

"You think?"

"Could be," I said.

"I'm never sure," he said. "Sometimes I think she couldn't be any older than I am, and other times I think she helped bury Abel." He shook his head. "From one minute to the next, you just don't know."

Even though I was trying to listen I was pretty tired of hearing about it already. To tell you the truth, I kind of hate having people tell me how fascinating other people are. It's goddamned obnoxious. It's like the conversation is being dominated by somebody who isn't even there. And even if you have something to add, or something to say, you can't say it because if you start talking about you after someone has been talking about someone else you come off looking self-centered, while everyone else is being so goddamned altruistic and selfless in talking up somebody behind their back so they never have to give anything away to that person's face. That's the truth of it. Plenty of people will compliment someone behind his back who will never compliment him to his face, and when you do that you're just trying to show what a hell of a guy you are for being so selfless. It's faux social charity, and it gives me the creeps. Canasson wasn't doing that, exactly, and I guess it wouldn't have bothered me so much, except that it bothered me that it bothered me, and that made it ten times worse. I mean, really, I should have just said to hell with both of them, and her portraits, and whatever the hell else, but I couldn't.

We sat outside for a while, not talking, and then I went inside and took a shower. I felt like hell and after the shower I didn't feel any better. Canasson was still outside when I left the bathroom. I saw him through the glass in the kitchen door as I crossed the hall to the stairs and then I went up and went into my room and got dressed. A while later I heard Canasson coming up and he knocked on my door.

"It's open," I said. I was laying on my stomach on the bed with my face turned to the wall and I didn't feel like getting up. I heard the door open and then I heard Canasson come into the room. He pulled a chair over next to the bed and sat down.

"Look," he said, "maybe it isn't a good idea, me staying here anymore."

"What makes you say that?" I said.

"I don't know," he said. "You seem bothered that I'm here."

"I'm not bothered," I said, "I'm just hung over as hell and I don't want to talk about June."

"It feels like more than that," said Canasson.

"Oh for god's sake," I said. I pushed up onto my elbows, and looked at him. "Do you want to stay? Do you like it here?"

"Sure," said Canasson, "I like it here. But I don't want to stay if I'm encroaching on you."

"Well, you're not," I said. "So stay if you feel like it." I dropped back down onto the mattress and faced away from him. I waited for him to say something, but he didn't. So I said, "did you have anything planned for today?"

"I was going to go play tennis with June this afternoon," he said, kind of soft, like he was worried that I would get upset because he was talking about her. "Not for a couple hours, though. We could do something beforehand. Or if you want to just sleep we could meet up after, or something. Why don't you meet us at the clubhouse after our game? We can all have a drink together. How does that sound?"

"Sounds fine," I said. It did sound fine, but I said it like I didn't give a damn about it, like I was just saying it to get him off my back. It did sound pretty good, though. I was already feeling bad about the way I was acting but I couldn't do anything to stop it, and I hoped that now he would just go away and close the door and I could go back to sleep and wake up and later, when we all had a drink together, things would be normal and pleasant and it would be as though none of it had ever happened.

"All right, then," said Canasson. "I'll call when we're done playing. Does that sound all right? I'll call from the clubhouse when we're finished with our game. June is going to pick me up so you don't have to worry about the car, or anything. I'll call when we're finished playing." He stood up but he hovered over the bed, like he wasn't sure whether to say something else or just leave me alone. I opened my eyes to look for his shadow on the wall, but the only light was from the sun coming in through the window beside the bed, and there was no shadow.

I could feel him standing there, anyway, so I said, "all right, that sounds fine. I'll see you in a few hours. I'm just going to go back to sleep and try to feel better. I'm sorry about this morning. I feel lousy and I didn't mean to seem upset. I just need a couple hours sleep and I think I'll be all right."

"All right," he said. "That's fine, then. I'll just let you sleep. Goodnight, Elliot."

"Goodnight Arthur," I said. "Sorry again about this

morning."

"Never mind," he said. "Just go to sleep. I'll see you in a little while." Then he pulled the door closed behind him, and I listened to his footsteps go down the stairs and, a little while later, the muted warble of the radio in the living room, the horn section blurred together and the woman's voice a warm organic hum. And then I fell asleep.

VIII.

I woke up with the sick panic feeling that I had slept through something important, and no one had bothered to tell me. But when I checked the clock I saw that I had only been asleep for a couple of hours, and I figured that Canasson had probably only just left. I felt a little better after that, but not much. Sometimes it takes a while to get over waking up like that, even when you find out that what you woke up panicked over hasn't happened. So I figured what I would do was go for a swim, and then take a walk up to the courts and catch the end of their game. I felt pretty bad about the way I had acted that morning, and I felt like maybe I could make it up by going to watch them play. Besides, I was curious to see how Canasson would do against her. So I changed into swim shorts and went downstairs and out the back door and across the yard and down the dock and dove into the lake. Then I started swimming straight out, not really looking where I was going. I got going pretty well, but then I started to cramp up. I had to stop and tread water for a minute. I sort of stayed out there, just kind of spinning around, and I tried to pick the condominiums out of the row of buildings along the north shore. It was pretty easy to see where they were, but they were too far away and I couldn't quite make them out. At least, I couldn't really see if there was anybody there working, or anything like that. So I gave up on it and started swimming out again. My cramp was pretty much gone, anyway. But I didn't swim too much farther out, because I was afraid it would come back. I felt much better but I didn't feel quite right and I could still feel myself sweating booze. So after a little while I turned around and headed back in.

From up on the dock I heard the phone ringing, and I ran up to the house to get it. But when I answered it wasn't Canasson, but a lawyer looking for Canasson. I said he wasn't there, and the man said he'd call back and didn't leave a message. I figured it was about the divorce and I thought I would tell him when I got to the clubhouse, but then I thought maybe it would be better not to say anything in front of June, and then I thought the hell with it because he said he would call back. So I went and took a shower and got dressed. Canasson hadn't called by the time I came back downstairs, so I left and started walking north along the shore, thinking that I would catch the end of the game.

I showed up just as they were finishing. Canasson served and faulted, and then he served and faulted again, and while I was walking around the fence to their side I didn't watch and by the time I reached them the game was over and they were both walking off the court.

"You're just in time," June said when she saw me.

"Hello, Elliot," Canasson said. "I was just telling June that I needed to go and call you, and here you are." He wiped his face with his sleeve, pulling his upper arm over his face. "You weren't kidding about this one," he said, nodding towards June. "She's a regular shark with a racket."

"I told you," I said.

"Arthur is just being modest," June said. "I got lucky, that's all. He was a gentleman, and played with the sun in his eyes the whole time. Wouldn't let us switch sides." Her face was red and she wiped her cheeks with a towel. "My god, it's hot, though," she said.

"Let's get a drink," Canasson said.

"Give me a minute," she said. "I have to put my things away."

We waited for her to put the tennis things away. She did it slowly and deliberately and I think a little bit to make Canasson uncomfortable. She had beat him at tennis and now she was controlling what they did afterwards. It was really a thing to see. Of course she wanted a drink, but she didn't want to have one because he had suggested it. Canasson stood there watching her, and when she took Bernard's racket from him he didn't know what to do with his hands. She loved doing it, and you could tell that he was loving it, too, because

it was him she was trying to make uncomfortable, and not
somebody else. After a while I almost couldn't stand it, so I
said, "I feel like a rum screwdriver. Is that all right with
everyone else? I'll go order them so they're ready when you
all are finished here."

"That sounds fine," said Canasson. "June?"

"I won't be another second," she said. She was putting
the racket into the bag, and then she took it most of the way
out and then put it back in again at a different angle. She
didn't do it by turning her hips at all, the way a lot of girls
would. A lot of girls would make a big show of how hard it
was to get it in at that angle by moving their whole body to the
side to show you what an effort it was to do it. But June just
pulled it out and then twisted her wrist so that the head turned
and she got it in. It was direct and powerful and I appreciated
that when she was finished there was no glance up to see if her
effort had been noticed like I assumed there would be.

"All right," she said, "I'm ready now. I don't feel like
rum, though. Elliot, lets order something else."

"Come to think of it, I don't feel much like rum either,"
Canasson said. We were walking through the gate and then
we were walking along the fence, back towards the club
house. "What was that drink you made last night?"

"Perroquet," she said.

"That's right, Perroquet," he said.

We walked down between the pool and the grass and
down through the clubhouse and out the back door to the
fenced-in bar. A couple of people were sitting in the far
corner against the fence, but beneath the umbrella their faces
and shoulders were in shadow and only their hands and wrists
showed in the thin moon of table that caught the light beyond
the shade and shone yellow on their skin and lit the ice in their
glasses. They stopped talking when we came in, and didn't
start again until the gate was closed, and even then only in low
voices, huddled down beneath the cover of their bodies and
mouths. We sat down at the bar.

"Perroquet," said Canasson. "Three, please."

"I don't know how to make that," said the barman.

"Oh," said Canasson. And then, to her, "June, how did you make the Perroquet?"

"It's *pastis* and *sirop de menthe* and water," said June, settling her tennis bag against the bar.

"I don't have any pastis," said the barman. He said it without any accent.

"What did he say?" said June.

"He said he has no *pastis*." And then, to the bartender, "It's fine." Canasson had a roll of bills out and was peeling a couple off onto the wood. "Three rum screwdrivers," he said. And then, to June, "to start. We can order something else for the next round, when we figure out what can be made."

"All right," she said. She turned to me. " Do you have a cigarette? I think I left mine in the car."

"I have some," said Canasson, but he was busy counting out the bills.

"It's all right," I said. "I've got some." I opened my pack and she took one and I lit it for her. She was sitting between us, Canasson standing and she on a stool and me half on one, too, and she turned her back to him and leaned an elbow on the bar as she blew smoke up over my head.

"Rene has been asking about you," she said. "Maybe next time we could get together and play doubles, you and Arthur and Rene and I."

"It wouldn't work," I said. "Arthur and I would have to take turns with Bernard's racket."

"We could dig another one up for you, I'm sure," she said.

"Sure, Elliot," said Canasson, putting his money away. "We could find you another racket, no problem. I may have one back in my things, come to think of it." He laughed. "I don't know why I didn't think of it before, actually."

She spun around on her stool. But instead of turning to face him she took the nearest of the three glasses the bartender set down and turned back to me. She slid the drink down to me, and didn't turn as Canasson moved hers around beside her.

"Don't worry, Arthur," I said. "I think I'm done with tennis. For this year, anyway."

"I hope not because of me."

"No," I said, "I just don't feel much like playing."

"Well that's all right," Canasson said. "Rene seems like a fine girl, I'm sure she'd be game for something else."

I lifted my glass and touched it to June's. We both drank, and June drank until her ice was bare. She winced and turned on the barstool, sliding her glass towards Canasson.

"Another?" he said.

"Christ, no," she said. "Something else. Anything but that."

He laughed, and sipped his own, but seemed to enjoy it less. I sipped at mine and held it in my mouth for a while before I swallowed it. Then the bartender came over and June ordered us three tall beers. I lit a cigarette and offered one to Canasson behind her back. Then I offered one to her. Hers was still going, but she took another anyway. Canasson lit his and blew smoke over the bartender's head as he brought the beer. I still felt a little bit sick from the night before, and for a while I sat facing straight ahead and listened to them talk. After a while June excused herself, and Canasson ordered three more and then slid down onto June's stool and elbowed me in the shoulder.

"What do you think?" he said.

"Of what?" I said.

"Of June," he said. "Of me and June. Of June and I. Of us."

"She's married," I said. "She's married to Bernard Hautdesert."

"They have an arrangement or something," he said. "I mean, not an arrangement. They have an understanding about it."

"They have an understanding," I repeated. The bartender set my beer down and I took it and sipped off the top.

"An understanding," he said. "They have an understanding. They have the same friends and everything. I don't know. I didn't really ask about it."

"What did you ask?"

"I don't know," he said. "I asked her wouldn't Bernard mind, and she said it was all right they had an understanding and besides he was out of town."

"That's a hell of a thing to say."

"If the son of a bitch paid more attention to her, instead of his work all of the time, it wouldn't be an issue," he said. "Do you know what she told me? Do you know how many times he has played tennis with her in the past five years? Hmmm? Twice. He's played her twice. And you can see how much she wants to play. I mean, look at her for God's sake. She was born to play goddamned tennis."

"Oh that's good," I said. "It's practically his own fault, when you look at it that way."

"I'm not saying it's his fault," Canasson said. I lit another cigarette and he slid the ashtray towards me. "You don't even know Bernard," he said. "And you know what Diane is doing to me. You know what a nightmare this has been. I mean, I wasn't sure I would be able to talk to another woman, after Diane. After the way she has tried to hurt me."

"I hadn't noticed," I said. I blew smoke out through my nostrils. Then the gate opened, and we both turned and watched June come in. She had undone her hair, and it hung down over he shoulders. She moved with the same forceful sway and her eyes fixed on Canasson and she smiled. I looked at him, and watched him watch her cross the empty bar, coming towards us.

We finished our beers, and then June drove home. She offered us a ride, but Canasson suggested that we walk, and I said that sounded fine. The day had cooled while we were in the bar, but the sun was still high and hot as we walked along the water back towards the house. Canasson asked what I had done while he was with June, and I told him about Bill and Nick and Gill, and about stealing the beer, and the broken windows and the fire, and the girls at the fair. He listened to all of it and laughed when I laughed but it was pretty easy to see that he was thinking about something else. I figured it was only that he was thinking instead about June, and what he did Friday night, but to tell you the truth I didn't want to hear about it and so I didn't ask. I kept talking and he kept laughing when I laughed until we were home. By then we were both covered in sweat and tired and whatever high had come with the rum and the beer was gone. We changed and went swimming, and then Canasson said that he was hungry and I said I was too, and we got changed and went out to dinner. When we were finished it was almost dark, but I could see a dozen or so boats out on the lake, and hear voices coming in from across the water. The fair had started again for the night, and across the bay the Ferris wheel was going around, but I couldn't hear the merry-go-round music. Canasson suggested we take the boat out, and see how far we could go. Out on the water there was great yelling between boats, and behind it was the gurgle of laughter and other voices. I said that sounded fine and we walked back home and down the dock and Canasson took the oars as I undid the lines and then climbed in, and we rowed out across the black water towards the bobbing lights and sound.

And then it was all a great blur. We rowed alongside one and came aboard and there were drinks handed around and then, before we were finished with those, other drinks. I pointed out our house to a young woman and then to a young man and then introduced myself and pointed it out to a half dozen more and during all of this, more drinks, and then other drinks before those were finished. I watched Canasson from across the heavy crowd and felt the boat reeling with the weight of so many bodies in the water. Then there were lights and another boat, and then that boat was very close, and then it was tied alongside, and the railings were lifted and moved so that one could climb the stairs and go over the side and then down into the other and the bumpers between always squeaking as the water and the motion of the people onboard moved the boats together and apart and I glanced back at the rowboat tied far to stern, hoping that it was still there and that it would not swing around and strike the sides and then a splash as someone went over and screaming and yelling and laughter and it was Canasson and he came up waving and someone jumped in after him, and then three more, men and women in their shorts and tee-shirts and the heavy rolling sound of half-empty beer cans knocked over and moving along the planks with the sway of the boats, and people calling out to them and yelling and laughing and Canasson already pulling himself up and out of the water and the sound of cheering and then the untying of the boats and the engine roaring and going out far out across the water and watching the line twitch and throw mist while far out on the end the rowboat danced and skidded on the wake and not knowing where were going and calling to Canasson where are we going and he only lifting his arms and another drink thrust into my hands. And then the engines cut and the dark shape of an island on the horizon and the anchor dropped and then many small splashes as they jumped over and swam to shore and the panic when I hit the water and it closed in over me and then I came up feeling naked and cold in only my shorts in the darkness. And then onto shore on sand and the smell of wet sand and somebody calling for a dry lighter and soon a fire going and people appearing out of the woods carrying logs and branches between them. Out across the water the fair was only a glow and I realized suddenly that we were outside of the bay, out into the lake, now, and the sudden panic when I looked around and couldn't see Canasson anywhere, in the sudden drunk fear but then another drink, and Canasson by the fire, and the bright shapes of bodies lit by the fire in flashes in their dash from the darkness of the woods to the darkness of the water, screaming and whooping through the bright orange glow of the fire amid cheers and whistles and the shore soon churning with bodies sporting in shallow water and Canasson beside me and then gone and then the sound of his voice and coming towards me, the thatch of hair on his chest melting into the shadow beneath his arms and across his ribs and down between his legs and then suddenly past and the two long lit strands of muscle down his back orange and yellow and his long arms pumping out wide from his body and then the splash as he hit the water and I watched the place into which he had disappeared and then fell back upon the sand, feeling the heat from the fire and that something was rising up and soon would be over me, like sleep, rising up from the voices and light to linger for a moment in passing beyond the tips of my fingers before it vanished into the rising embers and the stars, shining cold and bright above.

Later, when the drinks were gone, we swam back to the boats and the captains turned them and headed back through the broad mouth of the bay, steering by spotlights pointed down at the water, and I watched our rowboat from the stern with Canasson beside me, smoking someone else's cigarettes. Canasson lifted a beer can off the deck and shook it, then dumped a few drops over the side.

"Lets go home," I said. "I can't stay awake any longer."

"It's not far," he said. "Just pretend you're already there."

A while later I felt the captain cut the motor. We pulled the rowboat up alongside and climbed down in. We said goodbye and Canasson rowed us in towards shore. I leaned my arms on the side and put my chin on my hands. A minute later we were there. I tied us to the dock and climbed out. Canasson climbed out behind me. The house was dark and my clothes were still wet. I said goodnight to him at the top of the stairs and then went into my room and got undressed. I left my clothes in a pile on the floor. I got into bed and fell asleep, feeling happy.

IX.

A week went by, and not much happened. Greene and Finnerty both thought that I was asking to get canned and was probably going to get canned sooner or later, and I held out that I didn't give a damn. Canasson said the divorce was moving forward, and that pretty soon, next week, maybe, he would have to go into the city and sign some papers, and then a few weeks later he would have to go in and go to court. He talked about it like he would talk about any other business deal that called him back to the city, or made him spend the morning on the phone, and I knew it was because of June, and that it didn't seem bad, now, because there was someone else. It was kind of strange to watch, knowing that it couldn't last forever, and might not last any longer than it took Bernard to finish his business with the galleries and come back. And it was also strange because Canasson knew it too, that pretty soon she wasn't going to be there when he hung up the phone, when he signed the papers.

It didn't matter to him, I guess, and I could see getting behind an idea like that, since nothing really lasts forever, anyway. Still, I knew that if it were me I would have closed myself to her a week before in the name of the distant date of separation the minute I saw it coming. I guess maybe it was noble of him to hold onto it, but maybe it wasn't. Knowing now what happened later, it seems like either would have been as good. After lunch he paid the bill and said he would see me later, and disappeared for hours, and came back grinning. Nights we went fishing, or to the movies, or with June to the bar, where Canasson told jokes and stories, yelling them over the jukebox and the crowd and I laughed huge and loud so that he would know that I had heard. But even then it was obvious that his jokes and stories weren't for me. But I was still very happy and those nights when I walked home from the bar with them and they left me at the doorstep and continued on I was still very happy and I called after them goodnight, goodnight, I will see you tomorrow I was very happy as I watched them weave into the shadow of the willows down by the water beyond our lawn and then into the light again, beyond where they thought I could see them, and turn to each other, even then I was happy as I watched them, watched him stoop to her and I told myself that I was very happy and very happy for them and very happy for him and I was sure that it was the same thing as being very happy.

Then, Bernard came home. Canasson and June played tennis the first Tuesday he came back and afterwards Canasson came home and had a half dozen drinks by himself on the porch. The next day she called and I answered, but Canasson didn't answer when I called up to his room to tell him that she was on the phone. June said could I have him call her when he got a chance and I said sure and then I went upstairs and knocked on his door. He answered after a minute.

"Would you please tell me," I said, "what the hell is going on with the two of you? You've been like a goddamned spook for a week, now."

"It's nothing," he said. "Anyway I don't want to talk about it."

"You not talking about it is fine," I said. "It's goddamned perfect, actually."

He sort of shook his head. "You don't understand," he said.

"I don't understand?" I said. "What am I supposed to understand?" He didn't say anything, so I said, "well how the hell am I supposed to understand, anyway? You don't tell me anything about it. I have to guess at goddamned everything."

"I'm sorry, Elliot," he said. He sighed. "I know. I know I've been acting like a bastard for the past week. "You're a good friend, for putting up with me." Then he didn't look at me, but kind of looked at the floor. He didn't look very good. He looked kind of sick to his stomach. Then he walked past me and stood looking out the window. "I'm in love with June," he said, not looking at me, "and she's in love with me."

I don't know why, but for some reason seeing him standing like that and saying that made me pretty mad. I knew he couldn't be in love with June and it seemed pretty unlikely that June was in love with him and the whole things felt shot through with that kind of fake heaviness that people use in church. I didn't really give a good goddamn about how he felt about June and to be honest I was sick of having it hanging in the air. I don't know. The thing is that when he said it, I kind of felt like pushing him right through the goddamned window. But instead I just said, "you're joking."

"I've never been more serious about anything in my whole life," he said, with that same heaviness, and I almost pushed him through the window again. But then he turned around and walked towards me, and he wasn't by the window anymore, and anyway as soon as I started feeling angry I started feeling tired of the whole thing.

"Does Bernard know?" I said.

"Of course not," said Canasson. "He doesn't know *yet*. June and I are going to tell him, but we're waiting for the right time, that's all. As soon as my divorce goes through we're going to tell him"

"You're going to what?" I said. I was sort of laughing by now. "Jesus, listen to yourself."

"You don't understand, Elliot," he said. "June and I love each other." He tried to move around in front I guess to look me in the eye, but I turned around and started going down the stairs. Then he said, "you said you were happy for me. You said you were happy for us."

"Oh for God's sake," I said. I stopped and turned around. "I was," I said. "I mean I am. But for Christ's sake, realize that it's over when it's over. If Bernard doesn't know now then you are damn well better off to let the whole thing drop and pray that he never finds out."

"No," Canasson said. "We're going to tell him. We already decided it. I have to tell him." He had his hands on his hips, looking down the stairs at me, but then his face kind of fell and he started crying. "I need her, Elliot," he said. "It's not like it was before. We meet for tennis but it's not enough. She – she keeps saying that we can go back to her place, that Bernard is always out in the workshop, but I just can't do that. I mean, I tried, once, but it felt wrong. It makes our love feel wrong. It makes it feel like something we have to hide, and it's not, it's not something we have to be ashamed of. It's too pure. That's why we are going to tell him. We've got to tell him."

It was pretty pathetic to watch. I mean it was sort of surprising, too, but then it was just sad and I felt like I wanted to be pretty much anywhere else. For a minute all I could think about was being somewhere else, but then I started thinking that I didn't really know what it was like for Canasson, with Diane leaving him, and maybe he was in love with June. I didn't know a whole hell of a lot about it, so it kind of got easy to imagine. I never really understood people falling in love anyway, and I guess Canasson crying didn't make sense in the same way falling in love didn't make sense. But it still kind of bugged the hell out of me, seeing him make a scene like that and not really being able to go anywhere, so after a while I said. "All right. Maybe you're in love with June. I don't know. All right? I don't know. Just don't put me in the middle of it. I don't want anything to do with it." Then I turned and went down the stairs, kind of wishing that Canasson wasn't there.

But I guess I was just angry at him, not really sick of him, because pretty soon I started wondering what we were going to do for dinner, and I wanted go up and figure it out. But I thought I'd wait for him to come ask me first. But it got dark, and he never came down. I guess he fell asleep.

On the day of the party I had to be in at work and I made the drive early, before Canasson was up. I didn't feel like listening to the radio, and I rode with only the wind noise drowning out the engine's rattle. I got to the newspaper a half

AURIC ADAMS

an hour late, but the place was empty, and I kicked around the break room drinking coffee and reading through the day's print. What I mean is, nobody saw me come in late. A while later Ranks and a guy named Rafferty who worked sports came into the lounge and we sat around talking.

"The way things are going, I'm surprised you don't wear a goddamned army helmet around here," said Rafferty. "I'm surprised you don't wear a goddamned flak jacket."

"What do you mean?" I said. "Ranks, what does he mean?"

"They're pissed at you in the editors booth," he said. "They're upset about the arrangement. Say they can't even get you on the phone, half the time. Like you're on summer vacation from school or something. They think you're not taking your job seriously."

"I am taking my job seriously," I said. "And besides, if they didn't like the arrangement, they didn't have to take it."

"You didn't give them a hell of a lot of choice, Elliot," Ranks said. "I mean, they needed you on staff, and then you tell them that you're moving out to the lake and you need to cut your time in the office in half? That's a hell of a lot to ask if you're a big shot, and it's a hell of a lot more than anybody thinks you should get away with as a beat guy."

"Give my hours to Greene," I said. "Why don't they give my hours to him? He needs the money, and it'll give him some time away from his kids."

"They're already giving extra shifts to Greene and Finnerty," said Ranks.

"They're not even calling you, half the time," said Rafferty, "when the calls come in."

"Why the hell not?"

"Why would they?" said Ranks. "By the time you got there, there would be nothing left to see, nobody left to talk to." He leaned forward, kind of concerned but serious. Ranks kind of bugged the hell out of me, if you want to know the truth. "It's a job suited for a guy who's in the action. You just

169

can't do it from an hour away, unless you plan to commute every day."

"I'm doing fine, the way it is," I said. "You telling me I'm not doing it fine?"

"We're not telling you anything," said Ranks. "There's just talk, that's all."

"Yeah," said Rafferty. "It's just talk."

"The hell with this," I said. "They don't want me, then fuck them."

"If that's the way you feel about it. Is that the way you feel about it?"

"What do you think?" I said. "I'm here, aren't I? I send in copy, don't I?"

"Sure," said Ranks, "you send in copy."

"It's just talk," said Rafferty.

I hung around with them for a little while longer, but we didn't talk any more about me living out at the lake. Then Rafferty started running down the baseball rankings and after that I excused myself and went back to the beat office. I felt like everybody was watching me as I climbed the stairs and when I was inside I shut the door and took papers out of my desk and spread them around. Then I smoked a couple of cigarettes and while I was doing that I went through Greene's desk and found a couple of things he had been working on and followed up on them with calls to the police. But they didn't know anything new, so I went to lunch. I felt lousy because I hadn't done anything all morning and because everyone expected me to do exactly that, so I figured the thing to do was to lay low and not talk to anybody, and hope that I could avoid catching anybody's eye and getting called into an office. I figured it would be pretty easy to do because it was Friday and people had other things on their minds. So I went back and laid low. Then I figured I had to get cleaned up before June's party, so I left early. I felt lousy about the whole thing, to tell you the truth, but driving back towards the lake I felt better. I tried to forget about my worthless day. But the funny thing was, I don't think it would have made any difference, if I had gotten anything done. I think I would have felt lousy either way, having been there at all.

The entrance to the fair was crowded, and I had to wait for a while before people cleared off the loop and I had room to go by. There were a hell of a lot of people in town. When I got to the house Canasson wasn't inside, but I saw him through the kitchen window, sitting on the porch. He had a drink in his hand and there was another drink sitting on the armrest of the second chair and I went out and sat down beside him without saying anything and sipped the drink. It was a gin sea breeze, with enough soda to make the top fizz. Canasson didn't say anything, but it was pretty easy to tell that he was excited. He kept tapping the front of his armrest with the tip of his middle finger while he sucked on his ice.

"How was work?" he said.

"Bad," I said.

"How's that?"

"They don't like me working from here. They think I can't do the job. That it needs to be done by somebody close to the city. They've even been calling Greene and Finnerty on my days, because they think I can't get to the scene fast enough." I sucked an ice cube and talked around it. "I wouldn't even give a shit," I said, "if they'd just come up and say it to me, instead of hearing from guys who heard it from guys who heard it from guys, you know?" I was getting kind of worked up about it, just thinking about it.

Canasson bit through an ice cube and swallowed the chunks. "Don't worry about it," he said. "If they had a problem, they would have already let you know. How long have you been out here? And besides, you can get another job. One job isn't worth being unhappy over."

"You think?"

"Sure," he said. "I'll tell you what, if you get fired you can come work for me."

"All right," I said. "Thanks." I had never really

thought about working for Canasson but after he said that, I felt better. Besides, I figured, I had money. Not a whole lot, but enough for a little while, and more than I thought that I would have, because Canasson had bought and paid for almost everything since he had been staying with me, and there was no rent. So I relaxed and sipped what was left of my drink out of my glass.

We had another drink, and then Canasson went in to take a shower, and I sat out on the porch and read the paper and had another. I looked over Greene's piece, five hundred words on a robbery that went bust and the standoff that followed, and found at least a dozen things I would have done differently, and better, and I started to feel like there was no way that they would fire me. While I was thinking about that I heard Canasson going upstairs, so I went inside and took a shower. While I was in the bathroom Canasson knocked on the door and said that he had promised June he would be there in fifteen minutes. So I said fine and hurried up and then got dressed and we left. My hair was still wet and I combed it back but it fell forward again while we were walking.

Their driveway was full of cars. They were fanned out on either side of the loop that led up to the house and then down to the road. From down beside the water I could see people out on the back lawn and patio and porch and then we moved onto the road as it began to climb and I couldn't see them anymore. It was hot and I opened my collar and put my tie in my pocket. The front door was open and the inside was loud with music and voices. There were a half dozen people standing around inside and another half dozen on the porch and I could see more people on the lawn below. A bar was set up on the kitchen counter, and the dining room table was pushed up against the back wall of the living room and covered with food. Bernard was standing in the kitchen and I waved and started towards him, but then I remembered Canasson and I stopped and looked back at him.

"Lets go to the bar," I said. I watched him look Bernard

up and down, and then nod.

We went over to the counter. Bernard was talking to a couple of people, a woman with a tight knot of black hair and a tall man in a blue workman's shirt. He excused himself and leaned over the counter to shake our hands.

"Welcome," he said. "Help yourself to anything you want."

"Where's June?" said Canasson.

"I don't know," said Bernard. He looked around. "I think I saw her down on the patio. She's around somewhere. Has my racket been working out for you?"

"Perfectly," said Canasson. "It's a very nice racket."

"Bernard," said the woman with the tight black hair.

"Excuse me," said Bernard.

"You smarmy bastard," I said, throwing ice cubes into a glass. "Well, you didn't waste any time with that one, did you?" I passed the glass to him and then filled another with ice.

"He doesn't know anything," said Canasson, pouring.

"He knows everything," I said. "He knows everything he needs to know to get jealous. You're just lucky that he trusts the two of you, the poor bastard."

"Shut up," said Canasson. "Here she is."

She was coming up the stairs from the patio. She caught sight of Canasson and came over. Bernard stepped between them but she kissed him on the cheek and then stepped past him to the bar. She took a glass and began to fill it with ice, and as she did she watched her own hands and Canasson watched her and you could tell that she knew that he was doing it.

"Hello, June," said Canasson.

"Hello Arthur," she said. "Hello Elliot."

"Hi June," I said. "Great party." She was filling her glass.

"Can't I do that for you?" said Canasson.

She was squeezing in the lime. "Already finished," she

said. "Thank you both for coming, but I am already being a terrible hostess. I've been downstairs since before these people showed up. I have to make the rounds. Will you excuse me?"

"Sure," I said. Canasson didn't say anything.

"I'm so sorry," she said. "Please forgive me. We'll sit down later, and have a drink. Will that do?"

"Don't worry," I said. She smiled at me and then took her drink and left. I looked back at Canasson, but Canasson was looking at his drink while he stirred in a twist. He took a long drink of it and then turned around and leaned against the counter. "Are you all right?" I said.

"Why wouldn't I be?" said Canasson.

"She was pretty cold to you," I said. He shrugged. I watched to see if he was going to say anything else, but when he didn't I took my drink and leaned against the counter beside him. We sipped at our drinks and watched the crowd.

Part of the crowd from the patio had followed June up, and now they stood around in a clump in the center of the room. Beyond them, over by the record player, a few people were dancing to *Ain't Misbehavin'*. I watched June detach herself from a group and walk through the open doors out onto the porch. I moved down the counter towards Canasson to make room for a man with an empty glass. He nodded to me and went for the scotch. I lost sight of June and then found her again, sitting in the far corner of the porch with two young men. Then the men got up and left and she stayed. I excused myself and went outside. She was facing out towards the trees that stood between her house and the next, with her back to the lake.

"Hello, Elliot," she said when she saw me. She sounded pretty tired.

"Hi," I said.

"Sit down, please"

I took a seat facing her, but she looked back out at the trees. She had her hair pulled back and piled up on her head, and I could see the short dark lines above the silver hooks of her earrings, where the hole had been stretched over time. It was that and the fact that she sounded so tired that made me suddenly think that maybe she was older than I had imagined when I first met her. But when she turned around to face me she was smiling again, and she looked young and happy and that there was nothing in the world that could touch her.

"I'm sorry," she said. "I'm just somewhere else tonight. I don't know why."

"It's all right," I said.

"Elliot," she said. "I feel like I haven't talked to you in forever."

"I'm here now," I said.

"I know," she said. "But it's almost no good talking now. You know how these parties go. As soon as we get talking someone will come up and I'll have to go talk to them… and besides," she stirred her the ice cubes in her glass with the tip of her index finger, "I'm a little bit drunk, if you want to know the truth."

"That's all right," I said. "I should be. I wish I was, actually."

"Do you know how it's been with us?"

"I think I know enough," I said. "He says he's in love with you."

"He's told me."

"He thinks that you're in love with him," I said. "Have you told him that you're in love with him?"

"No," she said. "Oh God, the poor thing. I really have been awful about it." She leaned in close to me. "What should I do, Elliot?" she said. "Tell me what to do about him, and I'll do it. You know him better than anyone."

"Break it off," I said. "It can't keep up forever, anyway. You know that."

"Yes," she said. "Of course, you're right. We should break it off now. I'm so glad you know, Elliot. It's like the weight of it has been lifted, to know that someone else knows.

I can't tell you what this has done to me, keeping it from Bernard like this. It's tearing me apart inside." She frowned, and the lines that ran from the curve of her nostrils down to the corners of her mouth grew deep and dark, and the lines around her eyes stood out.

It's pretty odd, but right at that moment I realized that she wasn't a hell of a girl, and never had been. It was her tone or the way she was playing the situation, or it was the lines on her face or the stretched out holes in her ears, but suddenly she wasn't even beautiful anymore, and I was ashamed for having ever thought that she was. The whole thing seemed sordid and dirty and meaningless. Canasson's professions of love only made the meaninglessness more obvious, in the same way that begging the dead to breathe makes them more obviously dead.

"It's funny," she went on. "When I first met Bernard I was so sure that I would never want anyone again, that he was all that I could ever hope for. But now that seems like so long ago, that I was a different person then. If I had only known how it would be, I could have saved us. I should have known. I was so much younger then, and so idealistic, and I had no sense of time or what it would do to me. Oh Elliot I don't know what to do." She put her face in her hands, and stayed like that for a while. Then she made this big show of regaining her composure and said, "could you – could you send Arthur out here? I think – I think I need to talk to him."

"Fine," I said.

I walked back inside. I felt kind of sick to my stomach, and I felt like leaving. I had the sense that they were all insufferable bastards and that Canasson was one of them.

"How is she?" he said.

"She's lamenting her lost youth," I said. "The great drama of being. She wants to talk to you."

"I appreciate you talking to her," he said. "You're a good friend."

He walked past me and through the crowd and out onto the porch and I watched him sit down beside her and then I turned back to the bar and made myself another drink. I didn't feel like talking to anyone, but I knew that I ought to. I was a little worried what I would say, so I decided to just shut up for a while. But standing there, not talking to anyone, I started to feel worse and worse. I started thinking about all of the times I had been jealous when Canasson was off with June, and I felt like an ass for having let myself care. That's the thing about caring: sooner or later you end up feeling like absolute hell. But after I stood there for a while I started feeling alone and awful, and I kind of wished that Canasson was there with me instead of off with June. I couldn't help it. Watching him talk to her I felt more alone than I ever had in my entire life.

"Elliot," someone said. I looked up to see Bernard leaning over the counter towards me.

"Hey Bernard," I said. "This is some party."

"You don't look to be enjoying it too much."

"I'm just tired is all," I said. "Are you enjoying it?"

He shrugged, and looked around. "I never feel like I have very much to say to these people," he said. "They're really June's friends. She's the one who talks to them whenever someone has a party. In these circles I think I'm just known as her husband." He reached across the counter and took a glass, then started filling it with ice. "You see him over there?" he said, nodding to the tall man in the blue work shirt I had seen him talking to earlier. "He's a photographer. He takes pictures of landscapes and then layers blueprint drawings over them. And her," he nodded to the women with the knot of black hair, "she does abstract watercolors. Just a few lines of these very pale colors on a blank page." He poured his glass half full with vodka and squeezed in a wedge of lime. He took a sip. "And him," he pointed with the index finger of his drink hand at a fat older man with small black-rimmed glasses, "he makes the most intricate pieces of jewelry you can imagine. Very minute little details, all done under a magnifying glass. It's amazing to see. All of these people," he made a circle with his drink hand, indicating the room, "all

177

of them make beautiful work, but we have nothing to say to each other."

"Why do you come, then?" I said. "You can sneak off, I'm sure."

"June asked me to be here," he said. "She doesn't feel like she belongs, unless I'm here, even when it's at our house." He laughed. Out on the porch, I watched her smile and then cover her mouth with her hand, then uncover it and laugh.

"She is something," I agreed.

"She really is," he said. He looked at her, too, then sipped his drink and looked away and said, "look, the real reason I came over was to ask you if you could help me carry something up from the boathouse. They want to see some of the new work and there's no way I'm having them all down there."

"Sure," I said.

"Wonderful," he said.

I followed him down the stairs and out onto the patio, and then down the steps set into the lawn. Down away from the party and the conversation noise I could hear Bernard's keys jingling and behind that I could hear the lake against the shore. The night was warm but there was a breeze blowing in across the lake that slapped the water against the dock boards. I followed Bernard into the shadow of the boathouse and then we paused as he unlocked the door. It was dark inside and I stood against the near wall as Bernard crossed the room to the light switch. Then he turned on the light. It was sitting between a pair of electric wheels on a rough palate and was covered in a white sheet stained with clay brown handprints.

"That's it," said Bernard.

"What is it?" I said.

"Uncover it," he said, waving his hand at it. "Take a look." I pulled back the sheet. "What do you think?" he said.

"It looks just like her," I said.

"We had better get back up there," he said. "They're

waiting on me."

We lifted the palate, and then carefully maneuvered through the doorway and started up the steps. I went first, and I walked in a half-crouch to keep the palate level. Then the ground leveled out as we neared the patio, and someone held the door open for us. We went in and Bernard called for someone to clear a table. Someone cleared away the plates and glasses. Bernard lifted the sculpture by its base and I took the palate out from under it and Bernard set the sculpture down and I put the palate outside and when I came back in Bernard was standing back from it, considering it, and I looked it over and said it looked fine and he agreed and we went upstairs to join the party.

Upstairs was crowded. I left Bernard and made my way to the bar. I made myself a drink and while I was doing that I felt someone tap me on the shoulder and when I turned around it was Canasson. His face was red from pushing through the crowd to reach me. He said something, but I couldn't hear him over the noise in the room from footsteps and voices.

"What?" I said.

"Never mind," he said, louder. "I'll tell you later."

Someone called that Bernard's new sculpture had been brought up, and everyone started moving towards the stairs. I waited until the room was almost clear and then I went out onto the porch. Out across the lake I could see light shining out on the point. I sipped at my drink and then I walked to the side of the porch, over out of the light coming through the glass doors. I set my glass down on the railing and leaned against the house and closed my eyes. I could hear voices from the room below me, but no words. I leaned forward and bumped my glass with my elbow and it fell off and landed in the grass. I looked after it and then went inside and made another. I was feeling like the only person in the world. So I went downstairs.

With everyone downstairs the room was pretty full. I pushed my way through to the center of the room, where the floor was clear. Most of the people were huddled around the sculpture. I caught sight of Canasson on one side, and June on the other. Then a couple moved from in front of me and I moved forward. Someone moved one of the lights in the ceiling to shine down on the statue, and the crest of her back and shoulders and the top of her head shone white. I watched Canasson. He was looking at the sculpture, and I watched his eyes work down it and then up and then work down it again. His mouth was open in this sort of half-smile. I looked over at June. She was watching him. I felt a hand fold over my shoulder, and Bernard stepped beside me.

"Enjoying the party?" he said.

"Yes," I said. "It's a terrific party."

X.

The fireworks started, and we went up on the porch to watch. June stood beside Bernard and Canasson stood beside me. The explosions traveled across the open water and echoed off the glass wall behind us. After a while I went inside to make another drink, and when I turned back I saw that Canasson had moved down the railing to stand beside her. I went out the front door and sat on the front step. I was feeling pretty tired, and something else, but I told myself I didn't care and I decided to think about anything other than all of them. But I didn't really know anyone else, and the world seemed empty without them.

People started to leave after the fireworks. I felt a little too obvious on the step and so I went back inside. I had drained off the rest of my drink and went to make another. Canasson and Bernard were standing where I had left them, leaning against the railing. I watched them for a moment but nothing seemed to be happening, so I went over to the table and picked through what was left of the cheese. I wasn't really hungry, but I suddenly felt like if I didn't find something to do, I was going to throw myself out the window. But while I was doing that, June came in.   "So this is where you ran off to," she said.

"Sure," I said. I turned around to lean against the table facing her, and looked at Canasson so she could see me doing it. "Ah well," I said, "it's just as well that you broke it off with him. It couldn't have gone anywhere good. You must feel better."

"Oh Elliot," she said. She looked at me and shook her head, like she was really sorry for me, but there wasn't anything she could do about it and she wasn't going to try.

That made me pretty angry, so I said, "fine. Fuck this. Fuck you. Fuck both of you." Then I took off across the living room and went down the hall and out the front door. I wasn't running or anything, but I was moving pretty fast, and I think it seemed like I was moving faster because I was pretty drunk.

But when I got outside I sort of lost momentum. I guess I felt better being outside, and I didn't want to leave without Canasson, since we had come together. Then I decided fuck him, because I was sure he had told June what I said, and because he had been ignoring me all night, and because of the way he had looked at Bernard's sculpture, so I started down the driveway towards the road and towards home. But then I heard Canasson calling my name from the house, and I stopped and he ran up beside me.

"Elliot," he said. "What's going on? Are you leaving?"

"Don't worry about it," I said. "Go back in there. Go back in there to June." I was waving him back towards the house, backing down the driveway. But the funny thing is, even while I was doing it I knew I was being stupid. I just kind of couldn't stop. "No, no," I said. "You go. You go have a good time. I'm going to just go home."

"Elliot," he said, following me down the driveway. "Elliot, hold on. Elliot come back. I'm sure whatever June said -,"

"Go back in," I said. "She'll tell you what she said. Go back in." I was still waving him back, but I started to veer off the driveway into the lawn, and I had to turn around for a second to see where I was going. When I turned back he had stopped at the edge of the light that fell onto the lawn from the house, and he grew into just a silhouette against the white façade as I kept backing up until I was sure he was not following, and then I turned and kept walking until I reached the road. I guess I had kind of hoped that he would follow me, but when I turned around at the end of the driveway the lawn was empty.

I didn't have a hell of a good reason to go anywhere, so I moved a little down the road towards home and then I walked off into the ditch and sat down in the grass.

Everything seemed really still, but like if I moved an inch in either direction a shit storm would start. That's how drunk I was. So I stayed put and smoked a few cigarettes, one right after the other. After that I felt a little lightheaded, so I decided to lie down. The grass was a little wet with dew and I felt it soak through between my shoulders and I got cold, but then I got used to it. The night was really clear, and since I was up on the hill, above the town and the lights, I could see a lot more stars than I could from the back porch. You could see a hell of a lot of stars from the back porch at Bradner's house, but you could see even more from up on the hill. There were stars and then there were more stars between the stars. After a while the world started to spin and I closed my eyes, but with my eyes closed I could still see the stars. The ones overhead were clear, but the other ones, the ones around me, all spun into long streaks that seemed to hold still and to also go back and forth and also to go around. Then I started feeling pretty sick and I thought I was going to throw up, but it passed. But even after I stopped feeling sick the stars kept on spinning, so I opened my eyes and sat up so I wouldn't have to look at them anymore.

After a while, though, I kind of stopped caring. What I mean is, I sort of started thinking about other things while I was laying there. I guess I was pretty upset with both of them, but I was too drunk to really think about it for very long. Then I started thinking that I didn't care. It seemed pretty simple and easy not to care until I thought about going home, and that the house would be empty. Like there used to be something but now it was gone and the house would only remind me of it. Then I got angry again, and I stayed angry until I got tired of feeling angry, and I began to repeat myself, and then I didn't care again. I smoked a couple more cigarettes and then I saw that I only had two left and I smoked those and decided to go for a swim and try to forget the whole thing.

So I walked back to the house. But I didn't go inside. Instead I walked around to the back lawn and down the dock.

I was walking pretty steady by the time I got there, so I wasn't too worried about swimming. I took off my clothes and jumped into the lake. The water was warmer than the air and made the air feel cold when I came up. I swam around feeling fine, and in control and also very sharp and sober.

But then, after I had been swimming for a while, I heard somebody calling my name in kind of a harsh, yelling whisper, and then footsteps on the dock. I didn't know what to do, so I didn't do anything. I just stayed afloat and waited. Then Canasson appeared over the horizon of the dock end. He walked down to the end and sat down right away.

"Elliot," he said, "I'm glad I found you." There wasn't much light, but by the way he was holding his head I could tell he wasn't looking at me. He sighed and clasped his hands together between his knees.

"This is it for me and you," I said. I felt pretty silly saying it because I was naked, but I was pretty sure he couldn't see me through the water.

"Don't be dramatic."

"I'm not being dramatic," I said. "I could actually give a shit. But we're through."

"You're just drunk," he said. Then he sort of stiffened. Then he threw up his hands and said, "all right. I guess I'll talk to you about it in the morning." He stood up, but I guess I didn't really want him to leave, because right away I started feeling bad and like the black water and black sky were empty without him.

"Why did you come?" I said.

He turned around and leaned against the dock post and said, "I don't know. I went back inside to tell June that I was going to leave, to tell her that I was going after you, but when I went back outside you were gone. I looked around for you on the road but I didn't see you and then I thought that maybe you had fallen into the lake and drowned. I don't know, I was thinking a lot of crazy stuff and June was crying and Bernard was standing in one spot turning around and around, asking me what he could do over and over again. It somehow got around to everyone who was left that something terrible had happened to you, and everyone wanted to go out and help and be part of it. By the time I talked everybody down and we decided not to call the police I had calmed down myself and I figured you had probably just come here, and by then I wasn't thinking about why I was doing it. It just seemed like what I was supposed to do." I saw him shrug against the lighter background of the sky, washed out hazy orange-gray from the lights of the town behind. "I acted like a jerk tonight," he said. "I've been acting like a jerk this whole time, about June and everything. I guess all I can say is that I didn't realize that it was hurting you until it had already hurt you, and by then, since you weren't saying anything, I guess I let myself believe that it was all right."

"I wasn't hurt," I said. "I mean I wasn't hurt so much as it was just obnoxious to deal with."

"I understand."

Neither of us said anything for a little while. I felt angry, the way I had sitting on the grass at the roadside, going over all of the things that I was upset about and having them bubble up and roll over at the back of my throat. But I could never get one to stick, or I could never think of how to say it to make it come out right, so I ended up not saying anything. After a while I started getting cold, and I tried to think of what I could say to make him go away, so I could get out.

"Look," I said, "it's not as bad as all that. I'm just being stupid. I don't really mind about you and June at all. I really don't."

But he didn't say anything for a long time. Then he said, "All right, then," and stood and turned and shrank into the black border of the sky made by the house and the trees behind.

"Where are you going?" I said.

"I'm going back," he said. He sounded tired and I guess sick of talking to me. "I told Bernard I would help him

185

clean up. And I didn't really say goodbye, only that I was going to go look for you. They're still wondering what happened to you."

"What are you going to tell them?"

"I don't know. Goodnight, Elliot," he said.

"Arthur," I said.

"I'll see you tomorrow."

He turned and his footsteps were fast and then went silent as he left the dock and stepped onto the lawn. I pulled myself clear of the water and felt myself cold and naked against the wood as I called his name again, and watched him disappear into the shadow of the house. Then I slipped back down into the water. The world felt empty and I felt drunk and like it would be a very long time until I was sober, and that, even though I did not feel it yet, soon I would feel terrible, and there was no way to avoid it, and that it would last for a very long time.

I floated on my back for a while, and then I got out and walked up to the house, carrying my clothes. I went inside and went into the bathroom and got in the shower. I was shivering and I thought that I would stop if I took a hot shower, but it took a long time, I guess because I was drunk. After that I toweled off and went upstairs and got into bed. I was still a little bit wet, though, and the water rubbed off on the sheets and then cooled and pretty soon everywhere I touched was damp and cold. I started getting cold again, but then I fell asleep. It was funny because I didn't think I would be able to, and then suddenly I was asleep. It didn't really feel like anything, it was so easy to do.

The sun woke me up. I didn't do anything but open my eyes, and for a second it seemed like somehow I would be fine, that I felt all right. But then, when I tried to move, I realized that I wasn't fine, and that everything hurt. My stomach felt like it was filled with sand. I closed my eyes and lay still for a long time and was very thankful that it was Saturday and that I didn't have to do anything or go anywhere and that maybe the day could just go by, and I could wake Sunday morning feeling fine. But somehow, I knew I couldn't. I wanted to know what had happened after Canasson went back, and, I thought, it meant that I had to find Canasson, because I did not think that he had come home, though I thought that he could have come in later and that I would not have heard him. But when I got up and went outside my bedroom I saw that his door was open and his bed was empty, and when I went downstairs I saw that there was no coffee made, and that he was not out on the porch where I always found him, and that he was gone. I guess it was because I felt so lousy anyway, but it sort of made me feel like crying. Not because I missed him or anything, or because I thought he was gone for good, but just because he wasn't there and somehow that fact seemed to demand of me more than I could possibly give. But instead of crying, I made coffee.

I didn't know it then, but the conversation on the dock was the last time I would see Canasson for almost four days. Somehow, for four days, we kept missing each other. I don't know if he meant it to happen that way. But I saw him again on Thursday morning. I came downstairs and he was there. I had been in to work on Wednesday and come home feeling lousy and that everything was ending there. At about noon Finnerty came in, and gave me a look that said that I didn't work there anymore, and everybody knew it but me. But for some reason, when I saw Canasson, I felt a whole hell of a lot better. I didn't mean to. We met in the kitchen and then went out onto the porch without talking. Out on the porch it was already hot and we watched the long reflection of the sun narrow to a singular point as it rose higher above the trees and shone directly down onto the water.

After a while, just because I was tired of the silence, I said, "How's June?"

"She's fine," he said, without looking at me. "She's in excellent tennis form. You really should see her. She says she's playing the best tennis of her life. She said she always thought that she had already peaked but she says now she can see that each of the times she peaked before it was only part of one larger climb towards something else. She says she knows herself and knows how to handle herself better now than she ever has before. You can tell watching her, too. You can really tell, just by the way she moves. She's graceful and she's powerful and there's always something more that she is holding back. It really is fantastic to see."

"That's great," I said, and I meant it, too.

"I know you don't like her, Elliot," he said. "It's all right. You don't have to pretend."

"I'm not pretending," I said. "I'm glad she makes you happy. I'm glad that you're happy with her."

He didn't say anything after that. I guess we both knew that I didn't mean it. Across the water, the hammering gave a staccato rhythm to the dull whine of the saws. They had been going all week. Beside the condominiums, another was going up. The yellow pine framing showed almost white in the sunlight, against the background of wood and mud. In a week, they said, the workers would begin clearing timber on the other side of the fence. They were going to float the logs around the point to the launch point on the far shore, where a backhoe would pile them onto a truck so they could be taken to be split.

"I have to go into the city today," he said. "I was wondering if I could use the car."

"Sure," I said. "In fact, I should go in too. I need to go to the office. I'll give you a lift."

"How is work going?"

"It's going all right," I said. "How's it going with the lawyers?"

"It's going."

"That's good to hear," I said. "Well, I guess I should go get cleaned up."

"I should too," said Canasson. "Do you want the first shower?"

"You take it," I said. "I'm going to sit out here a minute longer."

He stood up. "Thanks, Elliot," he said. "I wasn't sure you would want me back here, if we actually saw each other."

"Is that why you stayed away?"

"That's part of it."

"Christ," I said. "I'm sorry Arthur."

He went inside. I sipped at my coffee, but it had gone cold and so I threw what was left over the railing. I felt about a hundred years old, and that time had moved on without me. But then the feeling passed. I got up and went inside. The house was warm and pulsing with the sound of the water as the pump pushed it up through the pipes.

We rode together into the city. The car was starting to fall apart. We kept the radio off.

"So," I said, after we had been going for a while, "how are things really going with June?"

"Fine," he said. And then, I guess because he figured it was what I was really asking, he said, "Bernard doesn't know about us. Did you know that already?"

"I don't remember what I knew," I said. "It's all mixed up for me."

"Bernard doesn't know about us," he said again. He hardly ever comes out of his studio. You should see the things he is making, though. He's shown some of them to us. They're beautiful. The most amazingly delicate things you've ever seen. He just draws them out and draws them out until they look like they could fall apart in your hands, like ashes. He says it's the closest he's ever come to making with his hands what he sees in his mind."

"But he doesn't know?"

"He doesn't know." He shrugged. "His work is all he thinks about. I mean, he loves June, I know he loves June. But it's this kind of austere, chivalrous love. To him June is part of art. She's his muse, and he has to keep her separate, like that, like she's up in the air floating over him all the time, or something. I mean, that's part of the reason I don't feel so bad about it, because he loves her as a concept, but he neglects her."

"Well he's going to find out sooner or later," I said. "How long do you think you can keep this up?"

"I don't know," he said.

We didn't talk any more, after that. I dropped him off at his office, then drove down to the newspaper. The beat room was empty, and so I closed the door behind me and opened the windows and took off my suit jacket and lit a cigarette. I sat down at my desk, but after a few minutes I got up again. I was thinking about June. I had thought about her the whole rest of the way in and after I had dropped him off and walking into the office and I was thinking about her now, about what it would be like. I felt like I had been too hard on her. But then the phone rang, and it was the secretary telling me that the boss wanted to see me, and so I crushed out my cigarette and put my jacket back on and went down the stairs and across the floor to his office. He was sitting at his desk. He pointed to a chair and I sat down and he said, "Elliot, I have had an absolute hell of a time getting hold of you."

"Oh yeah?" I said.

He nodded. "Yeah," he said. "They tell me you moved. They tell me that you are staying at Bradner's lake house, since Bradner got called up."

"Oh?" I said.

"Yeah," he said again. "As a matter of fact, I talked to Bradner the other day. He got shipped out last month, and he called me from overseas. That makes him officially easier to get a hold of than you, and he's on the other side of the goddamned world."

"What do you want me to do?" I said. "I got a phone. You got my number."

"Do you have any concept," he said, "of how many times I have called you? Go ask Brianna." He pointed through the glass to his secretary's desk. "How many times

I've said to her, "Brianna, call Poulain and don't stop calling until he picks up." Go ask her how many times she's come in two hours later and said to me, "sir, should I keep calling?" Do you have any idea?"

"No," I said. "But I'm betting you don't either."

"I don't need to know," he said. "I know it was a whole hell of a lot."

"So what?" I said. "You can't get me on the phone. I'm here on my days. You got a call you need to make, why don't you call Greene or Finnerty? Or send one of the sports photographers. Christ, you don't need a man on the scene for everything."

"I have," he said, nodding. "I have been sending sports people. Christ, I even sent the guy who writes our weekly op-ed piece out to cover a story once. He threw up a half dozen times at the scene of a goddamned car accident." He shook his head. "The goddamn commanding officer called me up and asked me never to send him out again. And don't lecture me on how to run things, for God's sake."

I lit another cigarette. "What do you want me to do?" I said. "Say I'm sorry? I'm sorry, ok?" I looked at him through the smoke. "Look," I said. "Maybe when you're you, and you've got your own office and everything, you can afford to pass up a summer of free rent in a pretty damn nice location. Ok? I can't. Cut me a break, already. I'll hire a goddamned secretary, if it makes you happy. But if you think I'm going to give that up so I can lope around here all the damn day, waiting for some schmuck to off himself so I can run over and take some pictures, you've got another thing coming."

"I know," he said. He looked at me, then leaned forward and looked down at his desk. He glanced up at me through his eyebrows. Then he leaned back in his chair and said, real fast, "you've got two weeks. Have your desk cleaned out by then."

"What?" I said.

"I'm sorry, Elliot," he said. "I can't count on you anymore."

"You're joking," I said.

"I'm not," he said. "Trust me, I'm not. I've thought about it long and hard. To tell you the truth, if it makes you feel any better, my mind was made up before you even walked in the door."

"You can't do this," I said.

"I can," he said. "And I am. I don't want to. You forced me hand."

"Bullshit," I said. "I didn't force anything." He didn't say anything to that, so I stood up. "Fine," I said. "Fuck this. You want me out, I'll be gone by the end of the day. Fuck your two weeks."

"You watch how you talk to me," he said.

"Fuck you," I said. "Fuck you and this whole fucking place."

I went across the newsroom real slow. Nobody really looked at me, but everybody was pretty busy, so it might just have been that nobody saw me there. I went to the supplies closet and got a half dozen large envelopes, and then I went back to the beat office and I took everything I had worked on out of my desk. I put text in two of the envelopes and pictures in three of the others. I took the sixth one with me anyway and I left the building and went out and got into the car. I sat there for a while, with the envelopes on the seat next to me, and kind of wondered what time Canasson was going to want to leave, and what time he was going to be done with the lawyers, and if he would be free for lunch. Then I kind of thought that I had better go over to his office anyway, because we had left it that he was going to call me at the newspaper when he was finished, and now I wouldn't be there to get the call. So I started the car and headed over there. The car was still pretty warm, I guess, because the engine started right away and sounded all right going across town. About halfway across town a pickup stopped short in front of me, and I stopped short, too, and one of the envelopes, one of the ones full of pictures, slid off the seat and onto the floor, and when I tried to pick it up all of the pictures fell out. I couldn't pick them up because I was driving. So I left them there. Then, after driving for a little while, wanting to pick them up but not being able to, I realized that they were all pictures that nobody wanted, not anymore, and that it didn't matter if I picked them up, not ever. That was the first time it felt like I was really fired, and wasn't going back to the newspaper anymore. The rest of the way to the office I felt so low I figured if the truck ahead of me stopped short again, I might just hit the gas and try to drive myself right up under the rear axle, so the tire would bust through the windshield glass. But the truck didn't stop again before I reached the office. So I just got out and left the pictures on the floor.

I started feeling better as soon as I saw him, though. Part of it was I guess that he seemed really happy to see me, I guess because it meant that he could take a break from talking to lawyers. He hung up the phone as soon as I walked in.

"How was the morning at the paper?" he said.

"Not good," I said. "Well, maybe all right. I got fired."

"No," he said.

"Yeah," I said. "I guess it's not really a surprise. Or at least everybody else saw it coming. Christ, I guess I saw it coming, too. It's funny how sometimes it's not until after that you realize that you saw it coming all along. Or maybe it just seems that way. How are things with you?"

"The same," he said. "They're really taking me to it."

"You all right?" I said.

"I'm all right," he said. "Diane and me... it was never all that it was supposed to be. It was never all right. The parts that were good were good and the parts that were bad were bad, like everything else, but the parts that were bad were the important parts and we both knew it, and it made all of the parts that were good seem like a sham, or like a trap we couldn't believe because they'd hurt too much when the whole thing finally caved in. It was easier in the past few years to steel up against it, I think, for her, but in the beginning we both thought it would work, and that the good parts were the true parts, and that they were building towards something, and I guess the unforgivable thing is that I gave up on them a long time before she did, and saw them for what they were, and I didn't tell her, but let her go on loving me the way she had when we were young and believed that one day everything would be wonderful. God, it seems so awful, now, thinking about it that way. It seems like something I did maliciously. I guess it was, in a way. I guess I enjoyed it. But it also just happened that way. And for a while - I guess for a while I thought that it was something wrong with me, having lost faith in us, you know, and that sooner or later I would get over it, and go back to being the way I was, and she would never know that it had almost fallen apart then. And I wanted it to go back to the way it was, and believing that Diane still believed that it would…" He didn't look at anything for a second. Then he sighed and shrugged and said, "I don't know, Christ. What did I know? It was my fault, and she deserves everything she wants to take, and she deserves to want to hurt me, and I guess I deserve to be hurt. But… but I didn't want it to be this way. I feel like that should count for something."

"Sure," I said.

We went and had lunch. Then I spent the afternoon in Canasson's office, smoking cigarettes and reading and listening to him talk on the phone. At about two o'clock a fat lawyer named Derbyshire came in and the two of them hashed over details for a while. Then, when he left, Canasson sent his secretary out for a couple cups of coffee and when she brought them we took a walk around the building and down the street. Canasson didn't say much, but you could tell he felt better being outside. I felt pretty lousy about the way I had been about June. It was easy to see that the situation with Diane was harder on him than he had let show. He was pretty beat down by the end of the day and he didn't talk at all on the ride home. He turned on the radio, and when we lost the station somewhere near the outskirts of the city he just left it, and the white fuzz of static filled the car, and I finally had to reach over and turn it off.

Back home I made our drinks and we sat on the porch and talked about nothing and drank more until the sun went down and the lake got dark. After that he said he was tired and was going to go in to bed and I stayed outside alone and felt myself going. I was drunk and everything seemed right in the world. I didn't mind losing my job, and I didn't mind that the summer was halfway over. After a while the feeling of going merged into the feeling of falling asleep and soon I was asleep, and it was not until later, when it started getting cold, that I woke up and went upstairs to bed.

The next morning I lay awake and listened to him moving downstairs for a long time before I got up and went down. When I did he was sitting at the kitchen table with the paper spread out in front of him.

"What did you have planned today?" I said.

"I was going to meet June to play tennis this afternoon," he said. "She reserved the court for three, but I think we're going to stay after and have a drink. What do you have on for this afternoon? You should come."

"I think I'll just be in the way," I said.

"You won't be," he said. "Honest. We're just going to play tennis and have a drink. She is having dinner with Bernard tonight. They made plans for it weeks ago. She has to be home by six o'clock. If you're already down at the courts, we could go out after she leaves."

I shrugged. "Sure," I said. I looked out through the glass in the door behind him. "Have you been outside yet today? I was thinking of taking the boat out for a bit. Just a loop around the bay."

"It's calm out," said Canasson. "It should be easy rowing."

"I'll go out after breakfast, then. What time should I be here to meet up with you and June?"

"We probably won't leave until two."

"All right," I said. "I'll be back before two, then. June doesn't hate me, does she?"

"I don't think so. Why would she?"

"I was pretty rude to her at the party."

"It was a bad night," said Canasson. "I think we all would sooner forget it happened than anything. It didn't mean anything, anyway. We were all pretty drunk and there's no use trying to pretend that any of us said exactly what we meant. Beside, June asked me to invite you. She said she would like to see you. She doesn't want to leave things the way they were."

"All right," I said.

"Besides," he said, "this is one of those things we're going to look back on and laugh at, and think how funny it is that we were worried about it back then."

"Maybe it's just one of those things we tell ourselves we'll look back on and laugh at one day."

"No, it really is," he said. "I'm sure it really is."

"All right, if you're sure. What's for breakfast?"

"Coffee. There's nothing here. I don't know what you've been eating."

"I guess I haven't been hungry." I crushed out my cigarette against a dirty plate that was still on the table and blew the last of the smoke up towards the ceiling. It drifted past the kitchen window and the gray of the smoke merged into the gray of the flat water, and for a moment it seemed like one day we really would all look back on this and laugh.

We went to the Main Street diner and had breakfast. After breakfast we walked back and Canasson said he had some work to do. So I left him alone in the house and went down to the dock and took the boat out. The water was flat and pale and the sky was, too, and I rowed easily out and then turned and headed south, towards Bernard and June's house.

But then I turned and moved along the shore until I was far out away from our house, and the house and the fair were very small across the water. I felt tired and when I looked at my hands I saw that blisters had formed along my palms and in the groove between my thumb and my index finger. I hadn't felt them forming, but after I noticed they started to hurt. I washed my hands in the lake. After that they felt a little better, but when I started to row again they hurt twice as much and I had to stop. So I just sat and looked back at the house across the lake. Then I looked along the shore. There were fresh white frames going up beside the others, out far along the north shore. I tried to imagine what it would be like, when there was nothing but a long row of condominiums there, instead of trees, and the long arms of the aluminum docks, packed with boats, reaching out into the lake. I couldn't imagine it. It would probably be a lot like it was when the first summer cabins were put in, I thought: probably very much the same, and for a while they would seem foreign and inhospitable, and then slowly they become part of this town, as well, and it seemed, for a second, that nothing ever really went away but only became something else, and it is only because I couldn't see it that I always thought it is gone forever. But then, pretty soon, I started thinking about what they had said, that the forest would be clear cut to the point, and it seemed that it actually was different, this time, and that something would be lost, and that it wasn't something that had happened a million times before, happening again.

And what did it matter if the whole thing fell at the end of time, and the earth went back to Eden, and we all went to hell? I didn't know, so I rowed back to shore. The hell of it was, I was sure that I had known, once: that everything was everything else and everything was nothing new and that sooner or later everything went to hell and wasn't worth getting tied up with. My hands hurt like a bastard and halfway into shore I took off my shirt and wrapped the sleeve ends around my hands, and rowed back with the shirt on my hands and the clothesline of the collar and torso of it coming towards my face and then moving away again with each stroke.

XI.

I got back into shore around one. Canasson wasn't on the porch or in the kitchen, and when I went upstairs I saw that his door was closed. So I got undressed and took a shower, but I couldn't use the soap, because it stung in the blisters. So I just rinsed off. Then I toweled off and went upstairs to get changed. While I was in my room changing I heard Canasson go downstairs, and I hurried up and finished getting dressed and then left my room and went down after him.

He was out on the porch, standing at the top of the stairs, looking out at the dock and the water. The wind had picked up, and the pale sky had gone gray. There was a chop on the lake, and a hundred thousand needle points of water rose up and sprayed and fell back. From the doorway I heard the merry-go-round record and, behind that, the whine of a saw and the inconsistent beat of hammers. I didn't know if I only hadn't heard it when I was out on the water, or if it really hadn't been there. I walked out and stood beside him.

"How was your rowing?" he asked me. I showed him my palm. "Jesus," he said. "That looks like it hurts. Did that happen while you were out there, or did you manage to make it back before it got too bad?"

"Out there," I said. I let my hand drop to my side. "Have they been going all morning?"

"The workers? Yes they've been going the whole time."

"It's funny, but I didn't hear them while I was out there. I heard the carnival all right, but I didn't hear the saws or hammers."

"Did you see June?"

"No. Was she swimming?"

"Yes, out to the float and back."

"No I didn't see her."

"We should really be going," he said.

HERE GROAN THE DEAD

We went through the house and out and got into the car. Canasson drove. It took a dozen turns before the engine clicked over. We pulled out of the driveway and down along the loop, heading north around the bay. I wondered if they had intended on playing tennis at all, if June would be surprised that I was there, if it would change their plans, or if it really was only what Canasson said it was, and afterwards we would all have drinks like three old friends with no unpleasant history between us.

"We really should get the car fixed," he said. "You must know someone who can do it."

"I do," I said, "but there isn't any point. It doesn't have much left to it. If it gets through the summer that will be enough for me. I'll do enough to see that it does that, but there's no point in trying to fix it up. It's too far gone."

"I guess you're right," he said.

We pulled up in front of the clubhouse and Canasson parked the car. I could see June's car a few spaces down and when I got out and looked over at the courts I could see her serving into the net. Her body raised up long and then contracted as one muscle and her arm and the racket at the end of it blurred into nothingness to reappear in a different place, lower beside her knees. I watched her serve three times, and then she moved to the net to collect the balls and Canasson looked at me and we moved down the path towards her.

She waved big with her racket when she saw us coming. I watched her as we moved along the fence towards the court, and watched the muscles in her shoulders move under the skin and the sliver of pale skin over her hip that showed as she bent and disappeared when she stood to face us. Canasson opened the gate and we both went inside.

"Hello, June," Canasson said.

"Hello, Arthur," she said. "Hello, Elliot."

"Hi June," I said. "How have you been?"

"Exactly the same. Nothing ever changes. You think it will, or that it is, but in the end everything is almost exactly the same way it was, and you feel silly for having worried about it. Don't you think?"

"Yes," I said, "I know what you mean."

They played and I stood outside the fence, watching. Canasson led but June overtook him in the end. She laughed and said it was luck, and he said that it wasn't luck, and didn't laugh. June was the first to reach the bar, and she was already ordering tall beers when we caught her up. There did not seem to be any need to argue over what it was that we drank, because this drink seemed somehow to be one in an ocean of others and that there would be time to drink all of the drinks we could imagine together, and that this one held in its insignificance the promise of many others. The bartender brought them and June and Canasson toasted each other as opponents and I toasted them both as good players and they toasted me as their very welcome guest. We all drank and moved to a table and drank more in the shade and then called for other drinks that I do not remember and soon there was trouble because we could not find room among the glasses we had for the glasses that were coming, and everything was more than funny and impossibly ridiculous, and what were we thinking? And do you remember? And how funny it all is, looking back on it, now that it is gone and over and it could not touch us or hurt us, and we may love the past in ways that we cannot love the present, because there is no danger there, we all agreed. Can you love the present like you love the past, we asked, and one of the glasses slid into the other, and we said we must have more room, and we set them on the table beside us, and when did it get dark? And please bartender another round, I've never been so thirsty in my entire life.

Pretty soon we went back home. June came with us. Canasson wanted to drive, but June would not let him, and she begged me to help her stop him, and in the end I said I felt like walking, that somehow it had become a lovely night, with the sky very clear and a little blue, still, and Canasson said fine and we began walking. And then Jesus Christ Goddamnit because she had left her rackets in beside the table, leaning against the fence, and do you think that the clubhouse is still open? And walking back and the same walk seeming very new, and wondering if that tree had been there all along, and that fence, and the door Goddamnit is locked and those sons of bitches are in there and they won't open up, and then Canasson said let's sneak around back and hop the fence and we did and Canasson went over and I heard a table flip and cursing and laughing and then the rackets came over the fence and then Canasson came over, one leg and then the other, and onto the dirt, and cursing and laughing, and noise from inside, and we ran, and I was yelling, they're going to know it was us when we come back to get the car, and who the hell cares leave it and buy another one. Then the long walk that did not seem so long, past the entrance to the fair and should we go in again and yes lets but no should we, and Jesus Christ there are children, and keeping it together past the mean-faced policeman posted by the gate. Then the very long corridor lined with faces and Jesus Christ where do they come from, where do they come from? And someone said the summer people and it seemed for a moment a horrible injustice that those bastards could do it. Then, some time later, sick from the merry-go-round, staggering out to throw up in the bushes in the dark down by the water, and listening to their voices and then their silence and just go on without me, for Christ's sake, I'll be fine, it's plenty warm and I just need a minute to sleep, and knowing that I closed my eyes when the merry-go-round began, and kept them closed, and only opened them for a moment to see June before me, and Canasson before her, riding out ahead, and his face red from the lights and grinning and the teeth showing hungry like a wolf's teeth as he turned to look back at her. Then hands around my arms and up and moving, and feeling suddenly very sharp, that everything was very clear, as we walked along the road, and not needing to speak, but feeling only warm and happy and light with my arms around their shoulders, and both of them putting me to bed, and then the door closing, and the sound of their voices in Canasson's room, and then the long silence that followed.

I woke up late in the morning feeling fine and it was not until I tried to get up that I realized that I was still drunk. I was wearing my clothes from the night before, and so I took a change of clothes and left my room. Canasson's door was closed and when I went downstairs he was not in the kitchen, and I didn't see him out on the porch. The boat was gone from the end of the dock. I went into the bathroom and took a shower and then I got dressed and went out into the kitchen and had a drink. I started getting a headache in the shower, but after I finished the drink it was gone and I felt very sharp and like I would be all right. Then I made coffee and while I was making coffee I saw the boat coming back across the bay. When it got closer I could see June sitting in the bow and Canasson rowing. I watched them come into the dock while I waited for the coffee to brew, and then I watched them come up the lawn and they came up on the deck and came inside. June looked very pink and happy and Canasson looked pale and horrible.

"Good morning," I said to both of them. "How is the water?"

"Very calm," said June, "and very clear and beautiful. In some places you can see all the way down to the bottom. And Arthur rows very beautifully, very smoothly."

"You look like you could use another drink," I said.

"I'll have one if you are having one," he said.

"I've just had one."

"Do you have any champagne? We could have mimosas." She moved to the refrigerator, and looked inside. "No," she said. "We'll have to go to the store to get some."

"What have we got?" said Canasson.

"A little whiskey and vodka," I said. "A lot of vodka. There's enough orange juice left for a decent screwdriver, if you add enough ice."

"Sounds fine," he said. He went to the freezer and took out the vodka and an ice tray and I got him a glass down from the cupboard. June took the orange juice out of the refrigerator and handed it to him. He took another glass and filled them both a little way with vodka, then dropped in the ice and split what was left of the orange juice between them. It filled them both a little more than halfway. He handed one to June and took the other himself and spun the ice with his finger.

"We'll have to go to the store if we're going to make a day of this," I said. "What we have won't last us very long. And both cars are still at the clubhouse."

"I don't feel like walking all the way back there," Canasson said. "Let me finish my drink and think about it then." He sat down at the kitchen table and rested his head against his fist.

"I'll go," said June. "I'll go to the store. Just give me a second." She left the kitchen and I heard her going up the stairs, and she came back down a minute later, holding her keys. "It won't take me a minute," she said. It was the first time I noticed, because she had to go get her keys from his room, that she was wearing Canasson's clothes. She was wearing one of his shirts tucked into a pair of his pants. The shirt hung on her, and she had the pants pinched together in the back. She wore the outfit pretty well, though, and if I hadn't seen Canasson wearing those clothes before I might have thought that they were hers.

"How do you feel?" I asked him, after I heard the door close behind her.

"Lousy," he said. "It's funny. I felt all right when I woke up this morning. The trip out in the boat was my idea. But about halfway out I started feeling like absolute hell. I guess it's the heat. It's helping just to be in out of the sun."

"Have some coffee," I said.

"I don't want any coffee," he said. "Coffee will only make me feel worse. I think I'll just wait and see what June brings back."

"Do you want to go out on the porch? Or we could go for a swim while we're waiting for her. You'd probably feel a lot better after a swim."

"No," he said, shaking his head. "I'm just going to sit inside and try not to move. Christ, that came on me fast. One minute I felt completely fine, and then it just hit me. I guess I should have seen it coming. I just felt so good when I woke up, I couldn't quite believe that it wouldn't last."

"You'll be fine in a minute," I said. "Just finish your drink. You'll feel fine again pretty soon."

He finished his drink, and I drank a couple cups of coffee. After the coffee I started feeling tired, and wondering where June was, and when she was going to get back with the booze, and then when I was about to go out to look down the road to see if I could see her coming, I heard her pull into the driveway.

"See?" I said. "You'll be all right, now." The front door opened and then she came into the kitchen carrying a brown grocery sack.

"My poor baby," she said to Canasson. She slid her hand under the hair that fell across his forehead and held it there, the palm pressed against his skin. "Do you feel any better?"

"A little."

"Only a little?"

"Only a little."

"My poor baby," she said again. She went into the bag and came out with a bottle of champagne, a bottle of orange juice, a small bottle of gin and a glass bottle of tonic water. She lined them all up on the table in front of him and said, "what can I make you? What can I do to make you feel better?"

"I'm all right," he said. "Please, June, I'm all right."

"My brave little sailor." She stroked his hair back from his face. "I'll make you a mimosa. Do you think that will make you feel better? Or I could make you a gin and tonic. Or a whiskey sour. But please, let me make you something. You look so miserable and you put on such a good show about it for so long, coming in. Let me make you something."

"I'll have whatever you and Elliot are having," he said. "Elliot, would you mind terribly if I had one of your cigarettes?"

I handed him the pack. He took one out and lit it and then tucked his face down between his hands, holding his hands over his eyes like a visor with the thumbs pressed in at the temples. The smoke drifted up between his fingers. June uncorked the champagne over the sink and a little foamed over but much less than it seemed should have and I rinsed out all of our glasses and opened the orange juice. We set one in front of Canasson and held the other two ourselves and when we tried to toast Canasson would not respond and June said, "please, Arthur. Please. Just a little to take the edge off," and Canasson sat up and took his glass up between his fingers.

"I'm all right," he said. "I hate to ruin everyone's morning. Please, I really am fine. I just need a minute to collect myself, that's all. I'll be all right after."

"You poor baby," she said again. "Come on. Come on, lets get you into the other room. You can just lie down for a little while. I have some things to do this morning and then by the time Elliot and I are done doing them you'll have had some sleep and you'll feel worlds better. All right?" She was helping him up, and they moved through the doorway and into the living room. I heard her talking to him but I couldn't make out her words. I took one of my cigarettes from the pack that Canasson had left in front of his seat. His was still burning in the ash tray in the center of the table and I lit mine off his and then crushed his out. Then June came back in.

"How is he?" I said.

"He's going to sleep for a while," she said. "Lets go out onto the porch."

We took our drinks and went outside. June sat down in Canasson's chair and I sat down in mine. I watched a shallow-bodied sailboat cut across the water and then tack and come back, closer in. The wind was up and brought cool air in off the lake and the sail was full and taut. It felt good to sit outside in the sun with the air cool around and June there.

"It's nice here," I said.

"Yes," she said. "I always liked it here. I've always said that if there was anyplace on earth I could be happy, it would be here."

"You're not happy?" I said.

"I'm not unhappy," she said. Then, she didn't say anything for a while. I started to wonder if Canasson was asleep, and started hoping that he wasn't, and that he would come out because it felt like I was supposed to say something, but I didn't know what it was. Then June said, "for a long time I thought I could find something that would make me happy, and every time something didn't I told myself that it didn't matter, that happiness was still waiting out there for me. Then I got older and I realized that nothing was making me happy, and I started to think that maybe there was something wrong with me. I don't know why I've never been able to be… to be completely happy with any one thing or anything the way it is."

"Oh," I said. "Yeah. I can understand that. I mean, everyone feels like that, I think." Then I shut the hell up.

We finished our drinks, and then I took June's glass and my own inside and made us two more. I could hear Canasson breathing in the other room and I moved quietly so I wouldn't wake him up. When I went out she was sitting as I left her, and when I handed her the drink she smiled up at me, shielding her eyes from the sun. I sat down and closed my eyes, and there was no sound but the wind noise from off the lake, and the sound of the water against the boards, and in the silence I knew that she was there, too, and that made the silence seem full, somehow. I was still drunk and with my eyes closed the world began to spin or I began to spin in it, and it did not seem unpleasant and I did not want it to stop.

Out on the lake, a race was getting underway. A sailboat appeared around the point and then another and another. Soon a half dozen or more passed through. I watched for a while, and a while later they came through again. Then they came through a third time. One boat with a light blue sail had pulled out ahead and the others followed in more or less a knot behind him. The next time through, however, one of the others was out in front, and the one with the blue sail was falling behind. Then they were all through again and I couldn't see them anymore.

"They'll go like that for hours," said June. "It's a dozen laps or more until this thing is finished. At least they've got good wind today. That should make it go a little faster."

"Do they do this ever summer?"

"Every summer," she said. "Is there any champagne left? I think I'm ready for another."

I went inside and made us a pair of drinks, and while I was doing that I heard Canasson get up. He came into the kitchen, then went out onto the porch without saying anything. There was enough champagne left for another, so I made one for him, too, and then I took all three out onto the porch. He was sitting on the arm of June's chair, hunched forward, and when I held out the glasses he took two of them and I sat down. He looked pretty bad, I guess, but better than before. I watched him watch the boats go by.

"How are you feeling?" she said, rubbing his back. "Do you feel any better?"

"Yes," he said, softly, "quite a lot better, actually." He turned back to face June. "Will Bernard worry?"

"Oh dear," she said. "I hadn't even thought of it. Oh, I had better call." She set her drink on the arm of the chair and stood up. "I'll only be a second," she said. She went inside.

Canasson sat down in her chair, leaned his head back and closed his eyes.

"What will she tell him?" I said.

"She'll tell him something," he said. "He won't answer, anyway. I'm sure he's working."

She came back out, moved around in front of us, and sat down on Canasson's knee. She drained off the rest of her glass.

"Did you reach him?" I said.

"No," she said.

"Well," said Canasson, "I guess that's all there is to that, then. Who wants to go have lunch? Lets have one more drink and then go into town and have lunch."

"Sounds fine," I said, standing up. "What does everyone want?"

"Just gin and tonics, I think, for now," said Canasson, bouncing June a little on his knee. "I think gin and tonics will be fine at this hour, don't you?"

"Yes, that sounds fine," she said.

"All right," I said. I went inside to make them.

I watched them through the window while I mixed the drinks. June turned in Canasson's lap to face him, and put her arms around his neck to kiss him. I felt sorry for Bernard and I wondered if he knew. I wasn't sure if I was more sorry for him if he knew or if he didn't. It seemed like a hell of a thing to do to someone but, watching them, I was sure that I could do it if I had swum out first to meet her. And when the three of us were together, I felt all right not giving a damn about anyone else. So I mixed the drinks and took them out and didn't think about Bernard anymore. If he was worth a damn he would have figured it out already, and put an end to it, and if he wasn't then he wasn't worth worrying about. So I drank my gin and watched the boats. They seemed to be moving faster, now. But then I realized it only looked that way because I had begun watching the boats, and stopped watching the lake and the shore and the boats moving across them, and they really weren't going any faster at all. I wondered how many laps they had left to go, and I wondered if the captains knew, or if they had to keep focus only on the half mile of water ahead of them for fear that the whole thing would fall apart. I was going to ask June, because I thought she might know, but she and Canasson were talking together. I reminded myself to ask her later, but I never did.

"Can we please go have lunch now?" said June when our drinks were finished. "I think I'm about to fall over from hunger. I could practically eat your chair." We laughed at that. I was pretty drunk and it didn't matter that it wasn't funny because she was trying to be funny, and to make her feel unfunny would only make everyone sober again.

"Please," said Canasson. And then, "Darling, you're hurting my leg." She was bouncing on his thigh as she laughed. "June, please," he said, and when she went up the next time he moved his leg forward so that when she came down it caught her across the thighs high up near her knees and she jerked backwards. She caught herself against the arm of the chair and the deck, then slid her legs down and off and stood up.

"That wasn't very nice," I said. "Arthur, she could really have been hurt."

"I could really have been hurt," said June. "Why did you do that, Arthur?"

"I asked you to stop jumping on my leg," he said. "I asked you twice to stop bouncing on my leg." I watched him go red around the ears and then watched it spread around the line of his jaw, down his neck, but I thought it might only be marks from where June was holding him before she fell. "Besides," he said, more angry than sorry, "you're fine. And we were going to get up anyway." He stood up to show that we were all going to stand up anyway, but June moved a little bit away from him as he stood and Arthur put his hands in his pockets. "Well now," he said. "I guess we're about ready to go, then."

"Barely," I said. I stood up. "I need a dozen drinks or more, now."

"What does that mean?"

"I feel sober as the goddamned Pope." I moved over to them with my right hand in my pocket, and with my left I collected our glasses and pinched them all together between the rims. June put her arms around my right elbow and put her head on my shoulder, and I watched Canasson look us over.

He said, "I'm sure it's not as bad as all that. We'll find a place where we can have a drink with lunch, and everything will be all right, then."

"Fine," I said.

"Yes, fine," said June.

We went inside. June let go of me as we went through the door and I went to the sink and rinsed out the glasses. Then I put the bottles away. While I was doing that I heard June and Canasson talking in the hallway, but I didn't really listen. When I went out Canasson was halfway finished with what he was saying, but he looked up when I came in and stopped talking.

"All ready?" I said.

"Yes," said June. She moved over to me and took my arm again. I gave Canasson a look and he gave one back at me, and then I gave him one that said that he had better watch himself, or I was going to steal his girl. He gave me a menacing look and then rolled his eyes and turned around and opened the door and went out. I let June lead me out and I closed the door behind us. Canasson was out ahead of us, moving towards June's car. I felt a little foolish for the look I had given him, especially with her on my arm, because it made me feel comic, that her on my arm was just a parody of her relationship with him. But when I helped her into the car she pulled me down and kissed me on the cheek, and when I stood up Canasson was staring at me over the roof of the car.

So I gave him a look he couldn't do anything with and got into the back seat feeling much better.

We drove north past the fair, and then around the bend of the bay past the construction and into the woods along the point. We came out on the other side and headed down along a string of waterfront buildings and June said park somewhere and Canasson did. We got out. June moved first towards one of the buildings and Canasson and I fell in step behind her and I didn't look at him. Through the alley between the building I could see boats bobbing along the long hook of a wooden dock.

We went inside. The restaurant was crowded and we walked past the entrance to the bar and Canasson called for three whiskey sours. The bartender raised his hand in acknowledgement.

"Christ, I feel better," said Canasson. "That gin straightened me right out."

"And you drove so wonderfully," said June. "I've never seen anyone drive so carefully."

"He's an excellent driver," I said. "You should see him after he's had a few more. He could run a goddamned stockcar race. He'd probably win it, too. He's the only person I've known who gets sharper the more he drinks."

"My people are pickled people," he said. "What can I say?" June laughed. "It's true," he said. "The whole lot of them. To this day people see drunk worms staggering up from my grandparents" graves."

"God, that's awful," she said, still laughing. "Don't be morbid, Arthur."

A waitress came with our drinks and Canasson asked her for menus and she handed them around. The lunch specials were all fish. I asked her if the fish came from the lake and she said no, they were shipped in from out of town, and I said isn't that funny because you would think, with the boats out bobbing on the hook of the dock, and the deck overlooking the water, and the pictures of ships on the walls, that the fish would come from the lake, and she said she didn't see why, and I said oh for Christ's sake never mind. When the waitress left we toasted ourselves and all of the fun we were going to have, and I watched June as she drank feeling somehow that we were all at a great party that would not end for several days.

"Oh," said someone, "look at the boats," and we turned and the boats were going past again, close in to shore, and they turned at a buoy I had not seen from the bay and raced off south.

"They've been going around all morning," someone else said, "they can't have much more to go."

"They go for a good long while."

"They must get tired, going around like that. I should think that I would get tired."

"It's feeling like I am never getting anywhere that would tire me."

The waitress came back. We ordered lunch, and another round of drinks. Canasson talked about something, I don't remember what. June got quiet and after a while she got up and went to the bathroom and Canasson stopped talking while she was gone. Then June came back and he brightened up, but I couldn't tell if he was happy to see her, or just acting like it. We ate our lunch, and I started feeling very sober and very removed. It was that removal you get when you have been drinking for a long time and then you suddenly detach from what is around you and nothing that is happening makes any sense or seems to be there for any reason other than the fact that it was there already, and self-evident most of the time, but not now. It was like that, but I felt more sober than I usually do when I feel that way and so I thought that this was different, and probably had more to do with the place and the company than it did with the booze. But that was probably only an attempt to make it mean something, that feeling, and the truth was that I had been drunk or at least not sober for almost twenty-four hours by the time we finished lunch and everything did seem very arbitrary and also very funny and nothing seemed to matter very much. We drank another round with lunch, and I felt very warm and that I could stay at the table forever and never want for anything ever again in my whole life.

Then Canasson paid, and we went out. Outside it was bright and I closed my eyes and felt sleepy and I suggested that we all go for coffee and try to sober enough so that we could have a drink and watch the sun go down, and not all already be too drunk or tired to continue. June said that was a good idea, and that she knew a place, and so we got into the car and Canasson drove very carefully along through what remained of the town and then back into woods on the other side, and we came out along a bluff above the lake with a coffee and bait shop overlooking the water. Canasson overestimated the parking space and humped up onto the concrete guarder, and June laughed and I laughed too and Canasson cursed and said that if we weren't very careful the owner would know that we were drunk and would call the police on us. That made me stop laughing, but June kept laughing and when I saw that she was still laughing I started laughing again, too. It did seem pretty funny, and Canasson being upset about it made it seem even funnier, and then Canasson got even more upset and June and I laughed even harder.

We got out and went inside and had a few cups of coffee each, sitting up at the counter. The owner watched us but he didn't say anything. I drank my coffee and listened to Canasson talk to June without really listening to what he was saying. I was feeling pretty drunk all of a sudden. It was easy not to feel drunk with Canasson and June because they were also drunk, and it was easy to think that Canasson was driving very well because I was not driving and did not notice the things that made it obvious. But anyway there had been no one else on the road.

214

After a while we left and got back into the car. June sat in front and Canasson drove. He backed out very slowly and carefully and he waited for a long time before he pulled out onto the road, heading back towards town.

"Is it really that late already?" said June. "I have to go get ready."

"Ready for what?" I said.

"To go to dinner," said June.

"Wonderful," I said. "Where are we going?"

Neither one of them said anything for a moment. Canasson cleared his throat a little bit, and then June said, "Arthur made reservations for he and I at a restaurant we talked about. We made the plans a week ago." She waited for me to say something, but when I didn't she turned around and looked at me and said, "didn't you know? I was sure we told you. Besides, we were talking about it all the time we were having coffee. I thought you knew."

"I guess I wasn't listening," I said. I said it very indifferent, but I felt like hell about it.

"We can meet up after," said June. "I'm sorry, Elliot. It's just that we made these plans a week ago. Honestly, we'll call once we're done with dinner. We'll call right away when we're leaving and we'll make some plans to do something all together. All right? I'm sorry. It's almost impossible to get a reservation and I don't know how Arthur even got it and there's just no way that we can fit in another. Is there, Arthur?"

"No," said Canasson, not looking at me. "Sorry, Elliot. The place is always packed. I think they've got us sitting at a two-person table at the goddamned kitchen door as it is."

"Don't be upset," said June. "Please, Elliot, don't be upset or hurt, because if we had known we would have made the reservation for all of us, wouldn't we have, Arthur?"

"Of course we would have," said Canasson. "Of course we would have, Elliot. We just didn't know that there would be three of us, you know."

"It's all right," I said. "Honestly, lets just drop it. I don't mind."

"Only if you really don't mind," said June.

"I really don't."

We drove back along the north shore and down around through the town to the house. June took a bag from the trunk and I watched her walk inside. I got out and Canasson said to me over the roof of the car, "It isn't really how it seems. This place is very hard to get a table at and I don't think I could possibly get them to move us to a bigger table."

"It's all right, really," I said. And then, because I was sick of hearing about it, I said, "I don't even want to go. I was going to go have dinner by myself and then I was going to… oh Christ, Arthur, I just don't want to go, all right? I never wanted to go and I never said I wanted to go." I looked at him over the car, but he was watching me, and so I said, "you are going to call me after, right? And we'll go and have a drink, and it will be just like it was today, and all this fuss will seem like it's about nothing."

"That sounds fine," said Canasson. "If that's what you would like us to do then we'll do that."

"Don't do it because it's what I want to do, do it because it's what sounds like the most fun. Doesn't it sound like fun? It sounds like a hell of a lot of fun to me."

"Sure, it sounds fine."

"Good. Let's go inside and have another before you have to leave."

"All right."

We went inside. The bathroom door was closed and behind it I could hear the water running. We went into the kitchen and Canasson took down the glasses while I got the gin and the limes. We mixed in the tonic last. We went out

216

onto the porch to drink them and while we were drinking them I heard June moving around inside. She came out holding a drink and with her hair wet and tied back tight. She was wearing her bra and a white slip and she took a sip of her drink and then set it on the railing and undid her hair.

"We're going to be late," Canasson said.

"I have to let my hair dry first," she said. "It will ruin the dress I brought to get it wet. Aren't you going to shower?"

"I'm going like this," he said. "Besides, I showered this morning."

She smiled and then stepped forward, pressing herself against his back and snaking her arms under his to hug tight around his middle. I watched her do it and then looked away, over at the lake and at the entrance to the bay, and I heard her say, "Arthur you are so proper and wonderful. Promise me you'll never change."

We finished our drinks, standing on the porch. Then Canasson and I stood looking at our ice cubes and June went inside. She came back out wearing a black dress with broad straps that went over her shoulders.

"You look wonderful, June," said Canasson. "That's a wonderful dress."

"Isn't it?"

"We should really be going."

"Yes, we should be going. Goodbye, Elliot. We'll call you soon. I'm not even terribly hungry. We'll make a short meal of it, all right?"

"Goodnight, June," I said. "Please, don't worry about it anymore. Goodbye, Arthur."

"Goodnight, Elliot. We'll call when we're leaving the restaurant."

We all went back inside. I stayed in the kitchen and washed the glasses and I heard them leaving and then I heard the front door close. Then I heard the car start and I heard it move away and disappear and for a moment after the house seemed very quiet and for the first time all day I felt sober, and that all of the problems waiting in the shadows around us all day were finally going to come up, now that I was alone. I started thinking that very soon the summer would be over, and I wouldn't have anywhere to live, and everything seemed like it was ending more fantastically quickly than I had ever noticed before. Like the first time that you learn that the earth is always going around, and that if you were able to float above it for one moment in time, when you came back down everything you knew and loved would have moved on without you.

After a while, thinking like this, it was pretty easy to not care that the phone had not rung. They all seemed very far away and also very unimportant because I was looking at the world the way God looked at it, and I didn't give a shit, the way God doesn't, and also I didn't feel sober anymore. I wondered if they were thinking about me now that they hadn't called me, and if I was haunting them, and that was how I felt and it felt very good to be a ghost and to be dead and detached but also whole and not eaten through with worms and laying in the dark. I had another drink and felt good and I imagined myself floating from room to room and then I began to pretend that I was floating from room to room and then I started laughing because it was so silly, to be pretending to be a ghost, floating from room to room, and then I started crying because I was all alone, and the phone hadn't rung, and because forever was such a long time and I would be dead forever very soon, and because I had not made the most of every possible moment, and because I could not tell myself that I didn't care. They had left me and I cared very much that they were gone, and it was something that I hadn't thought about for a long time, and it seemed that I had never really thought about it at all.

Then after a while I felt tired and empty and I made another drink and went into the bathroom and shaved carefully because I had not yet shaved that day. While I was shaving I drank and I had to be very careful not to get any of the shaving cream on the lip of the glass. It got there anyway and I wiped it off, but the glass still had the taste of shaving cream and then I thought maybe it was only that I was smelling the shaving cream that made it seem that way. Then I washed my face and I studied it in the mirror and it seemed like a very strange face and that it was not a part of me the way sometimes things seem very strange when you are drunk, and all you can say is what the hell, because you know that when you wake up and are sober it will seem normal and that there is no strangeness, and that it is your face. But now for this moment it seemed not only that it was strange but also that it was the truth that it is strange, and you knew that you could never hold this truth for long. So after my face was washed I stopped looking at it I finished my drink and I left and walked north along the shore in the water, carrying my shoes in my hand. Then the ground grew rocky as I got to the pier, and I climbed out and up onto the grass and I sat and waited for my feet to dry, and then I put my shoes back on. It was dark already and I could see the stars beyond the lights of the Ferris Wheel. When I blinked at them they disappeared and then melted back out of the darkness, like if you hold a buoy under water and then release it and watch it slowly appear and then breach. I knew that it was the light from the Ferris Wheel and the fair that made it seem that way, but it also looked for a moment like the lake was above and the sky was below and everything looked strange the way my face in the mirror looked strange.

I sat there for a while waiting for my feet to dry, and then after I put my shoes on I sat there for a little while longer, and listened to the merry-go-round record repeat a couple of times. Then I got up and walked towards the bar where Canasson and I had gone our first night together in town. I was feeling pretty lousy, and I thought another drink would help. So I went in and stood at the bar and ordered a beer. The bar was pretty crowded, but not so crowded that you couldn't see.

Then, while I was waiting for my beer, I saw Bernard coming up. He looked worried. I waved to him and then I realized that I had waved to him and I pulled my arm down. But he had already seen me and he came over. The bartender came over too, holding my beer, and I started to pay him when Bernard arrived beside me and I said, "Hello, Bernard, can I buy you a beer?"

"No," said Bernard, and so I paid the bartender for mine and the bartender went away. Bernard said, "I'm sorry, Elliot. No, thank you. I was wondering if you've seen June."

"What?"

"I said have you seen June?" he said again, louder. "I thought maybe she had gone out with you and your friend or something and we just hadn't crossed paths. I've been working a lot." He said it like it was his fault that she was missing. "But you haven't seen her?"

"No," I said.

"Is your friend here? Maybe he's seen her."

"He hasn't seen her," I said, not looking at him. "He's been coming down with something. He's at home trying to sleep it off." I took a big swallow of beer. "Say, that was a hell of a party you threw," I said. "Did you find someone to help you move that sculpture back down to the boathouse? I would have, but I had to go, suddenly. I wasn't feeling very well." I wasn't making much sense, I guess, but he wasn't really listening.

"I'm sorry, Elliot," he said, "I've got to go. I'm going to go check the other bars around. I know it's silly, but I'm fantastically worried about her. The car is gone, and these roads are, well you know how these roads can be at night."

"All right," I said. "Good luck finding her. You're sure you wouldn't like a drink before you go?"

"I'm sorry, Elliot, I just can't. Another time, maybe."

He moved off past me, and I watched him go and then I watched him go out and I saw him stop outside the door with his hands on his hips and look both directions before the door

220

swung closed. I looked around the room, and then I turned
around to face the bar.

I didn't feel like talking to anyone after that. I felt like
absolute hell about it, for some reason. Maybe it was just
because he was so worried about her, and she was putting him
to it for nothing. It seemed like a hell of a thing to do to
anybody. I hoped that Canasson would just drop her off at
home and that she would be able to tell Bernard some story
that made it seem like an honest mistake. I knew it was going
to end badly one way or the other, but seeing Bernard made
me want it to end badly some other time, and I understood
how Canasson and June could continue on without putting an
end to it. It was easy to go one day without ending it and then
once that day was already gone and the next had come it was
easier to go another than to erase both that day and the day
before. Sitting at the bar, it seemed somehow possible that it
would never end, that we would never let it end, and
everything bad that we had coming would simply never come.

I stayed at the bar and had two more, and then a man I
had been talking to bought me two more, and by the time the
last was finished the bar was closing, and when I got down off
my stool I had to hold onto the bar for a very long time before
I could stand. I remember leaving and then I remember hitting
the pavement outside, and yelling voices, and I remember
arms under my arms and I remember that I was either laughing
or I was crying, but I can't remember which it was. Then I
remember somebody putting me into a car and seeing Nick's
face, and Bill's face, and going past the fair at great speed, and
the point of the Ferris Wheel and the whole sky turning around
it as we went down the road towards home. Then the front
yard and the doorway. Then laying me on the couch, and
many hands helping, and thinking that it had all happened so
quickly, and that now they were leaving, and leaving me
behind, and wanting very much to go with them, but being
unable to move properly. Then darkness coming, and

wondering if I would die, and then surrender, and then I was asleep.

XII.

I woke up a few hours later because I heard somebody coming in. I felt very drunk and also that any sort of action would require a lot of effort. But I sat up. Through the kitchen window I could see the edge of the horizon growing pale gray and pink, and I wondered what time I had finally come in. I heard the door close and so I stood up and went to the hallway. Canasson was standing by the door, leaning against the wall, kicking off his shoes. He looked up at me but didn't say anything, and then he came towards me and went past me into the kitchen and put coffee on. I watched him do it, and when he was finished I followed him out onto the porch. He sat down and I sat down next to him.

We sat there for a while, and the horizon went from gray to white and the air was still cold. After a while Canasson said, "I'm sorry we didn't call, Elliot. We took a little longer at dinner than I thought we would, and by the time we were finished June thought, we both thought, that you had probably already given up on us and had gone out."

"Who the hell would I have gone out with?" I said. I meant it to sound kind of funny, because I thought that it was kind of funny, but I guess it came out sounding mean because Canasson didn't say anything or laugh. So I said, "that's all right. I went out to that bar you and I went to way back when you first got here. You remember that one? I had a hell of a time. I saw Bernard."

"Oh?"

"Yeah," I said, watching him. He was looking away from me, out at the water. "I came in and he must have seen me because a second later I saw him coming over. He looked pretty worried, but I was so surprised to see him I didn't notice it, I guess. I had just ordered my beer and so I offered to buy him one, but he said he couldn't. He asked me if I'd seen June."

"What did you say?"

"I said I hadn't seen her." I watched him, but he didn't seem to think anything of it because he kept staring out at the water. "Then he wanted to know if you had seen her," I said, "and I told him that you were home sick and that you hadn't seen her either."

He didn't say anything to that, either, so I went inside and filled a couple mugs. I spilled some, but I kept most of it in the mugs. When I went back out I moved around in front of him and set the mug down carefully on the arm of his chair but he only glanced up at me as he took it. I had to do all of it pretty carefully because I was pretty unsteady. I felt tired and out of sync with time and everything else that was waking up now.

"So did you have a good time with June?" I said. "I mean, after all that, did you at least have a good time with her?"

He held out, then he seemed to surrender to it. "It's bad, Elliot." His voice was really quiet, and he sort of said it facing the water. "You were right. The whole thing went bad and I didn't even see it coming. I walked straight into it." He sounded pretty tired and like he was all talked out. "It's bad," he said again. He put his hands over his face and moaned through his fingers.

"Christ," I said, "what happened?"

But he didn't say anything for a while. He wiped his face with his fingers. Then he started talking, and while he talked he looked out at the lake, but he kept glancing back at me, like he was checking to make sure I was still there."

"All right," he said. "We went out to dinner like we said we were going to and the restaurant put us at this god-awful table near the back of the room. I mean I swear to you it was tucked practically into the hallway leading to the bathrooms. We ordered our drinks and started looking at the menu, but before we had been there ten minutes six or seven people had asked June to scoot in so that they could get past to get to the bathroom. I offered to switch seats with her but she wouldn't let me, and we drank our drinks just getting more and more upset at the restaurant and we couldn't find our waiter and June said lets just go, just go without paying for our drinks, and I said fine, you know, because the idea seemed to excite her and make her less upset and it seemed like they deserved it for where they had put us and the lousy service and all of that.

"So we left and as we were getting into the car this waiter came running out after us, and June said step on it, and I peeled out and bumped bumpers with a car parked on the other side of the parking lot. June just laughed, though, and she said go, and so I hit the gas and this waiter chased us out of the parking lot yelling and waving at us. That just about killed June, and she said lets go dancing, I feel like dancing now, and I said fine, where do you want to go, and she said lets go to that place, remember the one we went with you and Rene way back at the beginning of the summer. So we went back there and danced for a while. And then June said that she forgot her purse, and I said I'm sure it's just in the car, and she said no, she remembered that she didn't have it, and do you suppose that was what the waiter wanted when he chased us out of the parking lot? And she laughed and said yes I suppose it is and I guess we have to go back.

"So we went back to the restaurant. Christ, that was embarrassing. She made me go in and ask for it. They had it there at the front and the waiter who gave it to me just looked me over. I guess he didn't know, but as I was going through the door I heard somebody call to him and start to ask if that was the purse belonging to the woman who was seated in that table over there, and I got the hell out of there as fast as I could. Out in the car I asked her why she had to leave her goddamned purse in the first place. She said don't be angry and let me make it up to you. Where? I said. At the house, she said. She said Bernard was always in the boathouse at this hour, and didn't I know that already?

"So I said fine and I drove back to her house. June went in first, calling Bernard honey I'm home, and Arthur's here too, I offered him a drink after dinner, right, and when nobody says anything back to her she waves me in. So I say, Goddamnit June, I don't like feeling like your goddamned plaything. I mean, because that's what it felt like, being sent around and running into things, and her laughing. I said I don't like feeling like your goddamned plaything, and when are you going to tell Bernard about us, anyway, and you don't really love me, do you?"

"What did she say?"

"She said of course I love you, Arthur. You know, in this really obvious voice, like I was an idiot if I didn't already know that. I can hear her saying it. Of *course* I love you, Arthur. But Bernard is working very hard right now, and he needs me to be here for him. And you know I say but you're not there for him, you know? You're not there for him now, what the hell's the difference? And she said he needs to think that I'm here. So I said you're never going to tell him, are you. You're never going to tell him, and she said no I'm going to tell him, but the time is all wrong. The time is just wrong, now, to tell him. And so I say but you're going to tell him? And she's moving in close to me, and she says of course I'm going to tell him, you know, of *course* I'm going to tell him, just be patient, and then starts kissing me, and I push her back and make her promise that she is going to tell him.

"So after that we go upstairs and we're on the bed and I hear something behind her and I sort of lean and Bernard is standing at the top of the stairs. And Christ June doesn't even stop, because she doesn't know yet, and she's got her back to him, and so I yell stop, and then Jesus, and June turns around and sees him and she rolls over off of me and off the bed. And I scramble off the other side and into the bathroom and I wrap a towel around myself and I can hear June saying Bernard, what are you doing here, and Bernard just isn't saying anything. And so I come out and I start walking over to him, and I'm wearing this goddamned towel, and I'm saying, Bernard, I know it looks bad, but let me explain. You see, I'm in love with your wife. I love her, Bernard. And he looks at her, and I look back at her, and she's got the sheet pulled down from the bed and wrapped around herself and she just says, Bernard, and he says Jesus Christ, but real quietly, and he turns around and goes back down the stairs. And so I turn around to look at June, because I don't know what to do, and June is yelling Bernard, Bernard, and she gets up and goes after him.

"And I'm just standing there, and I've got no idea what's going on. And I hear them downstairs, and June is saying Bernard, stop, Bernard, wait, and Bernard is saying Jesus June, Jesus June, I thought we were through all of this. You said the last one was the last time. I guess it's my fault for believing you. And June is saying it's not like that, Bernard, you know it isn't like that, and he says well then why don't you tell me how it is, June. Why don't you just tell me. And I put on my pants and I go downstairs, and Bernard and June are sitting on the couch at the far end of the room, and they both just turn and look at me, and then Bernard says, why don't you make us all a drink. And I say sure and I go and do it and I bring them over and sit down, and nobody says anything while I'm doing it. And Bernard takes this really big drink and he says, very calmly, I was really worried about you, June. Elliot said that he hadn't seen you in a couple of days, and if you weren't with the two of them I didn't know where you were. It wasn't fair to do that to me, June. You could have left a note. And June is crying and she says, do you want to talk about what's not fair? You want to talk about not fair? How about living up here in this house and being your loving wife and being charming for everyone, and you're always off in your boathouse and you think that's fair? You think that's fair to me? And he just shakes his head and says we've been through this, June. You know we've been through this a hundred times already, and it's never gotten us anywhere, and she says well then I guess we're going to go through it a hundred and one times or two hundred times or a thousand times. And Bernard just shakes his head, and then he looks at me and he says, does he know? He doesn't know, does he. About all of the others? About all the other ones? And he looks back at June, and June just kind of covers her face with her hands and curls up into this little ball. And Bernard says to me she does this every summer, you know. Almost every summer. It's funny, I guess. Did she tell you that she loves you? That she is going to leave me for you? And I didn't say anything to that, so he said, I can't say I blame you for wanting to believe her. I understand that much. She didn't do it to hurt you, you understand. She just can't help herself, and the whole time June is right there, crying on the couch next to me."

"Jesus," I say. "Jesus, Arthur, I'm sorry. That's a hell of a thing to hear." He didn't say anything, so I said, "what happened after that?"

"Bernard said they play this game. Every year she starts one of these, and every year she keeps it on the edge between a legitimate friendship and an affair. And as the summer goes on she makes it more and more flagrant, she'll stay out longer and later, she flirt more publicly, and he pretends that he doesn't mind or that he doesn't notice because they play the game, and as long as their behavior stays within the form of normal social interaction, no one has cause to say anything. And then, at some point, it always gets too obvious, and he's forced to step in and corral her in. It's her way of getting him to pay attention to her. And June is right there, just sobbing, hearing all of this. And Bernard says, I'm sorry, Arthur, but now you know the way it is."

"What did you say to that?"

"I said what do we do now?"

"And what did he say?"

"He said I'm going to have to ask you not to see my wife anymore. I'll give you a few minutes to say whatever it is you would like to say to each other, but when I come back from the boathouse I expect you to be gone. Then he just got up and left."

"So what did you do?"

"I hugged June, and I got her to stop crying. And then I said is all that true? Is everything that he said true? And she didn't say anything. And so I said do you care about me at all? Did you mean anything that you said? And she didn't say anything. And I said talk to me Goddamnit, and she just started crying again. So I said that's fine, then. It was nice to have known you, and I got up and I went upstairs and got dressed. And I kind of figured that when I came back down she would be standing there, waiting to say something. But she wasn't. I think she was in the bathroom or something. So I just left. And then, as I was going down the hill, I heard this big crash coming from the boathouse, and I heard Bernard yelling and then more crashes. So I left and I came back here."

"Jesus," I said. "You had a hell of a night."

"Yeah." He yawned.

"How are you feeling?"

"Just tired now, I guess. I'm all talked out about it and I couldn't give a good goddamn about any of them. I'm too tired. I don't know. I don't know, Elliot. What do you think I should do? Do you think I should forgive her? I mean, if she wants me back, do you think I should forgive her? I guess that's a stupid question. If she never really meant to leave him, I guess that's a stupid question."

"Do you think she really meant to leave him?"

"I did," he said. "I did until tonight. Now, Jesus, I don't know." He stood up. "I'm going in," he said. "I'm going to sleep."

"I'll go with you."

We went inside and Canasson shut off the coffee maker. Then we went upstairs. Canasson went into his room and said goodnight without turning around. Then he closed his door and I went into my room and I took off my shoes and closed my door. I fell into bed with all of my clothes on and I knew that I should take them off and I knew that I would feel better once I did, but I couldn't quite bring myself to do it. Then I heard four short, hard bursts of noise from Canasson's room and it felt like the whole house shook and then I heard him crying. I lay awake for a while listening to him and then he must have fallen asleep or something because the sound stopped. I wondered if it was really over and I didn't think that it was, but I thought probably that was only because I couldn't imagine that something like that would end so simply. But then I thought if June really didn't give a damn about him, maybe it could, and I remembered that lots of things ended for no good goddamned reason and that this one had a better reason than a lot of them. But by then the sun was up and shining in my window, and I felt hot and hung over and miserable, and I decided it would be better to just go to sleep and not think about it anymore.

I woke up late in the afternoon and all of the feeling from the two days before that a party was coming and that everything was slowly building towards it was gone and what was left in its place was the feeling that I had missed everything and that there was nothing to look forward to ever again. But then I took a shower and I thought about going out for dinner, and I started feeling better. I wondered if Canasson wanted to go, but when I got out of the shower I couldn't find him, and I figured that he had probably already gone. I went upstairs to get dressed.

Then, as I was coming down stairs, somebody knocked on the door. I went to get it and it was a man I didn't know. He looked at me and then he walked past me into the hallway and into the kitchen. I stayed by the front door, and I watched him move across the hallway from the kitchen to the living room. Then he came back towards me. He had his hands on his hips and his eyes on the ground and when he was almost to me he glanced up at me through his eyebrows and then turned and went upstairs. I watched him go up, not using the railing or anything, his hands still on his hips, and I saw him open Canasson's door and stand in the doorway, looking the room over. Then he did the same to my room. I guess I had kind of expected it for a while, so I didn't say anything. He came back down and stood in front of me.

"For the record," he said, "it was never all right with me, Ted's decision to let you stay here. He never checked with any of us. It was his summer to have the house and it was his to do with as he saw fit, but I think we were all a little bit hurt that he didn't hand it over to someone in the family. I mean," he laughed, and looked at me, "how well do you even know him? How close were you?"

"Close enough that he offered to let me stay here," I said. Then I said, "look, you can't just come barging in here. I mean, Goddamnit, this is my home. I mean, I'm living here. Ted said that -,"

"Ted's dead, you asshole," said the man. He said it very flat and with nothing on it, with his hands still on his hips, and then he said, "I want you out of here. The family is getting together up here on Ted's birthday to scatter his ashes over the lake." He scoffed at me again. "That's the first week of August, in case you didn't know," he said. He looked at me malevolently for a second, and then he seemed to settle a little bit back into himself. "Anyway," he said quietly, "I want you out of here before then."

"Wait a second," I said. He was already moving past me in the narrow space of the hallway and for a moment we were face to face before he slipped past, towards the door. "I said wait a second," I said. I reached out and grabbed his elbow, and he turned fast into me and grabbed my wrist with his opposite hand. He clamped down hard on it, and I saw his teeth go set tight together behind his lips. I let go of his elbow, and he held onto my wrist for a second longer, both of us waiting to see if he was going to hit me. Then he sort of threw my own hand back at me. He looked at me and his face flinched, and then he thought better of it and turned and opened the door.

I followed him out onto the lawn. Out on the street there was a car waiting. There was a woman in the front seat and a man in the back, and the man was reaching between the seats to hold the woman's hand. She looked towards us as the man walked across the lawn.

"Wait a second," I said. "Come on, would you wait a second?" I ran down the lawn after him and caught him up. He stopped and for a second I thought that this time he was going to swing at me. I don't know why, it just seemed like what he was going to do. I guess me taking Bradner for his house was a little like somebody else taking him for his life. Not that there was a real connection, but at least I was there to be hit for it. But he didn't hit me. Instead he turned around and took a step towards me, backing us up towards the house.

"Look," he said, pretty quietly. "That's my mother in the car. That's Ted's mother in the car. Let's not make a scene and let's not give her a reason to get out and get involved so that when I drive away I can tell her that this is all taken care of and that she doesn't have to worry about it, all right?"

"All right," I said. "Look, I'm sorry, all right? I didn't know. I just – I didn't know anything about that people wanted Ted to give the house to someone in the family for the summer or any of that. I just – I mean I told Ted that I had a lousy apartment, and he offered me this place for the summer, you know, until I could find a better place. I mean, that's what a good guy your brother was. Ok? I mean, I didn't mean to insult anyone or anything. I didn't know that what I was doing was making people angry and if I had I would have done something about it, honestly. I just didn't even know, you know? But I mean you want me to go I'll go, ok? Don't worry about it. But can I have a couple of weeks to find a new place to live? I mean otherwise I'm going to have to live in my car."

"You're right," he said. "It's not your fault. I'm sorry I yelled at you before. You couldn't have known. It's just that, ever since we heard -," he looked up at the sky, then looked down at the ground. "Look," he said, looking back at me. "We're all coming up here the first weekend in August. That gives you almost three weeks. Just be out of here by then, all right?"

"All right," I said. "All right."

Then he shook my hand, I guess because he couldn't think of anything else to do. Over his shoulder I could see the woman in the passenger seat, Bradner's mother, watching. She was turned to face the window, and when the young man turned towards her she opened the door. But he waved her off, and she pulled the door back closed. I stood watching him go and I watched them until the car went around the bend in the Loop Road and I couldn't see them anymore. Then I went back to the house and I got my jacket from inside and then I left and locked the front door. The breeze was warm off the lake, but the air was cold and the sky was flat white haze and I wondered if rain was coming.

I went into town and ate dinner and then as I was walking home I turned and took a walk through the neighborhoods. I did it because I was worried that Canasson still wasn't home, and I didn't want to sit alone in the house. I felt pretty good, except for my stomach. My stomach was pretty upset. I walked down one street and then down another, and then I turned around and looked down a fence that bordered the sidewalk on one side. There were vines growing out between the polished iron uprights and streetlights every fifteen feet or so that showed the vines green and the iron black and shiny, and pools of sidewalk, and on the other side the near faces of the trunks of the young trees, all of them stretching down to the light point of the streetlight at the end of the block, and I knew that Bradner was dead, and in an urn somewhere, and I had that old feeling that nothing would ever be right in the same way again, and that there was a hole in the world that everything fell out of and that if I was not careful, I would fall out of the world, too. But this feeling passed, and afterwards it seemed more like a memory of a feeling than the feeling itself. So I turned back around and kept walking.

When I got home Canasson was there. He was sitting at the kitchen table. I walked in and sat down across from him.

"Bradner's brother was here," I said. "We have to be out by the first weekend in August." Canasson glanced up and me, then nodded, and I said, "Bradner's dead."

"Huh," said Canasson. "How did it happen?"

"His brother didn't tell me. I didn't ask."

"What do you think?"

"It doesn't seem real, somehow. It's too far away. It's not like a funeral or something. I don't know. I guess even a funeral doesn't make it seem real."

He didn't say anything to that. Then, after a while, he said, "I have to take the car into the city tomorrow. There are a few things I need to finalize with the lawyers. I guess I could start looking for a place while I'm there. I don't know. Christ." He rubbed his eyes with the heels of his hands. "I'll just have my secretary do it," he said. "I don't think I quite have it in me right now."

"I know what you mean."

"I saw June again."

"I was wondering where you were. What did she say?"

"Nothing, really. Nothing that mattered. Bernard smashed up a bunch of his sculptures last night, she said. He was down in the boathouse, gluing them back together or maybe he was just putting the shelves back together. I don't know. She only invited me in for a minute because she said she wasn't sure when he was coming back up. He had been coming up all day to check to make sure she was still there." He laughed. "It's funny, isn't it? The way it all turned around so fast. I can't quite keep up with it, I think. Don't you think it's funny? I think it's funny."

"It's not very funny."

"No, Elliot, tell me it's funny. Please, tell me it's funny. If I don't have someone else to tell me it's funny I'll think I'm cracking up."

"All right," I said, "it's funny. What happened when you saw her?"

"We sat in the living room and talked. I asked her if she loved me and if she had meant it all the other times that she said it and if she had ever actually meant to leave Bernard for me. Christ, it sounds so stupid now. It made so much more sense when we were together."

"What did she say?"

"She said she had meant it when she said it and that it was all more complicated than that. I said that it was only as complicated as we decided to make it and that if we loved each other then it was simple."

"Then what happened?"

"We went around and around about a couple of things. She said that I had wanted her to give up everything without being willing to give up anything in return. I said that I would have given up anything to be with her and that she never asked me for anything. She said that she never asked me for anything because I wanted her to give up everything she wanted, and that it only upset me when she talked about wanting anything other than what I wanted. Then I said that I only wanted her if she wanted to be with me, and it went back and forth and around and around. God I feel so goddamned stupid. The whole thing seems so damned stupid now." He looked up at me, and laughed. "I can't even imagine what you think of me, right now. You'd never let yourself get put in a position like this, would you."

"I don't know," I said. "For a woman like June, I don't know."

"You're just saying that to make me feel better."

I shrugged and said, "So it's over then, right? You're not going to see her anymore?"

"No," he said. "I'm going out with her tomorrow night."

"You are goddamned stupid, then," I said. He looked surprised and then he looked hurt, and then he looked angry. I felt pretty angry about it I guess.

Canasson said, "what the hell do you -,"

And I said, "you're fucking stupid if you think you can take June out tomorrow night. You got goddamned lucky that Bernard didn't see you up at the house. Christ, if I had seen you there I would have carved you in half with my bare goddamned hands. I can see going back today to get some closure but it's over, now, and you're going to have to deal with it, before the whole thing blows up in your face any more than it already has."

"Look Elliot," he said, "I appreciate your advice as my friend but I'll be goddamned if I sit here and have you lecture me on behalf of Bernard Hautdesert. I will be absolutely goddamned. Now I have lost my wife, I have lost my apartment, and I have lost more than you will ever know and more than you will ever own in this goddamned divorce. June is the one good thing I have left, and if you think I'm going to simply hand her back over because her husband is upset you have got things horribly mixed around. June has made her decision and it's me, and I'm sorry it's not Bernard, and I'm sorry it's not you, Elliot, but that's just the way it is."

"Fuck you," I said. "Fuck you, Arthur. I invited you out here. I invited you out here into my home, to help you when you were down. Fuck you, you snob shit. You've lost more than I will ever own. Fuck you." I stood up.

"Elliot," he said. He stepped between me and the doorway and I pushed him to the side as I moved past. He pushed me back harder and I turned and pushed him back into the counter. He caught himself against the edge and twitched like he was going to come at me, but then he didn't. We looked at each other for a moment. Then I went through the doorway and went upstairs and into my room and closed my door. After a while I heard him come up, too, and then I heard him go back down, and then the shower running. A while later I heard the shower stop and then a while after that, the front door open and close.

I went out to dinner and sat with my back to the door and didn't see anyone that I recognized. Then I went home and went to bed. When I woke up in the morning the car was gone. So I went downstairs and ate breakfast out on the porch. While I was out on the porch I saw June walk down her lawn and then down the dock and then dive into the water. I set my plate down and ran down our dock and dove in. I swam hard towards the platform, but I was a ways out when I saw her pull herself out of the water and up onto the raft. I was afraid that she would dive back in before I could reach her, but she must have seen me because she was still there when I reached the raft.

"Hello, Elliot," she said.

"Hi, June," I said. I was out of breath and I had to hang on the edge of the raft for a minute before I could pull myself up. I sat down next to her. "I wasn't sure you were going to wait for me," I said. "I thought I would be a better swimmer after living here for a couple of months."

"Have you been swimming much?"

"Not very much."

"How did you expect to get to be a stronger swimmer?"

"I don't know," I said. "I guess I just thought it would happen."

"I used to be a very strong swimmer," she said.

"You're still a strong swimmer," I said. "You put me to shame."

"But I used to be a very strong swimmer," she said. "I used to come out and swim back and forth between the dock and the platform for hours. When I was younger, when

237

Bernard and I were first married and he first took me here, I used to come out here every morning and swim back and forth and back and forth. I always imagined that I was swimming the English Channel, and that when I finally came out I would be in France. It's funny, isn't it? It's just like life. You think you're going somewhere, but really you're just going around and around in circles. Or maybe it's the other way around. Maybe you go around in circles and you imagine you're going somewhere because what is really happening is just too sad or something. Not sad just. I don't know."

"Well that's easy," I said. "Just make a point to swim every morning. You can start swimming again and work up to it. You're not in bad shape, and I'm sure you'll work up to an hour or so before the end of the summer."

"That is so horribly not the point."

"I know. I just didn't want to talk about the other thing."

"The other thing is all I think about anymore." She sighed. "Anyway," she said, "Bernard has cancelled his winter show, and he says without the show there's no reason to be here or to even be in this country, so we're going to take a trip. Bernard wants to. He says his work is getting too repetitive, that he knows too clearly what he is going to make before he makes it, and that if he makes things that come to him easily he is doing some disservice to art or to himself or I don't know."

"And what do you want?"

"Oh Elliot what does it matter what I want?"

"I don't know," I said. "I guess it's just something people say."

"People say a lot of things," she said. "People say a lot of things and people say a lot of stupid things and you can't spend your life doing things because people say."

"Isn't that what you're doing? Isn't that what you're doing with Bernard?"

"Oh Elliot just leave it alone."

"Fine."

We sat, not talking, for a while. We were facing towards the house, but I didn't think that June wanted to go back and I didn't want to go back, either. Then, I don't know why, I said, "I don't want you to go."

"Why?" she said.

"Because I think I'm in love with you," I said.

She laughed. "Oh *Elliot*," she said.

"I'm serious," I said. "I've never felt about anyone the way I feel about you." She laughed harder. I said, "Is it so hard to imagine that I might be in love with you? I mean, the thought of you and Arthur drives me crazy, I don't want you to leave, why couldn't that be love?"

"You don't want me to leave," she said, "because you are afraid that when I leave there will be nothing left keeping Arthur here. You are afraid that if I leave he'll leave too."

"Don't be ridiculous."

"I'm not claiming I'm the one in love."

"I am in love with you," I said. "What's so hard about that?"

"Nothing," she said. "Nothing is hard about that."

We didn't say anything for a while. I felt pretty stupid and I didn't feel like talking anymore. It made sense to say it when I said it but then immediately after that it didn't make any sense at all, and I realized that I wasn't in love with June. After I realized that I felt worse, but also like I didn't give a good goddamn one way or the other about what she thought about me.

"Fine," I said, "I'm not in love with you."

"That's much better," she said. "See how much better it is to not be in love and not to care one way or the other who stays and who goes? It's very much simpler this way. You understand it so much better than Arthur does. Sometimes it's much better and much simpler to love someone and Arthur understands that, but he doesn't understand that as many times, more times, it's better and simpler to love no one. People drift in and out of each other's lives all the time."

"That's true," I said. "I guess that's true. I suppose it is better to keep everything simple. Now that I know how it is for you, I suppose it's better to keep everything simple."

"You don't know how it is for me."

"I only know what you've told me and I can't be blamed for not knowing what you won't tell me about how it is for you. You can't blame me for not understanding."

"That's all the blame there ever is," she said, looking at the house and the lawn and then down the dock to the water. "That's all anyone is ever blamed for."

"Fine," I said. "Blame me."

"Oh Elliot don't be like that. I can't take it if you're like that. I couldn't stand you like that."

"Fine. How do you want me to be?"

"Oh, be however you want to be," she said. Then she said, "oh to hell with both of you," and stood up.

"Won't you please wait?" I said. "Won't you please wait and stay a minute and tell me how it is?"

"Oh Elliot there isn't any point. What's the point? There isn't any point." She was perched on the edge of the raft. She touched her hands to her face but I could not tell if she was crying or just wiping her eyes. I didn't say anything, but I could tell she was waiting to see if I would. Then, when I didn't, she pushed down on the lip of the raft. Her side dipped and then as it came back up she dove off. She cut into the water and did not come up for a long ways. She came up without breaking stroke and didn't turn around until she reached the dock. I watched her pull herself out of the water and I watched her walk up the dock and the lawn and when she went inside I stood and dropped off the side of the raft and started swimming towards home.

When I got home the car was sitting in the driveway, and when I went upstairs I heard Canasson moving around in his room. I went into my room and closed the door and read

240

for a while. Then a while later I heard Canasson going up and down the stairs. I waited for him to go down and then I opened my door and looked out. His door was open and I could see the wall of boxes was broken down in the middle and there were fewer boxes in the room than there had been before. The front door was open and when I heard Canasson coming back up the front walk I closed my door. I wasn't really upset at him anymore, but I also didn't really want to see him. So I let him finish what he was doing, thinking that when he was finished he would take a break and then I could go down and talk to him. But a while later I heard the car drive off, and when I went to look his door was standing open and most of the boxes in his room were gone.

A while later, he came back. I had started making a drink and when I heard him come in I took down a second glass and made another. He came in and I handed his to him and raised mine and said, "here's to the times we've had, I guess, since there aren't any times to come."

"Here's to that," he said. We both drank.

"Should we go out?"

"Lets."

We went out on the porch and stood by the railing, both facing the water. I was going to tell him about swimming out and talking to June, but I couldn't think quite how to do it, and then I decided to hell with it. So I said, "you found an apartment?"

"Yes," he said. "My secretary found it and then signed off on it. It was all pretty easy, actually. If I don't like it I can always move. But it's nice." Then he added, "I needed to do it, anyway. Just to have somewhere to put things." He guessed I was hurt that he had started moving and I was hurt, I guess. But I didn't really want him to know it, so I just shrugged and didn't say anything. We finished our drink and then Canasson checked his watch and said that he had to go. I felt like I should tell him about talking to June, if only so that he would know what she'd said, but I thought better of it.

241

It seemed over, and that him knowing wouldn't make much difference one way or the other. So I just let him go without saying anything.

I sat around for a while until I felt pretty sober, and then I went for a drive around the lake. I felt like I had to get out of town pretty soon, like everything good that had been would be spoiled if I stayed any longer. It was still good enough to keep, but it wouldn't be that way for long and pretty soon it would be too used up by all that it was weighed against. It took a while to go around the lake and it was pretty well past dark when I got back to town. I ate dinner in town and then went home and read for a while, laying in bed. Then I realized that I was falling asleep, and I thought that I should put the book away and get undressed before I did. But realizing that I was falling asleep woke me up. So I read for a little while longer and then the phone rang. It was Canasson.

"Elliot," he said. "We need a ride. Somebody stole June's car."

"You're joking," I said. "Did you call the police?"

"June wants to call from her house. It's too loud here."

"Somebody stole her car? Are you sure?" I was sort of half-asleep already, and was pretty surprised to hear from him. And I had a hard time believing that someone stole her car.

"It's not where we left it." He sighed into the phone. "Can you give us a ride back to her house or not? We're at the bar we went to with you and Rene."

"I'll be there in a few minutes," I said.

I drove around to the bar. They were standing outside, and I pulled up and they got in without saying anything. June got in the back and Canasson sat next to me but sat facing the window. I pulled out onto the road and headed west again. But when we got to June's house June leaned forward and said, "please, Elliot, let me call from your house. Do you mind?" and so I kept going, and when we got to the house she said, "would you mind just driving for a while? Do you think you could do that?" so I kept going. It was late and everything was dark and I could feel Canasson angry and hurt beside me. Anything that had been left undecided between them seemed decided, now, and the decision hung in the air around him. I watched her in the mirror, and watched her turn to catch the wind from the open windows on her face and through her hair, and did not wonder how someone could come to feel that their world would be destroyed if she vanished from it.

"I suppose you want to know what happened, then," said Canasson. "I suppose it's just killing you to know every little detail of what happened, isn't it?" He glanced back at June. "I guess maybe you already know. I guess you've got a little guess worked out about how it all went and you're not going to ask, you're just going to sit there and smirk and think how you were right all along. Aren't you. Aren't you? Aren't you."

"I don't know, Arthur," I said.

"Leave him alone, Arthur," June said. "Just. leave him alone." She sounded old and tired and like it had been fun before but now it wasn't and couldn't everybody see that it wasn't any fun anymore, and leave it alone?

"Why didn't you tell me what June said on the raft?" he said.

"I don't know, Arthur," I said. "I'm sorry. The moment never came up. You were in a hurry to go and I didn't think you would want to hear it." I glanced at him. "Was I wrong? Was I wrong to think that you wouldn't have heard me?"

"That's not the goddamned point," he said. "The point is that it was goddamned important and that you were my friend and were supposed to tell me before I saw her again so that I wouldn't make such a stupid ass of myself. That was the goddamned point of it, was that you should have told me and you hid from doing it like the little chicken shit that you are."

"Arthur," said June. "Arthur, leave Elliot alone."

"You did it on purpose, didn't you?" he said. "You've wanted June to yourself from the very beginning of this thing and you want me to look bad because you think you've got a shot with her if I'm out of the way, don't you?" He was leaning in close to my ear.

"Why don't you just calm down, Arthur," I said. I could smell beer and whiskey on his breath and I leaned away, towards the window. "Just calm down, all right? You've just had a little too much to drink, is all. You'll be all right in the morning. Don't say anything that you're going to regret, now."

"I regret everything," he said, leaning back into his seat. "I regret goddamned everything that I've ever done." And the next thing I knew he was crying, leaning forward against the dashboard and then sinking to put his head down between his knees so that the sobs were muffled in the close space by the floorboards.

"Arthur, Jesus Christ," I said. "Get up, Arthur. You're making a goddamned fool of yourself."

"So what if I am?" he yelled into the space between his calves. "So what if I am? Who is left to see me who hasn't already seen me at my worst? I can't look any more foolish to anyone than I already do to both of you."

"Christ," I said.

"Arthur," said June, "sit up. Arthur, you're making Elliot uncomfortable. Elliot is your friend and you're making him sorry that he came to give us a ride. You asked him to do you a favor and now you're acting like this. It's not fair to Elliot."

"Would you shut up already about Elliot?" he said, coming upright and turning suddenly to face her. "That's all you ever talk about is goddamned Elliot." He turned to me, in close and his breath hot and heavy with booze and his face wet with tears. "You hear that, Elliot," he said quietly. "Do you hear that? You're all she ever talks about anymore. She thinks you're goddamned wonderful. She thinks you're a goddamned peach. Should I tell her how I met you? Does she know what you did for a living, before you came out here?" He was talking loud, too loud for the car and too loud for as close as he was to me.

"Why don't you try shutting up for a while?" I said. "Why don't you try sitting back in your seat and shutting up for a while, Arthur?" I looked up at June in the rearview, and saw her staring back at me with the blankest expression I have ever seen. Canasson saw me looking up at her reflection and he looked at it, too, and then he brought his fist up and down against the curve of the windshield and knocked the rearview mirror off so that it shattered against the dashboard.

"Arthur!" said June.

I hit the brakes and swerved over onto the shoulder. Then I threw it into park and got out and ran around to the passenger side. Canasson saw me coming and tried to climb across the seat and out the driver's side door, but he didn't get the latch undone until I was around his side of the car and had his door open. June was yelling my name. Canasson dove across and grabbed the far side of the seat and I caught him by the ankle as he sprawled out lengthwise. He shook me but I held on tight and then he turned over on his back and kicked me in the face with his other foot. I felt my nose crunch and push flat and for a moment I couldn't see anything. Then I felt the blood come fast and I pulled hard backwards. Canasson tried to catch the steering wheel as it went past but he missed and then I reached inside the car and grabbed him by his collar and pulled him up so that he was sitting on the edge of the seat with his feet on the ground. June yelled for me to stop and I pulled back to punch him, but my arm caught in the window frame and so I only pulled back halfway. I was aiming for his nose, but he jerked when he saw it coming and I ended up hitting him in the forehead. His head snapped back and then came forward again and I grabbed him by the collar with both hands and pulled him out and dumped him onto the ground. Then I started kicking him. And while I was kicking him I was talking and I was saying, "You. Goddamned. Son. Of. A. Bitch. Who. The hell. Do you think. You are?" and Canasson wormed under the car and I had to stop anyway because I was out of breath. I sat down on the passenger seat and then pretty soon I lay down. There were black spots ringed in yellow light flashing in front of my face and they didn't stop when I closed my eyes.

I lay there on my back and felt the blood come out of my nose slide over my cheeks and down beneath my ears and across my neck. After a while I heard Canasson climbing out from under the car. I was going to sit up, to try to cover myself, but I decided that there wasn't any point because I didn't care if he hit me and I was too tired to do it anyway. But he didn't hit me. He just stood there. None of us moved for a little while. I reached up and switched off the engine. In the silence I could hear the lake beyond the trees standing between the road from the water.

After a while I sat up and pulled myself across to the driver's side. Canasson got in and we closed our doors and I started the car and drove us back the way we had come. I did it so we could drive past the fair. It seemed like a hell of way for everything to end, and I guess I wanted to remember the gazebo where we had all met for the first time. But the lights were off at the fair, and we couldn't see the gazebo from the road. I guess it wouldn't have meant anything if we could. I guess you always try to turn a thing like that into something meaningful. Anyways, nobody was looking. I could hear Canasson breathing shallow beside me. He was hugging his ribs and I thought of him shirtless in my apartment, and of how little there was of him behind his clothes, and I felt like crying for having tried to destroy something so small and so beautiful.

I pulled up in front of June's house. Her car was sitting in the driveway. I parked and shut off the engine and they got out and I got out, too. I knew I didn't have any reason to, but nobody protested and I think they understood that I had a right to know why the car was not stolen, now that I had given them a ride. So we all went inside. I went in behind June and ahead of Canasson. Down the hallway and through the living room I could see Bernard. He was sitting out on the porch, on one of the wooden chairs from the lawn below. He had a drink in his hand and his other hand was wrapped up in a white towel, soaked through at the end. He flinched when he heard us coming in. Then, with a lot of preparation, he stood up. He looked at us, testing his balance. Then he came towards us and through the doorway and went over to the line of bottles still out on the counter.

"Hello everyone," he said. He waved the towel hand. "Don't mind me," he said. "A little accident in the workshop just now." He set his glass down and then refilled it.

"Bernard," said June, "what did you do?"

"It's nothing," he said, filling the glass and not looking at her. "Nothing at all that you need to worry about." He glanced up at us. "Would anyone care for a drink?" he said. "There's plenty here, or at least there was when I started. If we run out we can always go and get more. Just jump in the car and go."

"Bernard," said June, "you really should have come inside and said something. We almost called the police."

"The police?"

"We thought the car had been stolen."

"I didn't want to interrupt your date," Bernard said, looking at Canasson. "I'm sorry, I'm not mistaken, am I? It was a date, wasn't it? I just want to make sure I've got my... my definitions clear. Some things are getting so very hard to define." He took a sip from his glass, then topped it off, then said, looking at Canasson, "wouldn't you agree, sport? Wouldn't you agree that some things are getting downright hard to keep straight? Don't look so worried, sport," he said, raising his drink. "I'm not going to do anything. It looks like your friend beat me to it anyway."

"Bernard," said June, stepping towards him. "Bernard, let me see your hand." She reached out and took the wad of towel between her hands but he pulled it away. Some of his drink splashed out of his glass and fell on the counter and he looked at it, studying it, holding his hand away from June.

June said, "You have to let me see it, Bernard. Let mommy see it. You have to let me see it," and after a long time Bernard seemed to surrender, and held it out to her. She took it in her own and began unwrapping it.

"Fix yourselves a drink, boys," Bernard said over her shoulder.

"Thanks very much," I said, and I went over and filled a glass with ice and whiskey and then I pressed the bottom of it to the bridge of my nose. While I was doing that June got the hand unwrapped and I heard her suck in her breath sharp and hard and then cut the breath short.

"Oh Bernard," she said, in a whisper. "Oh Bernard," she said again, looking at him. "Oh baby," she said. "Oh my poor baby. Oh. Oh Bernard. Oh my God Bernard," and she wrapped the hand up tight again in the towel and said "just. Oh Bernard just stay right here. Just don't move. Let me go change my clothes and then we'll go. Promise me that you won't move at all. Please just stay right there. Oh my God Bernard. Oh Bernard just don't move," and she turned and went up the stairs, and we all stood there staring at nothing in her absence.

"How bad is it?" I said. My nose felt numb and huge and I lifted the glass down and took a sip.

He looked down at the towel. "It's pretty bad," he said. "I don't know. It looks pretty bad. I would have driven myself to the hospital, but I'm too goddamned drunk to drive.

It's funny, isn't it?" He looked at Canasson. "You know, don't you? You know how funny this is."

"That's all anybody says anymore," Canasson said. "It's all you all ever say is, isn't it funny? I wish to God you'd all give it a rest. All of this "we'll look back on this and laugh." I'm tired of it."

"You never look back and laugh," said Bernard, very serious. "Not about these things. Nobody ever laughs about what they think they are going to laugh about when they're older. Nobody ever laughs about anything important. Nobody ever laughs at the things they're supposed to."

"I don't know what you're saying," said Canasson.

"Never mind me," said Bernard. "I'm drunk."

"How did it happen?" I said.

"She's always been like this," said Bernard. "She was like that for me, too, and I don't have any right to be surprised that she's still like this. I wouldn't have married her if she wasn't like this." He looked at Canasson. "But I did marry her."

"He means your hand," Canasson said. "He means how did it happen to your hand."

"Was moving that great damn sculpture of June," he said. "It started to go and it caught my hand against the kick wheel." He looked down at the towel. "Now tell me that isn't funny," he said. "I dare you to tell me that that isn't funny."

"Does it hurt much?" I said.

"Yes," he said. "It hurts a hell of a lot. Even when I decide I don't care about the pain, it still hurts a whole hell of a lot." He shrugged. "I can't sculpt anymore, anyway. It's been coming for a long time. Everything has been coming out all wrong for a long time, even the things I get into with the best intentions and then especially the things I get into with no intentions. If I can't sculpt anymore it is just as well. I wish it hadn't happened, though."

"I'm sorry it happened," I said.

"Thank you." He said. He turned to Canasson. "I guess you know that June and I are going away," he said. "I'm sorry, Arthur. I'm sorry it worked out like this, although I'm not sure that it could have worked out any other way. Still, I'm sorry that it worked out like this. If we had more time, we could have become friends. If we had become friends before I found out that you were a rat bastard it might not have bothered me so much." He laughed. "See?" he said. "I told you that the whole thing was funny."

June came down the stairs. She had changed her clothes, and looked about a thousand years old. She looked at me and then at Canasson and then at Bernard. He smiled when he saw her, and raised his glass. Then he set it down and moved towards her and she took him by the elbow and led him down the hallway to the front door. I heard them go out and then I heard the car start and then a moment later I heard the door open and June came back in. She walked over to Canasson and kissed him on the cheek.

"I'm sorry, Arthur," she said. Then she walked over to me and kissed me on the cheek. "I'm sorry, Elliot," she said. She looked at both of us. "I'm sorry for the way everything happened. I suppose I won't see you anymore, either of you. Goodbye. I've had a hell of a lot of fun. Please keep in touch. I'll write you when we get back to the states."

Then she turned and went back down the hallway and I heard the door close and then the sound of the engine and gravel under the tires and then the quiet when she was gone.

I sat down on one of the barstools and filled a second glass with ice and poured it full of whiskey, and set it on the counter in front of the other barstool. After a moment Canasson sat down and took it up. I filled a third glass with ice and pressed it to the bridge of my nose. The blood had stopped coming, now, and the blood that was already on my face and inside my nostrils had grown dry and sharp.

"That's a hell of a thing," I said, after a while.

"Please don't talk about it," he said, not looking at me. "I don't ever want to talk about it again."

"That's the problem with the world," I said. "How can you give a damn and get through it?"

"Find someone who gives a damn and ask them," he said. "I don't give a damn. Not about anything. Not anymore. I'll never give a damn about anything ever again."

We drank our drinks and then went out to the car. I drove. But when we got to the house and got out Canasson didn't go inside. Instead, he walked across the lawn. I watched him and then I followed him. We walked across lawns in the dark and then down behind the bars and I watched him climb up and over the fence and then I went after him. He went down the empty causeway in the dark, down past the mural of the strongman pushing the great iron boulder up onto the stand and the one of the escape artist, up to his neck in the Chinese water cabinet. I watched him climb the stairs leading onto the dark platform of the merry-go-round and then climb onto one of the horses and sit there in the dark, slouched against the pole. I stood a hundred feet away, and watched him. He was staring out at the lake, facing away from me, and after a while I turned and went down the causeway without looking back and went home.

I went into the bathroom to wash the blood off my face. It took a long time to get it all off and then I realized that there was more that I could not see around the back of my neck and in my hair, and so I got undressed and took a shower. When I got out I washed my face again in the sink and when I looked at it in the mirror it was my face and it did not seem like it could ever be funny or strange. Then I went upstairs and got into bed. I was still wet from the shower and the sheets got damp and then got cool and I pulled the blankets up over my head and lay there shivering in the dark. My window was open, and I could hear the crickets and behind that the slap of the lake water against the dock boards. Then I thought

HERE GROAN THE DEAD

I heard the merry-go-round record start. But after a while I couldn't hear it anymore. Pretty soon after that I fell asleep.

XIII.

I woke up because someone was in the driveway pumping their car horn. I didn't get up. Then I heard Canasson get up and go downstairs, and the front door open, and then I heard two sets of feet coming back up. Then more steps going back down. I got out of bed and went to the doorway and watched the cab driver, carry one of the boxes from Canasson's room, go down the stairs and out the door. Canasson had taken most of them already, but there were still a few left. Then Canasson came out with one and carried it down, too. I saw his face over the top of the box. He had a bruise on his left cheek and a knot high on his forehead, up by the hairline. He looked at me as he went past but didn't say anything. I closed the door and got dressed quickly and then went back out and went downstairs and outside. While I was doing that I heard them both coming down the stairs, and then they came out. Canasson stopped next to me on the step and the driver went and closed the trunk and got into the cab and started the engine.

We stood there, not saying anything for a little while. Then I said, "I guess there isn't much to say, is there?" and we agreed that there wasn't much to say.

"Goodbye, Elliot," Canasson said. "I'm sorry about everything."

"Me too," I said. "Goodbye, Arthur."

"We did have a hell of a lot of fun, didn't we?" he said. "It wasn't all bad, was it? Didn't we have a hell of a time?"

"Sure," I said. "I had a hell of a time. I'll call you when I get back to the city."

He nodded. "I guess we don't need to make a big goodbye, then," he said.

"I guess not."

"Well, goodbye then," he said.

"Goodbye."

HERE GROAN THE DEAD

He stepped down onto the front lawn and crossed to the cab and got in. I stood on the front step and watched the cab back down the driveway and then turn out onto the road towards the route back to the city. Then I went back inside. Standing on the front step after he was gone I had had the feeling that I had come home before him, or that he had just gone out, for ice or something, and that he was still there. But when I went back inside the house felt different and big and hollow and I knew that he was really gone and that I was not going to call him and that I most likely would not see him ever again and the rest of my life became a very long time, and death went on forever after that. So I made a drink and sat out on the porch and stared out at the water.

Sitting on the back porch, staring at the lake, I thought a lot of things and I thought those things were true and very important, but afterwards I couldn't remember hardly any of them, and all I remember thinking is that there is really very little difference between a lake and the ocean, if the lake is large enough so that you can't see the opposite shore. After a while I walked down off the porch and down the dock and got into the boat and started rowing. I rowed out even with the end of the pier and then I rowed out even with June's house, and then farther out even with the point and out of the bay and out into the open lake. I watched the house as it grew smaller and smaller. I felt my arms go tired and the blisters on my palms hurt but I kept rowing and I was far out into the lake when I decided to turn around. But then the house seemed impossibly far away and I rowed for a while and then gave up and let myself drift. I drifted in towards shore and then I rowed to a dock and tied off and walked back to the house. It took a long time. I went up and over the hill past June and Bernard's house. Their car wasn't in the driveway, and then the house was past and I walked without thinking or feeling anything until I got back to Bradner's house and saw June's car in the driveway.

She was standing in the living room with her back to me, backlit against the windows on the far wall. She turned around when I came in. I sat down on the couch and lit a cigarette and said, "he's already gone."

"I saw," she said. "Is he coming back?"

"No," I said.

"You're leaving too?"

"Yes," I said, "I'm leaving."

She nodded. "It's a silly thing about Bernard, really. He does these things, sometimes. Not really on purpose or anything like that. But these things seem to tend to happen this way. When he's upset with me. The doctors say he should recover, anyway. It looked pretty bad, but they say that in a year he won't even be able to tell that it happened."

"We're a real admirable lot," I said. "The whole bunch of us. We're a goddamned American classic. You find more decency in your average wolf pack."

"Don't say that," she said. "We can't help who we are."

"I guess that's some comfort, if you can believe it. I supposed next you'll tell me we were all just kids and none of us knew any better. That none of us can be held accountable for what happened to any of us, and that we'll all laugh about it someday."

"I don't think I'll laugh. I don't think I'll ever laugh ever again."

"That's not true," I said.

"You're right," she said. "I guess it just feels that way. Can I have one of those?" I lit a cigarette for her and she came across the room and took it from me. "Oh Elliot," she said. "It did go horribly wrong, didn't it?"

"It went wrong," I said. "That probably says enough. Saying anything more would reduce it."

"I guess it can't end well, if two people love each other," she said. "Did I read that? Or hear it somewhere?"

"Don't call it love," I said. "And don't call it tragedy, and don't say that it was doomed."

"I won't call it anything, if you don't want me to."

"Let's not call it anything, then." We finished our cigarettes and then I lit another and gave June another. "So when are you leaving?" I said.

"Next week," June said. "But we're going back to the city first. Bernard wanted to leave today, but with his accident we decided to go back tomorrow. There are things to do, closing up the house. I really should get home and pack. I just wanted to see if he was here so I could apologize for last night. Or not apologize. I don't know. It just doesn't seem over, somehow, yet. Although I guess there really isn't anything more to say. Can you think of anything more to say?"

"Me?"

"Yes," she said. "Say something that sums it up and makes it all right. Say that it all went the way that it did, and that it couldn't have gone any other way."

"I can't say that. Things like this don't get finished in any way that means anything and nobody ever feels like they said the right thing or that it's all over."

"I know," she said. "I guess I know that." She sighed. "Are you coming back next summer?"

"I don't know. I don't know where I would stay. It won't really be the same place anymore then, anyway. And besides. It will probably just feel like I'm trying to recapture something that I never really had in the first place. Like I'm just trying to relive a memory or something."

"I guess you only realize you care about things after they're gone, when you've got nothing left but the place where they used to be."

"You're not talking about Arthur."

"No, I'm not talking about Arthur."

"It's none of my business." I blew smoke towards the ceiling and watched it hit and then roll out in a broad ring. "I guess eventually the only things that you have are the things that you've already lost," I said.

"What are we talking about?"

"I don't know."

"Let's stop then."

"All right."

"I don't know what happened," she said. "I wanted so much out of life. When I first married Bernard I thought he could give me everything I wanted. It seems pretty silly, thinking about it now. I really believed it, though. I don't know why. I wanted to, I guess. Tell me, Elliot. Were you really in love with me?"

"I thought I was," I said. "I don't know."

"Would you just tell me that you were? It would mean an awful lot to me."

"Even if you knew I didn't mean it?"

"Yes."

"I was in love with you," I said. "For whatever that's worth."

"In some ways I wish you had swum out first," she said. "I think things might have gone differently."

"Most likely they wouldn't have," I said.

"I guess not. It's funny that it almost seems like it, though."

"Sure," I said. "I guess that's funny."

"Well," she said, "I guess I should be going. It's been nice spending time with you, Elliot. Hopefully we can see more of each other in the future. I'll look you up when we get back."

"Sure," I said, though I knew then that she didn't mean it, and that she wouldn't. "Give my best to Bernard."

I walked with her to the door. She kissed me and then turned and I stayed behind in the hallway as she stepped out into the yard. I watched her walk and watched her get into her car and watched her drive away. For a minute I was pretty sure that I had been in love with her, that she really had broken my heart. But that wasn't right. I knew that it wasn't right and pretty soon I figured out that I knew it, too. I stood there, trying to figure out exactly what it was that I was feeling. I was feeling something, but it wasn't really about June. I didn't know what it was about.

I still don't, but I don't give a damn. The whole thing went rotten and that's saying enough about it. What does it matter? What does any of it matter? I praise the dead which are already dead more than the living which are yet alive. I don't care. I really don't.

About the Author

Auric Adams lives and works in Cleveland, Ohio.

He is the author of everything you will find at
www.AuricAdamsBlog.BlogSpot.Com

Here Groan the Dead is his first novel.

www.ingramcontent.com/pod-product-compliance
Lightning Source LLC
Chambersburg PA
CBHW050021180626
46810CB00002B/520